"Kiss me again, Noah. No one's ever made me feel that way."

Sabrina stood on tiptoe and pressed the full length of her body to his.

He stood motionless, tormented.

Her breath whispered across his lips. Her mouth brushed his. Her tongue touched his lower lip.

With a moan, he swept his arms around her and claimed her mouth. He drank deeply of her sweetness, desire ripping through him as she moved against him. He skimmed his hands down her back then lower to cup her bottom.

She drew back, face flushed, lips round and tempting. Slowly she pulled the tie of her robe until it loosened. Arching her back, she parted her robe. "Touch me."

Noah's gaze riveted to her breasts. She was more beautiful than he'd imagined. He ached to touch her, to taste her. Closing his eyes, he set her on her feet.

"Sabrina, if I do, I won't be able to stop."

She leaned close to whisper in his ear, "Maybe I don't want you to stop."

Dear Reader,

I can't relate how excited I am to be a part of the new Blaze line! These books combine two of my favorite elements—a hot read and lots of romance. Thanks for joining us in the fun.

When I brainstormed this story, I got hooked on the irony of transforming a romantic virgin into a sexy seductress and a womanizing cynic into the defender of her virtue. On the night of her twenty-fifth birthday, Sabrina Walker feels like the last virgin on earth. When she learns it took a bimbo as a bribe for Noah Banks to take her to dinner, she decides to lose her virginity.

But after a night in his arms, Sabrina realizes that Noah may have claimed more than her body. Bent on proving that the disturbing emotions he stirs stem from the fact that he was her first, she heads to the beach in search of a weekend fling. Noah follows and spends the weekend staving off her would-be suitors.

Little does he know that one is married, one too young and none are as sexy as he. Can he maintain his role of knight in shining armor when Sabrina targets *him* for seduction?

I hope you enjoy this romantic journey as much as I enjoyed writing it.

Best wishes,

Dorie Graham

THE LAST VIRGIN
Dorie Graham

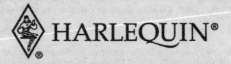

HARLEQUIN®

TORONTO • NEW YORK • LONDON
AMSTERDAM • PARIS • SYDNEY • HAMBURG
STOCKHOLM • ATHENS • TOKYO • MILAN • MADRID
PRAGUE • WARSAW • BUDAPEST • AUCKLAND

This book is dedicated to Larry, for loving me,
inspiring me and supporting me through all the craziness.
Thanks for always believing in me.

ISBN 0-373-79043-0

THE LAST VIRGIN

Copyright © 2002 by Dorene Graham.

Visit us at www.eHarlequin.com

Printed in U.S.A.

1

"NOAH, I'M DESPERATE!" Panic laced Mona Freeman's voice.

Noah Banks swallowed in discomfort. His stomach tightened. Normally women spoke those words to him with a sultry breathlessness, something he felt more capable of handling.

He'd stepped into his partner, Cliff Walker's office with nothing more on his mind than reviewing the day's trading and their clients' portfolios over their nightly shot of tequila. The last thing he'd expected was to walk in on a tiff between Cliff and his wife-to-be.

Noah's gaze swung from Mona to Cliff. Cliff sat rigid behind his massive walnut desk. His expression reminded Noah of his own father facing off with his mother, back in the days when they tolerated being in the same room.

Mona lunged toward Noah and he stiffened. Her small hands clung to his arm, eliciting a sense of frustration. Why did he have this desire to help her, when he'd never been adept at defusing domestic squabbles?

Reluctantly, he placed his hand on hers. He was almost afraid to ask, given Cliff's stormy expression. "What's the trouble?"

"No!" Cliff burst from his chair, sending it listing at an odd angle. "I told you. He…" his finger shook as he pointed at his partner "…is *not* an option."

Noah shot him a glare. What was up with Cliff? Though

he had no idea what his partner was referring to, the words stung. Noah opened his mouth to protest, then shut it.

Cliff was right. Whatever it was, they could work it out without him. Cliff could take care of his own hysterical woman. Noah took a step toward the office door he'd unwittingly entered.

Mona swung along with him. "Cliff, Noah's your best man, and our only hope."

With a tight smile, Noah patted her stiff fingers. "I'll come back later. Looks like you two need to work this out alone."

"Oh, no." Her eyes widened, turned pleading. "We need you."

"No!" In an instant, Cliff stood before them, his dark hair sticking out at odd angles as though he'd literally tried to yank it from his scalp. "We'll just have to tell her and let her get there on her own."

"But, Cliff…" Mona's bottom lip trembled. She blinked. "That will spoil it. I've been planning it for weeks. She has to arrive precisely at nine, or the whole surprise will be ruined. You know how much I have riding on this. She hates me and I need this party to win her over. I think she resents me for scheduling the wedding so close to her birthday. Oh, please." Huge tears rolled down her cheeks. She let out a choking sob.

Noah intensified his hand patting. The tightness in his stomach rolled into a knot. What was it about a woman's tears that made him go all soft inside? Damn it, he'd never been able to say no to a female in need. "Who has to get where?"

"S-S-Sabrina." Mona sniffed. "She has to get to her surprise birthday p-party."

"Sabrina?" Noah asked, unable to place the name.

"C-Cliff's sister."

Noah glanced at Cliff where he stood rigid and sullen. He'd mentioned a sister when they'd been at Auburn five years ago, but Noah had never met her.

"That's it? That's what all these waterworks are about?" Women were such emotional creatures. He swung his gaze from Mona's tear-streaked face to Cliff's stony expression. "You just need someone to play chauffeur?"

"It would mean the world to me to win her over. I think this might do it." Tears still glistened in Mona's eyes as she stared up at him, but a grateful glow lit their blue depths. "You can't let on about the party."

She let go of his arm to move beside Cliff. "Cliff will help you work out the details." She tilted her face up to her fiancé. "Okay?"

"No." His voice had lost some of its earlier vehemence.

Her fingertips traced his cheek. She brushed her body against his. "For me?"

He shut his eyes for a moment, then scooped his arm around her in surrender. "I really don't like this."

With a happy squeal, she threw her arms around him. "I love you. They'll be in a public place. Then we'll all be there to chaperone. It'll be fine."

She placed a fat kiss on his lips, then broke away to find her purse, her tears reduced to an occasional sniffle. "I've got to go see about the flowers for the wedding. You explain to Noah." She swept from the room.

Noah turned to Cliff with a grin. Now that the disturbance had passed, the tension in him eased. "That's showing her."

Cliff shook his shaggy head. "You have no idea." He turned to stalk back to his desk. He lifted a legal pad, then slammed it onto the blotter. "I'd never agree to this if it wasn't a last resort."

"It's six o'clock. Time for a shot." Noah ignored Cliff's

comment and brought the conversation back to his original purpose for coming to Cliff's office. He moved to a cabinet behind the desk and lifted two shot glasses from a shelf.

The six o'clock shot was a ritual they'd started during their college sophomore year. It was a time-honored tradition Noah had inherited from his father, who'd adopted the custom after a week in Mexico with his college buddies. During that trip, his dad had developed a lasting taste for José Cuervo tequila, and now it was the only brand used for the ritual.

Noah handed Cliff one of the glasses. Cliff set it on the desk, then retrieved a bottle from a low drawer. He splashed golden liquid into the two glasses.

"Thanks." Noah raised his glass in a toast, while Cliff followed suit. "Here's to work. Here's to pleasure. Foster both in equal measure."

Noah tossed back the drink in one gulp. He set down the empty glass, then paced to the far window to look out over Atlanta's downtown skyline. The sun slanted low, casting long shadows across the rooftops. Six floors below, a long line of cars snaked through the street.

He turned back to Cliff. "So, I finally get to meet your sister."

Scowling, Cliff stabbed his finger across the room at him. "Get her to her surprise party, but keep your hands to yourself! She's a nice girl."

Annoyed, Noah narrowed his eyes. "What are you all tense about? I haven't got any designs on your sister. I've never even met her, I might add, which seems a little strange. I can see when we were at Auburn, but we worked together here for years before I moved to Denver. I've been back all these weeks, she lives in Atlanta, and I still haven't met her. Why not?"

Cliff gaped at him. "I just told you. She's a nice girl. I

didn't want her exposed to your…your personal habits. Believe me, I've tried everyone for this party. No one else is available."

"Personal habits? I was thinking along the lines of a simple introduction, not a roommate situation." Noah tilted his head, his aggravation with Cliff growing. "What's wrong with my personal habits?"

With a sound of exasperation, Cliff gestured with his hand. "Blondes on Monday, brunettes on Thursday and redheads for the weekend. Sabrina's not like that. She's the romantic type, believes in love and happily-ever-after. I don't want you corrupting her."

Noah scowled. "I resent that. Just because I enjoy women doesn't mean I'd pounce on your sister." He twisted the blind pull. Atlanta's skyline disappeared.

"Just get her to the party, none of your funny business or…or you and I are gonna go at it!"

"Go at it?" Noah chuckled. He had a hard time taking Cliff seriously with his hair mimicking electrotherapy. "You're making too much of this. I can control myself. Besides, I haven't said I'd do it."

"Of course you'll do it. You have to. And you *will* control yourself." He blew out a breath. "I wouldn't ask if I wasn't desperate. I've got that trip to Boca for the Shoreland quarterly portfolio review.

"You heard Mona. She hired caterers. She's going all out. For some reason she has the silly idea that Sabrina doesn't like her."

All this to please a woman. Cliff had lost it. Noah squeezed his eyes shut. At the age of thirty, he'd learned the hard way there was no pleasing women—at least not in that sense.

Two years ago, he'd left his partnership with Cliff to follow Rebecca to Colorado. He'd given her everything—

his time, his money, even offered her his name. Thank God she'd refused the last. No matter what he offered, it hadn't been enough. He'd left that relationship without any illusions. It had almost cost him his career.

Cliff would have to learn that lesson for himself, but how could Noah get out of pinch-hitting for his partner?

He turned to Cliff. "You can take your sister to her party. I'll go to Boca for you. Old lady Shoreland likes me."

"No way. Her granddaughter's visiting with her fiancé, not that that would stop you."

"Wait a minute. I am *not* the sleaze you make me out to be. I've never stolen another man's woman."

"No, you've never had to. For some reason women flock to you. It's disgusting."

With a grunt, Noah moved to the desk. "Not all of them."

"Oh?" Cliff turned, his brows raised. "You mean one of them hasn't fallen swooning into your arms?"

"That blonde on the fourth floor. I think she's with the insurance agency." He shrugged. "She's been a little elusive."

A smile spread across Cliff's face. "Darcy. I had lunch with her yesterday. We kind of dated in high school." He cleared his throat. "Of course, I've got Mona now. I mean, it was just lunch. There she was alone in that big booth—"

"You put moves on her?" Noah stared, surprised. Cliff's cheeks resembled a red light district. Good old Cliff had been lunching with Noah's pick of the month? How could that be?

"No! No, nothing like that. Darcy's more your speed. She...well, kind of got around in high school. Of course, people change...."

Noah perked at the news. Darcy sounded like what he

needed—a nice unencumbered relationship. After the disaster with Rebecca, he didn't think he'd ever want anything else from a woman. "I can work with that."

With his hands jammed into his pockets, Cliff faced his partner. "Look, are you going to help me, or what?"

Noah pulled his mind from Darcy's long legs and bountiful curves. He'd rather spend Friday night with her than with a "nice" girl. "Can't you find someone else?"

"There isn't anyone else! I wouldn't have asked *you* if someone else was available."

With a frown, Noah scooped the legal pad off the desk. He scanned the page-long list of scratched-off names. "You asked Fred, the mail guy?"

"I told you I was desperate."

Noah tapped the pad. "My name isn't even on here."

Cliff glared at him. "Okay, what will it take? How much?"

"What? You're bribing me now?" A chuckle rose from Noah's throat. "No go. You couldn't pay me enough."

"Darcy!" Cliff's eyes widened. He moved toward Noah. "That's it. You take Sabrina to dinner, then get her to the party. I'll put in a good word for you with Darcy. I'll even invite her to the party."

Visions of Darcy's full bosom and rounded backside flashed through Noah's mind. Anticipation raced through him. How bad could one dinner with Cliff's sister be? Besides, he had lost most of his client base with the move, and Cliff was giving him a chance to rebuild his career. He owed his old roommate.

After another moment's hesitation, Noah thrust out his hand. "Deal."

Relief flowed over Cliff's face. Even his hair seemed to relax. He clasped Noah's hand. "Deal. You take Sabrina to dinner, then bring her by the house. My flight gets in around ten, but Mona wants you two there at nine sharp. I'll tell Sabrina Mona's going to Boca with me and we won't be back until Sunday. You can say you're feeding the dog.''

''Dog?'' Noah narrowed his gaze. ''That German shepherd wannabe who hates men?''

Cliff blinked. ''Opal is part shepherd, and she doesn't hate all men. She's gotten used to me. She's just protective of Mona. Anyway, you won't have to deal with her.''

''Right.'' With a nod, Noah moved toward the door.

''Wait.''

Noah stopped, then turned back toward his partner. Cliff paused, staring hard at him. ''There's something else you need to know about Sabrina. She isn't the kind of woman you're accustomed to.''

''Right. You already told me. She's the romantic type. Don't worry, I'll take her someplace nice.''

''Good.'' Cliff's jaw bunched. ''But that isn't what I'm getting at.''

Noah drew an impatient breath. ''So what are you saying?''

A cool warning slipped into Cliff's gaze. ''I'm saying…she's a virgin. And I want her to stay that way.''

SABRINA WALKER GROANED. She yanked the wall calendar from its place beside an old fuse box and stared at the big squares representing the days of the week, zeroing in on the upcoming Friday. The thirteenth. This Friday was the thirteenth. What kind of day was that to have a birthday?

''This is a bad omen, Walker,'' she murmured to herself. ''A very bad omen.'' The depression that had hovered over her for months descended. Everyone she knew was engaged or married and working on the second or third child.

Everyone but her.

She plopped into the rickety desk chair she'd picked up secondhand to go with the metal desk she'd inherited when she bought this bookstore four years ago. After a minute of searching through the pile of catalogs and order sheets on her desk, she unearthed the phone. She punched in a number, then waited through three rings.

"Hello?" Bess Anderson, her best friend, answered.

"Life is passing me by, Bess."

"Sabrina?"

"I know I vowed at sixteen to wait for The One, but I thought I'd find love by now." Sabrina twisted the phone cord around her finger. "I'm in a rut. I'm sitting here and nothing is going on in my life. There's no one to greet me at the end of the day." She swallowed. "No hope of having a child."

"Aw, Bree…you can borrow one of mine, or how about all three?" One of Bess's daughters shrieked in the background. "Excuse me a minute." The phone made a clunking sound, then Bess yelled for her offspring to quiet. "Sorry," she said as she came back on the line.

Sabrina's finger purpled. "All I need is a jump start."

"Tom has this new guy working for him—"

"I'm seriously thinking of going for it—"

"Really? Great, we'll have you both over—"

"Popping the cork, losing the old cherry—"

"What?"

"Maybe it's time I lost my virginity. Had a fling. Walked on the wild side." Sabrina squared her jaw. Saying the words out loud sent a wave of satisfaction coursing through her. She pulled her finger free, shaking the blood back into it.

"Now, hon, who is he? You're not going to do anything hasty, are you?"

Sabrina laughed. "I've been celibate for nearly twenty-five years. What's hasty about that?"

"You know what I mean. Who is he? Do you love him? Why haven't—"

"I don't know who *he* is, or will be. The way I feel, the next available male I come across might get lucky."

"Sabrina?" Toby Baxter, a high school student she'd hired to work afternoons, poked his head around the office door. "Could you cover the front? I've got to take a leak."

"Sure, Toby. Just a minute."

He smiled his thanks, then withdrew.

Grimacing, Sabrina turned back to the phone. "Okay, well, maybe the *next* available male."

"Look, Sabri—"

"I've gotta go. Thanks for helping sort this out, Bess."

"Wait, don't—"

She hung up. Nothing Bess could say would change her mind. Besides, Bess was no paragon of knowledge. Look at the mess she'd made of her own life. Sabrina sighed and shook her head.

Poor Bess. At sixteen, they'd cried together when she discovered she'd gotten pregnant by Tommy Anderson, her first "real" boyfriend. To Sabrina's horror, Bess, with her runway model looks, tossed aside her future in high couture to marry Tom and have his baby.

Nine years and three children later, Bess was still stuck in Atlanta, still stuck with Tom. Sabrina's heart twisted. Sure Bess loved her kids, but what a life she could have had. How many nights had they stayed up planning her career as a high fashion model, her New York apartment and her picture on the cover of *Vogue?*

Sabrina stood. For herself, all she'd ever wanted was a career, a husband who loved and appreciated her, and children. Professionally, she was doing exactly what she wanted, but her personal life was lacking. Sure, she'd dated, always on the search for The One. Bess's tragedy had taught her not to settle for less. Unfortunately, it never took long to realize when a man wasn't The One, so her relationships tended to fizzle before developing into anything serious.

With one last glare at the calendar, she pushed away from her desk. Friday the thirteenth! Of all the days to have a birthday!

She paused at her office door. She needed to do something to get out of her funk. Closing her eyes, she imagined herself basking in the sun along crystal-white sand. That was it! She'd go to her favorite resort in Destin, Florida, and treat herself to her own birthday celebration.

As she pushed through into the shop, her mind raced with the list of things she had to do to prepare for the trip— make sure the store was covered, call the resort and schedule her flight. With luck, she'd have everything set by the end of the day.

The resolve firm in her mind, she went to relieve Toby. The front door of the shop stood open, catching the May breeze. Sunlight flooded the row of floor-to-ceiling windows that graced the shop's front. Plants hung in baskets near the windows, and topped the many bookcases, lending a cool touch of green. The brassy strains of jazz drifted from overhead speakers.

With a sound of relief, Toby raced for the back room, leaving the small bookstore empty, except for Sabrina and Libby Conrad, one of their regulars. A flowered scarf held Libby's dyed red curls back from her face. She stretched to reach a high shelf in one of the many bookcases.

"Need help?" Sabrina asked.

With a wave of her hand, the older woman dismissed

her. "Don't mind me, dear. I'm fine. I know you've got work to do."

Sabrina smiled a small smile. She was so distracted right now, she'd hate to inadvertently snap at the dear woman. Picking up a watering can from behind the counter, Sabrina went to work on a basket of Creeping Charley. Caring for her plants usually calmed her.

Libby seldom bought or traded books. Mostly she browsed and chatted with other customers. Though Sabrina had grown fond of the elderly woman, she sometimes wondered if Libby was becoming senile. She often talked nonstop, wavering in and out of a long-ago past.

Done watering, Sabrina pulled out her customer request notebook to check it against her recent book shipment. She still carried a generous assortment of new product, though with all the mega-booksellers moving into the area, she'd expanded her used section. She needed an edge that allowed her to compete. Cliff had been appalled when she'd told him she was veering in that direction, but otherwise, she wouldn't last long against that kind of competition. So far, her strategy had paid off.

Toby emerged from the back, heading for a carton of used books on the counter. "I've logged these already," he said, scooping up an armload. "Some of this old stuff is rad." He hummed something Sabrina didn't recognize as he disappeared down a book-lined aisle.

Libby made a sudden beeline for the counter.

Sabrina braced herself.

"Has Henry called for me?"

Sighing, Sabrina mustered a smile. "No, Libby. I'm sorry, but no one's called for you."

The woman's hopeful expression sagged. "Well, he will. He promised," she said in her usual raspy voice.

Sabrina squeezed the woman's hand. Without fail, they

played out this scenario whenever she came to the shop. Normally, Sabrina controlled the inevitable tug on her emotions. Today, however, her heart lurched and her eyes stung. What had happened to Libby's Henry?

"Yes," her voice caught. "He will." She blinked back embarrassing tears. This ridiculous birthday disaster had her tied up in knots.

Libby shook her gnarled finger. "He's an incredible lover, you know."

Sabrina straightened. This wasn't part of the routine. "I'm…I'm sure he is."

"Has all the right moves."

"How…how nice for you."

"He plays his harmonica," she rasped, "and I do this dance. I'll show you."

"That's not necessary." Sabrina glanced around. No other customers had come in and Toby was probably lost in the bowels of the sci-fi area. "I wouldn't want you to go to any trouble."

"Oh, yes, dear. You must learn, so you can try it on your own young man." She threw her hands in the air and swiveled in what she must have meant to be a seductive motion. The music curled around them. "Gets 'em in the mood, you know."

Not sure how to handle her, Sabrina cleared her throat, then came around the counter, and reached futilely toward the woman. "I don't…I don't have a young man."

"No? Maybe…that's…because…you…don't do…the dance." The older woman's rasp intensified and her breathing became labored. "Gets the…blood pumping."

"Libby…please, why don't you sit down and rest a minute? I think I get the gist of it."

"No…no…you must!"

Sabrina frowned. The woman looked ready to have a

stroke and seemed determined enough to keep at it until Sabrina joined in. "Okay," she said, raising her arms and swaying. "Just for a minute." She glanced around again to ensure no one saw.

"More...hip." Libby's hips pivoted in exaggerated circles.

Sabrina chewed her lip in concentration. After a few moments, her muscles warmed and she smiled. The music flowed over her. Her body moved in tune with the sax's sultry strains. "There. I think I've got it."

"Oh, you've got it all right," a deep masculine voice sounded from behind her. "The question is, are you giving any of it away?"

Embarrassment flooded Sabrina as she swung around to face a tall stranger. He stood a few feet inside the shop's door. The light breeze ruffled his dark hair. His eyes, as black as coal, shone with undisguised admiration. His gaze ran over her hips, then up, pausing a long moment at her breasts, before rising to meet her eyes.

A shiver ran through her. Men had noticed her before— more often than she'd cared for—but their attentions normally had little effect on her. This man's gaze sent butterflies flurrying in her stomach. His lazy smile showed he hadn't been fooled by her simple cotton dress.

"See, you caught one." Libby nodded in the newcomer's direction. "Not bad for your first time out."

The man chuckled and headed toward them.

Heat spread up Sabrina's neck and across her cheeks. She'd never been more mortified.

He moved with the grace and precision of a panther. Sleek. Sensual. His gray suit draped him as if it were tailor-made, his broad shoulders and tapered hips filling its precise lines.

"So, are you?" His voice rumbled through her.

Another shiver struck her, this one in the pit of her stomach. The dancing must have made her dizzy. "Excuse me?"

"You go on!" Libby swatted his arm. "Sabrina doesn't give a thing away." She eyed Sabrina. "Maybe that's the problem."

Sabrina stared at Libby. Words refused to form on her tongue.

The man in turn stopped short. He drew up straight. "Sabrina?" He stared at her with disbelieving eyes.

"Yes." She offered her hand, grateful to have found her voice, though it held a strange, breathless quality. "Sabrina Walker. Was there something I could help you find?"

"Well, actually..." He sandwiched her hand between his big palms. "I came to find you."

"Me?" She blinked. Her heart beat triple time, as the warmth of his hands melted into hers. A little tremor ran from her fingers up her arm. She fought the alarming urge to lean into him. What could a gorgeous man like this want with her?

"That's right." Releasing her, he spread his arms wide. "I'm Noah Banks. I work with your brother."

Bewilderment swirled through her. "Noah? Oh, my... this *is* a surprise. Cliff's told me so much about you." Like how she should run the other way if she ever chanced to meet him.

Noah's eyes shone. "I can just imagine. Probably only half of it was true."

"I don't know. I have a feeling he wasn't too far off the mark." She'd always doubted Cliff's stories about his college roommate's sexual prowess. Until now. Cliff had been right to warn her. Noah emanated danger...and excitement.

She stepped back and nearly knocked over Libby. "Goodness, I'm sorry. Where are my manners?" Sabrina gestured to the woman. "This is Libby Conrad, my most valued customer. Ms. Conrad, Noah Banks, lady-killer."

Noah put a hand to his chest. "You wound me!" He took Libby's offered hand, kissing it with a flourish. "I always leave a woman smiling, and very much alive."

"I'll bet you do." Libby snatched back her hand. "You're a handsome rascal, but I'm afraid I'm spoken for. My Henry'll be here any moment and he's the jealous type."

Sabrina's heart gave another squeeze.

Noah darted a look over his shoulder, as if he were afraid of encountering the elderly woman's lover. "Henry?"

"Henry Thomas Watson, of Decatur, a real man's man." With shaky fingers, Libby extracted a golden locket from between her breasts. She flipped it open and held it toward him.

Despite herself, Sabrina crowded beside him to catch a glimpse of the infamous Henry. Two tiny portraits, one of a young woman with flaming red hair and a familiar smile, the other a wavy-haired man, handsome, but serious, stared back at her. She sighed. They must have been terribly in love.

Noah straightened, releasing the locket and brushing against her. "A hell of a lucky man, your Henry."

"Damn right." Libby dropped the locket back into her cleavage.

Sabrina swallowed and tried to calm the hundreds of butterflies that had stormed her stomach at Noah's accidental touch. She had to get a grip. He was just a man.

An available man.

She drew in a breath and let her gaze drift over his broad shoulders, trim waist, then lower. That fluttery feeling spread. He cleared his throat. Her gaze flew to his. Though he stood ramrod straight, the heat in his eyes pierced her.

So, this was desire.

"Listen, I'm going to get out of your way and let you two get acquainted." Libby patted Sabrina's arm. "Live a little." She winked, then wandered off after Toby.

Noah shifted beside Sabrina. Her brother had to be wrong. No way was she a virgin, not with the way she moved, or the way she looked at him with her hungry eyes. Her body had called to his with her siren's dance and her throaty voice alone was enough to do a man in.

"Cliff has kept you such a mystery, he'd gotten my curiosity up. I've been trying to figure out how to meet you." His gaze swept the crowded rows of books. Somehow, he couldn't look at her and tell his half truth. "I was grilling Tiffany, at the office, about what to get him and Mona for a wedding gift and she mentioned that I should ask you."

He glanced up and was again caught in her blue gaze. "So, here I am, come to humbly ask your advice, and to check out the mystery woman, of course."

She cocked her head. "Does Cliff know you're here?"

"Uh, no. I didn't announce where I was going."

She smiled and her eyes lit with pleasure. "Well, I won't tell him if you won't."

"My lips are sealed."

Her hair shone deep mahogany in the sunlight slanting through the open door. He knotted his fists to keep from reaching out to touch the lock draped over her shoulder. "You don't look like your brother, except for your hair color."

His traitorous hand rose. His fingers threaded through her dark strands. Satin and silk. He leaned forward and caught a whiff of wildflowers. His pulse kicked up a notch.

"Um…wedding gift." Her voice floated to him, soft and hesitant.

He met her wide gaze. Clear and bright, her eyes pulled

him in, until he felt he was drowning in them. They held a purity he'd never known.

With a mental shake, he dropped his hand and straightened. It was true. She *was* a virgin. Innocence radiated from her. A confirmed bachelor who didn't believe in fairy tales or happily-ever-after had no right going near her.

"Yeah." He cleared his throat, attempted to clear the haze from his mind. "I know they've got a registry going, but I was thinking I'd like to get them something different."

"Different," she parroted, as her brows drew together in concentration. "Let's see." She tapped her fingers against her chin, then suddenly brightened. "I know. Mona likes that new gallery in Buckhead, the one with the stick figures out front. Contemporary art. The owner knows her. She can help you pick something." Her mouth twisted in a wry curve. "As long as you please Mona, Cliff'll be happy."

"Well, great. Contemporary art." He nodded. He knew the place. That done, his palms moistened. He had to ask her out for Friday night, but his usual confidence and finesse had fled. He stood like a schoolboy ready to ask out his first crush. What if she said no, or worse, what if she was seeing someone?

He grimaced. He'd never before concerned himself with details.

"So, I'm glad you stopped by. It's interesting to compare the myth to the reality." Her eyes sparkled.

Noah fisted his hands. For some inexplicable reason, he hated that she knew of his exploits. "Funny how reality can sprout into such tall tales." His voice ground out rougher than he'd meant, but she smiled, nodding thoughtfully.

A moment of silence fell. She glanced over her shoulder

as a new customer entered. "I guess I'd better get back to work."

He gritted his teeth. His tongue felt too thick for his mouth. When had he ever had trouble asking a woman out?

She turned toward the counter, stopped, then faced him again. His gut tightened. Her cheeks flushed. "Maybe we could get together sometime," she said.

"Friday night…" He shook his head, then tried again. "Could I take you to dinner…Friday, this Friday night?" His heart pounded. "I mean, I just thought that since you're Cliff's sister and all, and with the upcoming wedding, it wouldn't hurt for us to get to know each other…" He snapped his mouth shut. Why was he babbling?

"Okay."

"Okay?" His heart lifted and he wanted to smack himself for the relief flowing through him.

"Yes." She raised her chin. Her eyes gleamed. "I'll go out with you Friday night."

"Great. About seven then?"

"Seven's good. Here, I'll give you my address." She moved to the counter, scribbled something on a piece of paper, then handed it to him. "My phone number, too, in case you need it." A spark lit her eyes. "I'll be looking forward to Friday."

Her voice held a sultry tone. As he grabbed the paper her fingers drifted over his. He swallowed hard and crammed the paper and his fist into his pocket. With supreme effort, he kept from turning tail and running. What in God's name was wrong with him?

With a mumbled farewell, he stepped back, then strode toward the door. He forced himself not to look back, but the weight of her intense gaze followed him all the way to the sidewalk.

Once out of sight, he stopped to wipe the sweat from his

brow. He hadn't had much exposure to virgins. It made sense that he'd suffer some adverse reaction. That sense of happily-ever-after and white picket fences that seemed to hover around them just didn't sit well with him. He was allergic, that was all. He blew out a breath and relaxed. Surely in the three days to come he'd regain his composure.

One evening, a few short hours. He could manage that long with Cliff's sister. Once he got her to the party, he'd be done with her.

Then he'd claim his prize.

He smiled, forcing Darcy's image to replace Sabrina's in his mind. Dinner with Sabrina would be a walk in the park. He just had to remember to avoid her eyes and not touch her. A dark cloud passed over the sun. He frowned and hurried to his car.

2

MUSIC PLAYED SOFTLY overhead as Sabrina fingered the price tag of a clingy black dress. She sighed and glanced at Bess, her shopping companion. Thank goodness her friend had come along to help. Nothing in Sabrina's assortment of flowing skirts and dresses would do for her date with Noah. She needed Bess's discerning eye to pick just the right outfit.

She pulled the black dress from the rack, then draped it over her front. "Sexy. That's what I want. No flowers, no pastels and no ruffles."

"Well, I never thought I'd see the day." Bess laughed. She held up a wine-colored sheath for Sabrina's inspection. "Sexy I can help you with."

Sabrina nodded. Bess added the dress to the pile on her arm. "So, tell me more about Mr. Tall, Dark and Gorgeous," Bess said, shaking her head. "I still can't believe you're considering taking the big leap. You *are* going to get to know him first, make sure you like him, right?"

"Oh, I like him all right." Sabrina drew in a long breath. Her gaze drifted over the colorful racks. "He has these dark eyes. They're so intense, like he's looking into my soul, and his voice sent shivers up my spine. And that mouth of his—"

"Listen to you. I've never seen you like this."

Sabrina met Bess's gaze. "I think he's The One."

A small crinkle formed between Bess's brows. "Oh, hon,

I hope so. No one deserves to be happy more than you, I just…''

"You just don't want me over-romanticizing this." Sabrina laughed. "Just because you don't believe in love at first sight doesn't mean it doesn't exist. Plenty of studies have documented the physiological changes associated with love. All it takes is the right mixture of pheromones and bang!''

She smiled at her friend's wry expression. "Don't give me that look. This could be it. This could be the real thing.''

Bess gave her a worried glance, then held up a pantsuit, turning it to reveal a nonexistent back. "How's this?''

"Definitely sexy, but I'm betting Noah's a leg man.'' Sabrina added one more dress to her stack, then glanced over the number Bess held. "This should do for starters. We'll be here all night at this rate.''

"No problem." Bess sighed. "When I left, the girls were fighting, and Tom was glued to the TV, oblivious!'' She frowned. "I wonder if they've noticed I'm gone.''

An all-too-familiar empathy filled Sabrina. Shaking her head, she followed her friend past a row of faceless mannequins to the dressing area. Though motherhood had proven a blessing for Bess, who loved her children, a certain wistfulness sometimes filled her eyes. That look tore at Sabrina.

"I wouldn't have missed this for the world." Bess handed her several items from her pile as they reached the changing area. "It's about time you decided to dress like a woman.''

"What does that mean?" Sabrina hung up the garments. "I dress like a woman.''

"Yes, everything you own is feminine, in a flowing kind

of way, but in this…'' She picked up a plum-colored dress with a plunging neckline. "In this you'll be all woman.''

Sabrina snatched the dress, then closed the dressing room door.

She turned to the full-length mirror gracing one wall. Frowning, she surveyed her long, loose blouse and black leggings. Bess was right. One dress wouldn't be enough. Sabrina's wardrobe needed an overhaul. She sighed. Her *life* needed an overhaul.

She slipped out of the blouse and leggings. She'd had to dig deep into her drawer to find the matching black panties and demi-bra she now wore. The satiny fabric caressed her as she reached for the plum-colored dress. She slid one hand over the curve of her breast, rounded by the push-up bra. Tingles of sexual awareness shot through her and she sighed. Her cotton underthings had never made her feel this sexy. It was as though her encounter with Noah had freed her to explore her sensual self.

She bit her lip as the memory of his heated stare washed over her. How would he react to seeing her in her scant lingerie? Warmth spread through her. Her heart quickened the way it had when he'd threaded his fingers through her hair. That one innocent gesture had sent her hormones tripping. What would happen if he really touched her?

He filled her mind with fantasies that grew more stimulating with each passing day. She flushed at the memory of waking in a sweat that morning, the sheets tangled around her legs, and the dream of Noah's lovemaking fresh on her mind.

With a groan, she cupped her breasts and squeezed, while pressing her thighs together. The sexual ache only intensified. Could she make love with Noah?

She turned and her dream Noah, golden skin gleaming

in all his natural glory, grinned his sexy grin. "Have you missed me, my sweet? Do you ache for me again?"

He moved before her, so close his warm breath fanned her cheek. "Here, allow me."

She let his hands replace hers on her breasts. His palms cupped and squeezed her, while his fingers teased her taut nipples through the lace. A moan worked its way from her throat. His hot mouth covered the lace. He suckled her long and hard, the pleasure so intense she bit her lip to keep from crying out.

The ache between her thighs had become almost unbearable. She gasped as he pressed her to the wall, then wedged his knee between her legs, urging her to straddle him. He claimed her mouth, his tongue hot against hers, his hands coaching her hips to ride him, sending more pleasure burning through her.

Once she'd caught her rhythm he continued to kiss her, while rolling her nipples between his fingers, pushing her to a faster and faster pace.

"Yes," she murmured as the tension peaked inside her. "Yes, yes, yeeesss…"

Sabrina slumped against the dressing room wall. These fantasies were getting more intense. She *needed* to make love with Noah. She peered again into the mirror. She didn't look so innocent now wearing her sexy lingerie and flushed cheeks. Doubt assailed her. She may not look innocent, but she was. She'd never measure up to Noah's more experienced partners.

Setting aside her misgivings, she put on the plum-colored dress, then turned to the mirror. "Oh." She stared in wonder.

If possible, the dress proved more provocative than her lacy underwear. The fabric floated over her, skimming her curves and drifting in a silky sheen over her thighs. The scooping neckline exposed cleavage nonexistent without the demi-bra. As she slowly turned, confidence blossomed in her.

In this dress, Sabrina *was* all woman.

"Sabrina?" Bess called, then knocked on the door. "How's it going? I'm dying to see…"

Sabrina swung the door open, smiling at her friend's slack jaw. She stepped out and moved toward a three-sided mirror.

"Oh my." Bess stood beside her. "Sexy definitely works on you." She rubbed the satiny fabric between her fingers. "Did they have one of these in my size?"

Laughter bubbled from Sabrina's throat. "I don't even feel like me. I feel so…so exhilarated!" She spread her arms and spun. When she stopped, she grinned at her reflection. Her eyes sparkled and pink flushed her cheeks. "I almost feel like I could do anything in this dress."

"Like win the heart of a dedicated playboy? I know that look of yours, Sabrina—"

"Stop." Sabrina held up her hand. "I refuse to listen to any dire warnings." She caught Bess's eye in the mirror. "I'm a big girl. I'm tired of waiting for my life to happen." She squared her shoulders and turned her gaze back to her own reflection. "It's time I made my life happen."

"Honey, believe me. With that dress, things are going to happen. The question is, are you really ready? And can you do this without being emotionally involved?"

Sabrina stilled. The thrill of those few moments with Noah had sustained her for days. If she closed her eyes, she could see the appreciation in his dark gaze, feel her heart race and her soul lift with an instant recognition. It was as though meeting him had jolted her into awareness.

"He's The One, Bess." She let the quiet statement settle over them, then she turned with a smile. "You know, with the weather heating up I could use a new swimsuit and a sundress or two. So, let's see what else we can find. I think we're onto something here.''

THE SUN FILTERED through the garden window of Sabrina's compact kitchen, showering light on her assortment of begonias and miniature roses. A curl of steam drifted up from her big coffee cup. She glanced up and frowned at the date on her kitchen calendar. Friday the thirteenth, her big day. She lifted her mug in salute. ''Happy birthday to me.''

Ignoring a vague sense of impending doom, she focused on the night to come. The wall phone rang beside her. She swallowed the hot brew and lifted the receiver. ''Morning, Mom.''

''Happy birthday, darling. You aren't moping about, are you?'' Gabriella Walker's voice held its usual note of censure.

''Actually, no. I was just toasting the grand occasion.''

''Sabrina, it's nine in the morning. Surely you're not drinking?''

''Just coffee.''

''Decaf?''

Sabrina grimaced. ''No.''

''That caffeine will age you, dear, mark my word. You're such a beauty now. And young. Oh, to be young again. To have your figure, your skin. I'd take good care if I were you, I would. Unfortunately, men notice the package first, you know.'' In spite of her nagging, warmth laced Gabriella's words.

''You're still a beauty, Mom. I know Dad thinks so. You'll always be his Buttercup.''

A short silence stretched across the line.

''Mom?''

Her mother cleared her throat. ''Yes, dear. Our other line

is beeping in. I'll have your father call later. You enjoy the day. Close that shop of yours. Take some time off. I love you, Sabrina, my girl.'' Her voice trembled with emotion.

"I love you, too. Is everything all right?"

"Fine." She sniffled. Though her mother was all the way in West Palm Beach, Florida, Sabrina could almost see the tears in her eyes. "Gotta go. We'll see you next week."

Sabrina hung up and stared at the phone. Her mother had been practically sobbing. Sabrina shook her head. It was just like Gabriella to get all choked up over Sabrina's birthday.

She rinsed her cup, then grabbed her purse. Well, it was a special day. A smile tilted her lips. And tonight…tonight would be a night to remember.

ARE YOU REALLY READY? By late Friday afternoon, Sabrina had had plenty of time to mull over Bess's words. She pinched some brown leaves from a fern hanging by her bathroom window. Earth tones accented the pedestal sink and spacious garden tub that had sold her on this apartment.

She'd pamper herself, taking time to get ready. As she soaked in a lavender-scented bath, she closed her eyes. Her fantasy Noah came to her, his eyes glowing with desire.

"Ah, Sabrina, you mustn't keep me away so long." He stripped off his shirt, then knelt beside her. The muscles of his torso rippled as he leaned toward her. "Mmmm…" While nuzzling the tender spot behind her ear, he ran his fingertips along her collarbone. "Your sweet scent drives me wild."

His palm slid down to cup her breast. Her heart sped in anticipation as he lowered his head. He ran the pointed tip of his tongue over her nipple, then covered it with his mouth and suckled her long and hard. She moaned as the

*sensation swept through her, igniting that intimate ache
between her thighs.*

*As he moved to lave her other breast, he swept his hand
down into the scented water, over the trembling curve of
her stomach. She raised her hips and parted her thighs as
his strong fingers sifted through her thatch of curls, to the
hidden folds of her femininity.*

*Her blood pounded in her ears. Heat engulfed her.
"Noah!"*

The pealing of the phone brought her upright with a start.
Water sloshed over the tub's edge. Grumbling, she stepped
from the bath, then wrapped herself in a fluffy white towel.

She grabbed the antique phone beside her bed on its third
ring. "Hello?"

"Sabrina?" Noah's unmistakable baritone sent goose-
flesh skittering up her arms.

"Noah. Hello." She stopped, frowning. He was supposed to pick her up in less than an hour. Why was he
calling?

"Hey. I wanted to let you know I'm running a little
late."

"Oh." Relief swept over her. He wasn't canceling their
date. "No problem." Heat rose in her cheeks as she
glanced at her towel-clad figure. She'd spent too much time
in the tub. "Take as long as you need. I'm not quite ready
myself."

After confirming the directions to her apartment, she
hung up, then raced to get ready. A little over an hour later,
she touched up the lipstick that was shades darker than her
usual hue. An unprecedented boldness filled her as she
stood before her full-length mirror.

Cliff and Mona were out of town and no one else knew
of this special day. Other than that call from her mother,
and a subsequent one from her father, Sabrina's birthday

had gone unremarked. But rather than wallow in her earlier depression, she savored the coming night.

No doubt, Noah thought of their evening together as a simple dinner date, but to her it was much more. Whether they parted tonight with a chaste kiss or progressed to greater intimacy, one thing was certain. She'd enjoy a birthday gift of her own—the gift of pretend.

Tonight she'd dine with her dream lover.

The doorbell chimed. Sabrina's heart skipped a beat. She spritzed on perfume, a unique floral blend, then sauntered to the door. Noah stood on the other side, devastating in pleated slacks, a collarless shirt and sports coat. She dragged her gaze up his length, marveling that he'd actually come for her.

"Hello," she said. Her fingers itched to trace the firm contour of his jaw, to see if it felt as smooth as it looked. Her gaze stopped to admire his mouth, with that little indent in the middle of his full bottom lip. Would his kisses be as thrilling as she'd imagined?

"You're wearing that?"

Her gaze flew to his. His eyes shone, dark and piercing as before, but without a trace of the approval she'd expected. He almost looked angry.

She gestured for him to enter. "You don't like my dress?"

He stood unmoving for a moment, his jaw squared, his gaze fastened to her chest. Self-conscious, she glanced down at the cleavage she'd been so happy to discover. Was he disappointed?

"You'll freeze. It's going to be cool tonight." He moved past her into her apartment, bringing in his woodsy scent. "The restaurant is likely to be cold, too. You'd better cover up."

She stared at his back. This was Noah, the lady-killer?

He was supposed to drool over her and her new bustline. "Don't be silly. It's almost eighty degrees outside. I'll be fine."

With his hands crammed into his pockets, he turned toward her. "You're ready, then? We have reservations."

"Let me just get my purse." Frowning, she turned from him. The man could use a refresher course in finesse. She raised her chin, resolved to have a good time, in spite of him. Certainly, his smooth manners didn't keep the women coming back for more.

She smiled. Could it be, he made up for it in bed?

THE MURMUR of conversations surrounded them as waiters moved efficiently between white-topped tables. Noah gripped his glass of scotch and stared at the painted brick wall that noted the restaurant's noble conversion from a pre-Civil War warehouse. A wall sconce flickered above them, casting odd shadows across the rough surface.

Frustration swelled in him. He glanced around the room. Was it his imagination, or was every man staring at Sabrina? Stephen, their waiter, approached and Noah could have sworn the guy checked out Sabrina's breasts. Why hadn't she covered up, like he'd suggested? Not a single man in the restaurant had missed her entrance.

She shone tonight, turning heads wherever they went.

Stephen leaned toward her. "I suggest the blush, a fine wine for a fine lady."

Noah gripped a butter knife. Was the man flirting with her?

Her musical laughter filled the air. Her fingertips grazed the waiter's arm. "Well, I trust your judgment. The blush it will be."

Stephen left and she cast a sideways glance at Noah. His gut tightened. Why was it her every gesture exacted a response in him? He hadn't forgotten their first brief meeting. All week, she'd filled his thoughts. And his fantasies.

Sabrina scooted her chair forward and her breasts moved in sync. He suppressed a moan. She had no right sounding and looking the way she did.

She's a virgin.

He'd repeated those words to himself when she'd greeted him in that dress and his throat had gone dry. He'd silently said them again when he'd helped her into his car and her fresh flowery scent made him dizzy with need. Then, he'd recited the reminder as he escorted her to her seat.

Regardless, his hand had found the small of her back and the warmth of her skin through the thin dress. She'd moved against him in an inviting way, her hip brushing his. His pulse had kicked up a notch and he'd wordlessly chanted his mantra.

She's a virgin.

"Do you like working with Cliff?" She took a sip of water, then used her napkin to blot a stray droplet from her chest.

Noah forced his gaze away. "It's great." Still holding the knife, he drew circles on the linen tablecloth with its end.

She's a virgin.

"Oh. So, do you like being back in Atlanta?"

"It's fine."

"You miss Denver, then?"

"Not really."

"Well, I should warn you, this has been an unusually pleasant spring. For the last couple of years, the pollen seems to have gotten much heavier. I keep inside for days when the pines are in bloom."

He nodded and slipped the butter knife back onto his bread plate. Stephen approached with her glass of wine.

Without so much as a glance in Noah's direction, he set the glass before her. He straightened, remaining beside her chair as she took a tentative sip.

"Mmmm, yes, that's perfect." The pink tip of her tongue darted across her lips.

Stephen leaned closer to her. "And for dinner, may I suggest the roasted duck? It bastes in its own juices, until it's tender and moist. It is most succulent."

Blood roared in Noah's ears. Was he hearing things, or had the man drawn out the word in a disgusting way? He hovered over Sabrina, and it seemed that he was practically drooling on her. Noah tensed.

She wrinkled her nose. Even that gesture didn't distract from her beauty. She had to be the sexiest woman he'd ever come up against. "I don't know," she said. "I got sick the last time I ate duck."

The waiter pursed his lips. "Perhaps the prime rib?" To Noah's ears, the waiter's voice grew husky. "How would you like a great piece of meat?"

"That's it!" Noah sprang to his feet, flattening his hands on the table. "Just back off! She's a vir...go."

3

BLOOD POUNDED in Sabrina's ears as Noah sank back into his seat. His chair creaked in the sudden silence.

Stephen ran his hand down the front of his white dress shirt. "I'll…get you some fresh rolls." He looked curiously at Noah, then scuttled away without a backward glance.

Slowly, the tables around them returned to their former buzz. Sabrina stared at her date in stunned silence. He knew. Damn Cliff! Her brother had no right divulging such personal information.

Heat climbed her neck. Anger and embarrassment warred in her. Was her virginity the reason for Noah's brusque behavior?

"I'm…sorry." Noah heaved out a breath. "I didn't mean to cause a scene."

Not trusting herself to answer, she pursed her lips and counted to ten.

He had the decency to look embarrassed. "I may have overreacted. I thought he was flirting with you."

"Flirting with me?"

"You should have covered up, like I suggested. Everyone's been staring…." He stopped as Stephen returned. With careful movements, he presented a steaming basket of soft rolls, then left.

Sabrina stared after the waiter. If the man had flirted with her, she hadn't noticed. Even if he had, that didn't give

Noah cause to act like a caveman. He hadn't exactly paid her any attention.

She'd tried everything to raise some response in him. Her subtle glances had gone unseen. He'd been unaffected by her rapt attention and open body language. In growing frustration, she'd even brushed up against him. He hadn't noticed.

She reached over and fingered the bread basket. "He had no right."

"The waiter?" Noah froze with a roll halfway to his plate. "He *was* flirting?"

"I meant Cliff."

He set down the roll. His gaze met hers. "Oh."

Despite the heat in her cheeks, she maintained eye contact. "Let me guess. He found out about tonight and read you the riot act. Of course, he made sure you knew *all* the facts."

Noah stared back at her for another moment, then dropped his gaze to his plate. "It's no big deal. Your secret's safe with me. It's your own business if you want to save yourself for true love."

Her heart thudded. "You're right. It's my business."

"You don't really believe in all that stuff?"

"Stuff?"

He waved his hand in dismissal. "Love and happily-ever-after." His chair creaked again as he leaned his elbows on the table. "It doesn't exist, though. I have seen enough relationships crash and burn to know that. This is real life, not some fairy tale."

She straightened. Indignation poured through her. How could she have ever thought he was The One? "Maybe to someone whose relationship aspirations peak with a one-night stand, true love is a concept too complex to grasp."

"True love is a myth. It's created by people who aren't

comfortable with lust. Half of all marriages end in divorce. What does that say?''

"It says half of all marriages work. My parents have been married for over thirty years, and their love is as pure as the day they met.''

The man had the audacity to laugh. "I'll tell you what I think. You're getting defensive here, because deep down you're afraid I'm right." He leaned back and folded his arms across his chest. "You're not getting younger, your internal clock's ticking and where's Mr. Right? Maybe he doesn't exist.''

She stared at him in mute outrage.

He leaned forward. "Look, I hope you find him, really.'' His gaze swept her. "He'll be one hell of a lucky guy.''

Horrified by the jump in her pulse, she reached for her purse. If she spent one more minute with this man, she'd scream. "I'm not very hungry. Would you mind taking me home?'' Craning her neck, she glanced around for their waiter.

For a moment, Noah looked as if he might argue, then he shook his head and stood. "I've got a quick call to make, then we'll leave.'' Without waiting for her to respond, he strode off toward the back of the restaurant.

SABRINA STARED out the passenger window, ignoring Noah and the strained silence hanging over them. She could not believe she'd thought that he was The One. Noah might look the part of her dream lover, but his qualifications ended there. Her dream lover didn't think love was just lust in disguise. Despite the physical attraction, she couldn't possibly consider making love with such a cynic.

A street sign flashed past. She straightened. "Where are we going? My apartment's back the other way!''

His big hands palmed the wheel. He lounged in the

driver's seat, seemingly unaware of the tense atmosphere. Clearly he didn't realize his rude manners had resulted in the worst date of her life—and the shattering of her fantasy.

He answered without glancing her way. "I have an errand to run."

"An errand?" She stared in disbelief. He'd planned an errand in the middle of their date? "What kind of errand?"

At last he met her gaze. A surprising mischief lit his dark eyes. "I promised to feed your brother's dog."

"Opal? She's Mona's dog." She folded her arms. This made no sense. "What about that neighbor that looks after her?"

"Out of town."

"Why did he ask you, then, and not me? I'm family."

Noah shrugged. "I offered." He shifted, focusing on the road. "Actually, I thought we could both do it." He threw her a half grin. "I need you to protect me from that maneater."

A short laugh burst from her. "What makes you think I won't just let her have you?"

He eyed her for a moment, before his lips parted in a full smile. "I'll take my chances."

Caught off guard by the sexiness of that smile, she could only nod. Chastising herself for the unwanted jump in her pulse, she turned back to the side window.

Sabrina squared her jaw. She'd have to stay on guard to keep from being fooled by Noah's nice packaging. She *definitely* wasn't interested.

After ten minutes of silence they pulled into Cliff's drive. Sabrina's gaze drifted over the pristine lawn fronting her brother's house. Well-tended flowers winked at her from window boxes set along the lower level of the two-story structure. It was a complete picture that reflected Cliff's life. He had it all—career, house, loving bride-to-be.

Longing welled up inside her. Hadn't she worked as hard as he to achieve that? So why didn't she have it?

Noah got out and moved around to her door. "Coming?"

She hesitated for a moment, then couldn't resist the image of him at Opal's mercy. "Why not?" Again, his easy smile sent ripples of awareness through her. She set her teeth and preceded him up the walk.

With a clinking of keys he unlocked the door, then motioned for her to enter. She stepped into the dark interior. "That's funny. They always leave a light on for that dog." Turning, she felt along the wall for the switch plate, alarmed by his nearness as he pressed through the door behind her.

Her heart hammered. How could she still react to him after his uncouth behavior? Her anxiety rose as the light switch eluded her. The last thing she needed was to be alone with this man in the dark.

She swung her arm in a wider search. Relief flowed through her as her fingertips grazed the plate. She let out her breath and flipped the switch. Light flooded the room.

"Surprise!" A chorus of voices greeted her.

Blinking, she turned, astonished by the sea of familiar faces filling Cliff's great room. A huge banner spread across one end of the room, wishing her a happy birthday. Balloons of every hue added spots of color throughout the lofty space.

"Bess? What is this?" She returned Bess's exuberant hug.

The stereo came alive with the strains of an old Jimmy Buffett song. Bess drew back, smiling as the crowd of well-wishers swarmed Sabrina. "It's your surprise party, silly. Happy birthday." She laughed and hugged Sabrina again.

"Sabrina." Mona pushed forward, her blond curls framing her flushed face. She pressed a kiss in the air above

Sabrina's cheek. "Were you surprised? Noah didn't give it away?"

"Noah?" Sabrina twisted around, but he'd melted into the crowd. She turned back to Mona, strangely disappointed. "No...I had no idea."

"He gave us a start when he called. We really had to scramble. We weren't expecting you so soon."

Heat again filled Sabrina's cheeks. "We finished early." Her traitorous stomach announced its emptiness at that moment.

Whether or not Mona heard the rumbling over Buffett's crooning, she took Sabrina's arm to lead her to a table laden with food. "Try these crab cakes. I'm working with a new caterer, and I need your opinion."

Sabrina turned to Mona. "I can't believe you had time to plan this with the wedding next weekend."

"I didn't want your birthday to get lost in the shuffle. I never had a sister, Sabrina. I wanted to get us off on the right foot."

"Thank you." Sabrina's gaze swept the room, while unwanted emotion clogged her throat. "This was very thoughtful of you."

Guilt tightened her chest. Maybe she hadn't given Mona a fair shake. It wasn't her fault that ever since Cliff had met her, Sabrina's emotional state had taken a downhill slide.

A smile lit Mona's face. "Actually, you'll have to thank Uncle John. This was his idea."

"Uncle John?"

"He's just dying to meet you. I've told him so much about how great you are with Cliff."

Shifting, Sabrina pressed her hand to her rumbling tummy. "It'll be my pleasure. He'll be at the wedding?"

Mona laughed. "He'd better be. In fact, he's flying in

early to help me tie up the loose ends. I'd never get through this affair without Uncle John's organizational skills. The man just knows how to get things done! He's a real planner.'' She gestured to the spread of food. "Eat!"

At her stomach's insistence, Sabrina put aside her questions about Uncle John and took Mona's advice. She ate her fill, then mingled with her friends. She'd caught little more than fleeting glimpses of Noah in the hour since their arrival. Putting thoughts of him aside, she lifted her chin and accepted a wine cooler from Pete Henderson, one of her neighbors.

Two years ago, Pete's wife had left him for another woman. Sabrina had gone out on one uneventful date with him. Though they remained friends, neither had pursued a second outing.

She eyed his thick auburn hair and ready smile. By most standards, her neighbor passed as an attractive man. Had she dismissed him too quickly?

She studied his lips and the shape of his mouth. How would it feel to kiss him?

He swiped a napkin across his mouth. "Have I made a mess with that dip?"

Her gaze swung to his. "No. You're fine."

"Oh…the way you were staring…"

"I just…" She shifted. Warmth spread across her cheeks. Why hadn't she ever learned to flirt? "You have nice lips."

A deep groove formed between his brows. "Thanks." He straightened. "There's your brother. Where's he been?"

She turned. "He had business in Boca." Cliff greeted Mona near the door. Sabrina narrowed her eyes. "Excuse me. I need to have a word with my dear brother."

A look of relief crossed Pete's face as she turned to

leave. She squared her shoulders, her earlier anger returning. Had Cliff shared her secret with Pete, too?

Making clipped responses to several greetings, she
crossed the room. Cliff moved off down a back hall, briefcase in hand. Sabrina followed, her anger growing with
every step. Brother or not, he had no right interfering in
her affairs.

He entered his study, leaving the door ajar. She hurried
her steps.

"Cliff! You made it." Noah's baritone stopped her in
her tracks.

"I see you two found each other. I hope I wasn't interrupting."

A low feminine laugh drifted through the doorway. "Of
course you were, but I won't complain, since you set us
up."

Sabrina maneuvered closer to peer through the opening.
Noah stood beside a high-backed chair, his arms folded
across his chest. A curvy blonde pressed into his side, while
her hand possessively climbed his arm. Outrage filled Sabrina.

The blonde ran her red-tipped finger along his chin.
"When Cliff told me I was your bribe to get his sister here,
I was flattered beyond words."

Bribe? Sabrina clenched her fists. Fury blurred her vision. Cliff used this blonde to bribe Noah to take her out?
Now, here he was, like some hormonal teen, hanging out
with the bimbo, while still on *their* date? Who did he think
he was?

She straightened. Why was she upset? The bimbo could
have him. They were probably made for each other. Noah
Banks was the last man Sabrina needed.

She turned and stormed down the hall. To think she'd
imagined herself falling for him. How childish she'd been.

Well, today she was twenty-five, old enough to put away her foolish fantasies. Maybe she'd never find Mr. Right, but that didn't mean she couldn't start living.

NOAH STOOD beside open French doors, and tossed back a long swallow of beer. Darcy leaned into him, continuing her one-sided conversation. He'd suggested they join the party at the first opportunity. His breath had come easier once they reached the bright lights, calypso music and festive atmosphere of the open great room.

He'd gone to Cliff's study to let him know he wasn't interested in meeting Darcy. It didn't seem right now that he'd met Sabrina. Unfortunately, Darcy had followed him and made the introduction herself.

Sabrina's lyrical laughter rose above the friendly ruckus. Straining, he glimpsed her through a crowd of men gathered around her. His gut tightened. The woman was an accomplished flirt. She had no right being a virgin.

Darcy rubbed against him. "Maybe we should slip away." She nodded toward Sabrina. "Your 'date' would hardly notice."

Gritting his teeth, he straightened away from her. "I should see that she has a ride home."

"Darling, really, I don't think you need to worry about her. Let's go to my place. It isn't far."

He faced the woman Cliff had dangled before him like a carrot. Somehow, her appeal had lessened. Her curves remained in all the right places and proportions, but his enthusiasm had evaporated.

"If you'll excuse me, I need to check on Sabrina." As Darcy stared at him with wide eyes, he turned, then headed across the room. He had brought Sabrina. In spite of their less than perfect start, she was his date. Common courtesy demanded he attempt to socialize with her. He squared his shoulders and moved through the crowd.

SABRINA LOWERED HER GAZE and smiled. She wasn't a bad flirt, after all. Pete and the half-dozen other single men around her all stared in rapt attention. Unlike Noah, they responded well to her candid glances and suggestive body language. With a gentle touch here, a smile there, she'd included each one in the conversation.

"Okay, who can answer this?" She leaned forward and they moved as one, shifting in, tightening the circle.

With deliberate motions, she lifted her wine cooler to her lips and emptied the bottle, then she eyed them one by one and smiled. A thrill shot through her. For once in her life she felt desirable. "What is your favorite means of seduction?"

"Seduction?" Pete blinked his hazel eyes.

"Mmm-hmm." She focused on him. "If a woman were to seduce you, how would you want her to go about it?"

"Well…" His gaze swept over her. "She'd wear something soft and sexy—"

"Something that showed off her breasts," said the redhead beside him.

"One of those teddy things," another added.

"No." Pete touched her hand. "It isn't what she wears."

"Right." Brendan, her brother's accountant, leaned forward. "It's the way a woman kisses that really turns me on."

"Yeah."

"Right."

"Oh?" Sabrina turned to Brendan. "How so?"

He grinned. "You know, she starts slow, with her lips—"

"No," one of Cliff's friends to her left interrupted. "I want her whole mouth—"

"With a full body meld," the redhead added. A movement behind him caught her eye. Her heart skipped a beat. Noah pushed through the crowd toward them.

The irrational need to prove her desirability to him rose in her. She cast a look around the group. "Maybe one of you should show me."

"Right."

"Yeah."

"Cliff won't like it."

"True."

"What about that big guy you came with?"

As one, the circle fell back.

Sabrina spread her hands in appeal. "Where's your sense of adventure?"

"Your brother's got a temper."

"Your date didn't look too congenial, either."

"Yeah, why can't he show you?"

Noah loomed closer. Sabrina bit her lip. She laid her empty bottle on the coffee table. "Let's see which one of you shows me." With a flick of her wrist, she spun the bottle.

Pete dove to the left. Brendan dodged to the right. The redhead flung himself over the back of the couch, out of the bottle's range. Sabrina pursed her lips. So much for feeling desirable.

The bottle rotated to a stop. She swallowed as her gaze traveled up the corded thighs and broad chest of the glowering figure standing before her. Dismay filled her. "Well, Noah," she said, "looks like you win."

4

NOAH'S ATTENTION SWEPT over Sabrina's scattered admirers. What had gotten into them? The lot looked as though they'd escaped a stint on death row. "Win what?"

"There." A guy with red hair peeked over the back of the couch. "I told you he should be the one to show you."

"Show you what?" Noah demanded.

A devilish spark lit Sabrina's eye. She stood, then moved around the coffee table, stopping inches from him. "We were discussing the most effective means of seduction."

Noah narrowed his eyes. An irrational anger swelled in him. "The hell you were."

"Oh yes." She leaned toward him. Her palm grazed his chest. His pulse kicked into gear. "The consensus seems to be that it's all in the kiss."

"Kiss?"

"That's right, but not everyone agreed on what constituted the sexiest kiss, so I thought someone should show me." Her glance fell to the table. "And I let the bottle decide who that someone would be."

He stared at the bottle, aimed at him. Adrenaline spurted through his veins. He'd won at spin the bottle. Maybe if his whole body hadn't tensed in anticipation, he might have laughed.

He inhaled her wildflower scent. Desire flooded him. She tiptoed, brushing against him, her luscious mouth a breath from his. He let out a stifled groan, made a move to grab her, then stopped. "Not in front of an audience," he murmured.

Taking her hand, he led her out the closest exit, a side door leading to a thankfully empty deck. She was in his arms before he had time to think. Whether he scooped her up, or she put herself there, wasn't clear. All he knew was that her sweet mouth beckoned him with an urgency he couldn't ignore.

He explored her lips with tiny nips and gentle caresses. Then, framing her face with his palms, he ventured farther into her welcoming kiss. She anchored her fingers in his hair and met the tentative stroke of his tongue. For long, drugging moments he lost himself in her warmth.

A small moan escaped her. She moved against him, her breasts pressed to his chest. His hands roamed over her back, then her hips, while he savored her firm contour. Sweet. She was sweet and wild all at once, like nothing he'd ever experienced. Some unnamed emotion rose in him, triggering an innate protectiveness.

Angling his head, he parried the hungry thrust of her tongue and slid his palms up her sides, past her waist. His heart hammered. She shifted, allowing him better access as his thumbs skimmed the lower swells of her breasts.

"Um, 'scuse me guys," Darcy's voice sounded behind him.

Noah jerked away from Sabrina. He caught one glimpse of her stunned expression, before turning to the blonde.

Darcy's gaze wandered sadly over him. "Guess this means you're not coming back to my place."

"Darcy, I—"

"It's okay." She held up her hand. "All's fair in love and…you know. I'll survive. I, um, really wanted to warn you that Cliff is looking for the birthday girl. Something tells me he might not be too pleased to find the two of you playing tongue hockey.''

''No, I don't imagine he would be.'' Sabrina brushed past Noah, stopping beside Darcy. She glanced at Noah and something hard glittered in her eyes. Then she turned to Darcy. ''Thanks for the reminder.''

Noah straightened as she turned back to him. God, she was beautiful. Her eyes flashed, pink stained her cheeks and her whole face glowed.

''Seems I lost my head for a moment.'' She turned, then pushed through the door, back into the party.

''Now wait a minute!'' Noah bolted after her, his heart thudding. He reached for her as she rejoined her group of admirers, but she twisted away, ignoring him.

Turning to one of her entourage, she asked, ''Pete, could you drive me home?''

Noah drew up to his full height. The man glanced his way. Noah stared evenly at him, sending a silent challenge. With a shake of his head, Pete shrank back into the sofa cushions.

''For goodness' sake.'' Sabrina glared at Noah.

He glared back. What was she mad about? A moment ago she'd nearly combusted in his arms. ''I'll take you home.''

She smiled a stiff smile and looked beyond his shoulder. ''Thank you, but I wouldn't want to keep you from your...bribe.''

A sick feeling hit the pit of his stomach. He turned to see Darcy at his side.

''Enough.'' Noah stepped away from Darcy and reached again for Sabrina. His throat tightened at the flicker of hurt in her blue gaze.

A tall, slender blonde pushed past Mona, who had just arrived, her wide-eyed gaze taking them all in. ''I'll take you," the slender blonde said. She gave Noah a curious look as she stepped to Sabrina's side. "Let's get you out of here."

"Thanks, Bess." Sabrina's hands opened, then closed into fists. Her gaze swept back to Noah. "And thank you, for a most…enlightening evening."

Noah swallowed. That sick feeling inside him grew. What had he done? "Sabrina—"

"Good night, Mona." Sabrina gave her a quick hug. "Thanks for the party."

Mona frowned. "Is everything okay? Are you sure you want to leave so soon?"

"Everything's fine. It was a wonderful party. Thanks for all your hard work." Sabrina glanced back again at Noah. "I'm sorry. I'm just really tired."

Her icy tone sent chills down his spine. Regret rooted him to the floor as she turned with Bess, then left.

Twenty minutes later, Sabrina sank into the pile of antique lace pillows strewn across her four-poster bed. She'd spent days scouring dozens of flea markets and antique dealers to find them. She captured one, bunching it between her palms. "That's it, Bess, the last straw."

The bed dipped as Bess sat beside her. "I can understand you're upset, but just because your brother and his partner are jerks doesn't mean you should toss aside your values."

Sabrina smashed the pillow into the mattress. "What have my values gotten me?"

"Bree, you've got a great life. You own your own business. At twenty-five that's quite an accomplishment. You have this wonderful apartment, and you're free to come and go as you please. No strings tying you down."

"Maybe I want some strings."

"And getting laid by the first willing male will do that?"

"Hah, willing, there's the problem. No one wants me because I'm a virgin, so how the hell am I supposed to lose my virginity?" She rolled over and tossed the pillow to the floor. "I don't know. I just know I can't go on like I have. Something has to change. *I* have to change."

"You're not the type to have a one-night stand, though. Think about it. When you take on a project, you always go all out. Remember when you wanted to repaint the dining room and ended up holed up in here painting every wall of every room?"

"And the ceilings. Boy, were my arms aching."

"Then what about the time you wanted to make a shelf for some of your knickknacks and you ended up with..." She gestured to the floor-to-ceiling unit gracing the far wall.

"Who would have thought I had it in me?"

"Then look at the bookstore."

Sabrina blew out a breath. She'd gone in for a part-time job, then ended up buying the place. "I'd always planned on owning a bookstore once I'd earned my business degree."

"But you see my point. You won't be satisfied with a one-night stand. You'll want a relationship, and trust me, that isn't the way to start one."

With a sudden movement, Sabrina sat upright. "See, that's where you're wrong. The old Sabrina may have felt that way, but the new me won't. He took a woman as a bribe, Bess. And did you see her? How am I supposed to compete with that? I'm reinventing myself. Drastic times call for drastic measures."

She drew herself up. "It's time I lost my virginity."

"Sabrina—"

"My mind's made up. In fact, I've already planned the rest of the weekend away. It's the perfect opportunity."

"So, you're talking about some type of affair, then, because I still don't see you having a one-night stand."

"A fling, I think."

"A fling?"

Excitement poured through Sabrina. "Yes, that's it. A weekend fling. That should do it."

Bess shook her head. "You'll get attached."

"Not if he's from out of town."

Bess's brows rose in question.

"Cliff's probably warned every single guy in Atlanta. I've got a reservation at a beach resort. I leave for Florida first thing in the morning. I'll find myself a weekend fling."

"You're not serious."

Sabrina swung her legs over the side of the bed, and waved to where her bags stood packed and waiting. "Oh, but I am."

NOAH GRIPPED the steering wheel and glared at the red traffic light. The air had grown heavy. Moisture swirled around the streetlights, distorting their glow.

Guilt gnawed at him. The memory of the look on Sabrina's face as she'd confronted him tightened his gut. When he'd made that deal with Cliff, he hadn't thought of the consequences. He hadn't thought of Sabrina. At the time, she'd been a faceless chore, a means to his selfish ends, not a flesh-and-blood woman.

The light changed. He whipped into a parking lot, then circled around toward her apartment. He had to see her, had to apologize—somehow explain how all that had changed once they'd met. Darcy meant nothing to him. Any fleeting attraction he may have felt for her evaporated once he saw her beside Sabrina.

He let his memory roll back over that incredible kiss. *She's a virgin.* The old mantra haunted him. Cliff had probably been right to keep him away from Sabrina, but now having seen her, met her...kissed her, there was no possible way Noah could stay away from her.

Closing his eyes, he groaned. The whole time she'd known about Darcy. She'd been baiting him, no doubt, knowing the memory of her hot mouth would torment him. Guess he deserved that.

Thunder rumbled in the distance as he sped down the interstate. The first fat droplets splattered his windshield as he turned the corner to her apartment. Tucked back off the main road, the complex rose like a dark fortress braced by tall pines, oaks and maples.

He glanced at the clock on his dash before he exited his car. It was after midnight. His pulse quickened as he climbed the short flight of stairs to her door. Light seeped through her front curtains. She was still awake.

Drawing on his resolve, he knocked. The curtains parted a fraction, then fell back into place. For one long moment he held his breath, willing her to turn the knob. The door opened, just enough for her to peer out. He exhaled.

"What are you doing here?"

The flat tone of her voice had him wincing. "May I come in...please?" He ground out the unfamiliar word.

She hesitated a moment, then stepped back and gestured him in. "Why not?"

Her floral scent surrounded him as he brushed past. She wore a thin robe that brushed the tops of her thighs. His blood warmed. He let his gaze skim the pointed tips of her breasts, outlined by the silky fabric, then quickly diverted his eyes.

He took in the main living space of her apartment in one glance. The glow of a ceramic lamp on a side table lent a warmth and closeness he hadn't noticed earlier, probably because he hadn't been able to take his eyes off her. The room had an inviting appeal. Picture frames and cat figurines dotted the area, and potted plants covered every available tabletop and shelf.

"What are you doing here?" she asked again.

"I came to talk to you...about tonight," he said.

"I would have thought you'd be otherwise engaged by now."

He drew in a deep breath. She wasn't making this easy. "As I said, I'd like to explain."

She stared at him, her brows raised and her arms crossed over her rounded breasts.

With an effort, he dragged his gaze upward. "Look, Sabrina, I'm sorry about that stupid deal I made with your brother. I never considered how you'd be affected. It was thoughtless and cruel."

Thunder rumbled in the distance. She narrowed her eyes, then let her arms drop to her sides. "Okay, apology accepted. It was good of you to come all this way. Now, I have a big day planned tomorrow."

He blinked. "That's it? You're not going to tell me what a jerk I was?"

"Since you're aware of the fact, why waste my breath?"

"What I did was rotten. I'd like to make it up to you."

She eyed him a moment, then shrugged. "That isn't necessary. I've accepted your apology. You can run along back to your bimbo."

He gritted his teeth and stepped closer to her. "I don't care if I never again lay eyes on Darcy."

"Well, that certainly isn't my business. It isn't as though you need to report your comings and goings to me." She picked up a brass picture frame from the end table. "Why not?"

"Why not what?"

Her fingers absently stroked the glass-covered photograph. "Why aren't you with her? I thought that was the idea—the reason you took me to dinner."

He swore under his breath. "It was, but I didn't know you when I agreed to that whole thing. It just wasn't right."

Sabrina set the picture back on the table. "Well, I'm sorry the night didn't work out for you."

"It wasn't all bad." His gaze held hers. "Parts of it are quite memorable."

She swallowed and closed her eyes. When she opened them, a warm glow illuminated their depths. "You didn't mind it, then—that kiss? I suppose I should apologize for it. I wanted to get back at you, to make you think I was desirable."

He couldn't take his gaze from her mouth. "How could I think otherwise? In case you didn't notice, I was enjoying that kiss far more than I had a right to."

Her teeth sank into her bottom lip. She set down the picture, then moved toward him. "I did it to make you jealous." Pink tinged her cheeks. "I mean, I meant for one of the others to kiss me." A sigh escaped her. "But none of them seemed interested."

"Fools."

"You were, then?" She smiled.

Desire beat through his veins. "I was what?"

"Jealous."

"Hell, yes."

Her lips parted. She placed her hand on his chest, over the place where his heart pounded. "You didn't need to be."

God, what was it about her that made him want to beat his chest and roar? Her simple statement sent euphoria tripping through him. He pressed his hand over hers. "Sabrina I—"

"Kiss me again, Noah." She held his gaze, her eyes

warm, but hesitant. "No one's ever made me feel that way."

He stilled. She tiptoed. The full length of her body hugged his. Her breath whispered across his lips, then her mouth brushed his. He stood motionless, tormented.

She made a soft, sighing sound, and touched her tongue to his lower lip. With a moan, he swept his arms around her. In a single motion he claimed her mouth, his tongue meeting no resistance in mating with hers. He drank deeply of her sweetness, somehow feeling redeemed by the power of her kiss.

He closed his eyes, desire ripping through him as she moved against him. He skimmed his hands up her arms, over her shoulders, then down her back. She threaded her fingers through his hair as he reached low to cup her bottom. She moaned softly into his mouth. He lifted her, kneading her firm buttocks and pressing her into his hardness.

She drew back, her eyes dilated, her face flushed, and her lips round and tempting. Slowly, she pulled on the tie of her robe until it loosened, then fluttered to the floor. Arching her back, she parted her robe. "Touch me."

Noah's gaze riveted to her bare breasts. She was more beautiful than he'd imagined. The creamy white of her skin accented her ruddy nipples. He ached to touch her, to draw her into his mouth and taste her.

His chest heaved. Closing his eyes, he set her on her feet. "Sabrina, if I do, I won't be able to stop."

She cupped his face with her palms. "Maybe I don't want you to stop. You want me, Noah. I can feel it."

A raw laugh burst from his throat. "I won't deny that, but it doesn't matter."

"It's all that matters. I want you, too."

Her words both provoked and halted him at once. He

drew a breath and willed himself to move away from her, but the heat of her body and the promise in her eyes held him.

He shook his head.

Moisture gathered in her eyes. "Please. I'm twenty-five and a virgin. In this day and age that makes me some kind of freak. I promise, no strings. I just need to know what it feels like to truly be a woman.

"It's time. If not you, then someone else." Her gaze pinned him. "I'm not sure why, but I want you."

He tamped down the swell of male pride that rose at her words. His chest tightened. Cliff couldn't protect her forever. The thought of another man touching her sent a different heat swirling through Noah. The determined jut of her chin confirmed her intent. She'd find someone else.

"I don't believe in love, Sabrina."

Her chin came up another notch. "I said no strings. I'm not asking you to love me, just to make love to me."

She shrugged her robe off her shoulders, letting it slip to the floor. She stood before him, clad only in lacy black panties that offered tantalizing hints of her true femininity. With one slim finger, she drew his face close to hers. "I don't want to be alone tonight. Do you?"

He inhaled, breathing in her soft floral scent and something more elusive, some essence that was hers alone. It was a potent combination, God help him. "No."

5

SABRINA SMILED. Relief rolled over her. Her own boldness amazed her, but she'd never yearned for anything more. Noah had instilled a great hunger in her, making her body ache with need. She took him by the hand. "Then come to bed."

He made no protest as he followed her to her bedroom, stopping her only when they reached the big four-poster. After pulling back the covers, he turned to her, then brought his lips down again on hers. He reclaimed her mouth with the steady thrust of his tongue, kissing her while he lowered her gently to the mattress. His hands kneaded her breasts, rubbing their erect centers until she moaned with pleasure.

She tugged at his shirt, pulling it from his waistband. He broke away to whip the garment over his head. Sighing, she let her gaze drift over his sculpted torso. Her pulse quickened.

His shoes and slacks joined his shirt on the floor, then he stretched out beside her. With one long finger, he traced the curve of her breast. "You take my breath away."

Blood pounded in her ears. She'd never been alone with a man like this before, but somehow, with Noah she felt safe. Excitement filled her. She trailed her fingers over his hard chest, toying with his male nipple. To her delight, he made a low guttural sound of pleasure.

"Tell me what to do," she said.

"Let me taste you." He lowered his head. The pointed tip of his tongue flicked across her nipple.

She nearly came up off the bed. Heat shot through her, settling in the apex of her thighs. He laughed lightly, then drew her into his mouth. He suckled her for what seemed an eternity, moving from one breast to the other.

Delicious sensations shimmered through her. Each pull of his mouth brought a new wave of pleasure. To her shock, her hips undulated in carnal rhythm. Sounds she'd never made before strained from her throat.

He blew on her erect nipple. It glistened with his loving. As his hand slipped low over her belly, her body jerked. He stopped, his palm warm and firm against her skin. "You okay?"

She nodded. She was more than okay. Every cell of her being vibrated with renewed life. "I think it was just a reflex. No one's ever touched me there."

His eyes darkened. He spread his fingers wide, covering the scrap of black lace. "I want to touch you everywhere."

Again, she could only nod.

He stroked her from collar to hip, tracing every curve, until his fingers brushed over her panties. He touched her through the lace, cupping her and pressing his fingertips into the sensitive juncture of her legs. A look of pure pleasure washed over him. "You're so wet."

Her cheeks heated. She swallowed. "Yes, I'd say I'm good and ready." She glanced down at his bulging briefs. She trembled in anticipation. "And you?"

"We shouldn't rush a good thing."

"Oh, but I feel so...needy."

His lips curved into that sexy grin. "Let's get you out of these and see what we can do about that." In one motion he slipped her panties from her hips, down her legs, then onto the pile of clothing on the floor.

"Here, is this better?" He sifted his fingers through her thatch of curls to the folds of her femininity. With deft movements, he found that part of her that ached to be touched.

"Ohh…yes." She clung to him while he worked his magic, circling her pleasure point until she moaned and her hips again moved in erotic cadence.

He kissed her, his mouth trailing over her neck, her collarbone, then again across her breasts. The steady pull of his mouth paired with the pressure of his fingers drove her to the edge. The exquisite tension crescendoed. She dug her fingers into his shoulders and rocked against him. With a startled cry she came, rocketing to the heavens with an intensity that left her gasping for breath.

He held her, gently stroking her back, until she calmed.

She burrowed into him, shaken by her extreme reaction. "That was…incredible."

His chest rumbled with quiet laughter. "*You* are incredible."

His eyes shone with approval. Her heart swelled. She kissed him, craving his heat, the stroke of his tongue.

He shifted and his erection pressed against her thigh. "Sabrina, I need you."

Desire swirled through her. "Yes." She rose to her knees and reached for his waistband. "Time to make you a little more comfortable."

With his help, she removed his briefs. He reclined, unabashed by his evident desire. Awed, she reached toward him, then stopped. "I'd like to touch you."

He watched her through heavy lids. "Just go easy. I don't know how much longer I can last."

The husky tone of his voice sent shivers of awareness through her. She focused on his erection, taking it gently in her hand, then running her fingers from base to tip, circling the blunt end. "It's so soft," she marveled. "Hard, but soft at the same time. Like velvet." Leaning forward, she brushed her cheek against the smooth surface.

Noah let out a strangled moan. She straightened, embarrassed by her impulsiveness. "I'm sorry."

"Sweetheart, you don't need to apologize." He pulled her into his arms, then rolled her beneath him, parting her knees, and settling between her thighs. His shaft pressed into her. She moved, rubbing against him experimentally, her body's reaction immediate.

He grabbed her hips to still her. "Wait."

To her dismay, he rolled away, to lift his pants from the floor. She sat up, distressed. He couldn't leave. "Noah—"

"I almost forgot."

Her gaze dropped to the square packet in his hand. She fell back against the pillows, chiding herself. She'd been so caught up, she hadn't thought of protection.

A moment later he stretched out on top of her. She cradled him with her legs as unbidden warmth for this annoying, impossible man filled her. He had a very caring way for a cynic. "I'll remember you forever for this."

He kissed her again, then rested his forehead on hers. "It's not too late to call it off."

In answer, she wrapped him in her arms and legs. "I don't want to call anything off. I've waited too long for this. Love me, Noah."

He touched her then, probing and stretching her with his fingers. His blunt tip pressed into her. He eased forward, then stopped.

She could feel him filling her, pressing against her barrier. "It's all right. Just do it quickly."

Nodding, he withdrew. He planted a quick kiss on her forehead, then murmured, "Happy birthday, Sabrina." With one powerful thrust, he sheathed himself in her.

She gasped as pain tore through her, but it eased almost instantly. He was inside her, fully inside her, and she was no longer a virgin. A sense of wonder and satisfaction rolled through her.

Then he moved. This time the pleasure radiated from deeper within and spiraled outward in a delicious heat. She moaned.

He stilled, bracing himself over her with his arms. "Am I hurting you?"

She shook her head. "No. Don't stop. It feels…it feels so good."

He chuckled softly, then words escaped them as he loved her the way she'd dreamed he would. His gaze held hers as he pleasured them both, and she'd never felt more connected to another living being. The beauty and tenderness of the moment lifted her to some higher plane, and he was there with her. She could see it in the depths of his eyes and feel it with every movement of their bodies.

Tears blurred her vision as wave upon wave of pleasure swept through her. Noah buried his face in her hair, his breath hot on her neck. Her orgasm hit with such force, she opened her mouth in a silent scream.

He collapsed on top of her. For a moment she lay stunned. Would she die right there, smothered and pleasured beyond the scope of human experience? Surely, no one had ever reached the lofty pinnacle they'd attained. This couldn't be ordinary sex.

With a soft groan, Noah rolled to his side, taking her with him so as not to disturb their intimate embrace. She let her gaze drift over his restful face, memorizing the curve of his cheek, the straight, strong line of his nose, and the shadow of his lashes beneath his closed lids. Warmth expanded her heart.

His eyes flickered open. He swept a strand of hair back from her face. "You okay?"

Sabrina had to swallow before answering. For some reason her throat had constricted. "I'm fine. And you?"

He grinned his sexy grin. Apparently, that was all she needed to get her wanting him again. Her blood thrummed as he cupped her jaw and brushed a tender kiss across her lips. "Sweetheart, I'm feeling no pain. *You* are a goddess."

"Now, don't go putting me on a pedestal."

"No, ma'am." He snuggled her closer, trapping her legs between his. "I like you where you are."

She stroked her fingers down his back, grazing him lightly with her nails. He nuzzled her neck, until she tilted her chin to give him better access. After nipping her gently, he kissed a trail down to the hollow of her throat, then slowly drew away from her. He placed one last kiss on her lips. "I'll be right back."

"Don't go too far," she said as he disentangled himself.

With a smile over his shoulder, he headed to her bathroom. She rolled to her stomach, smiling at the sight of this gorgeous nude man sauntering through *her* bedroom.

Satisfaction like she had never known filled her. She'd done it. She'd lost her virginity. And she'd done it in style.

"And a very happy birthday to me," she crooned softly to herself.

Noah returned in a moment, a wet washcloth in hand. "Miss me?"

Propping up on her elbows, she grinned at him. "Oh, yes."

He smoothed his hand down her back, then over her bottom, circling one cheek, before stopping. Awareness shivered up her spine.

"As much as I want to explore this side of you, I think I'd like you sunny-side-up for now. If that's okay," he said.

The warmth of his hand pressed into her and she wiggled against him. Who knew having her bottom caressed would feel so good? "Promise you'll pick up here where you left off?"

His eyes took on a glazed look. He gave her a little squeeze before removing his hand. "Promise. Anything the lady wants." He held up the washcloth. "But first, will you allow me to tend to you?"

"Tend to me?" She rolled to a sitting position.

He nodded, his dark eyes intense. His gaze ran over her, stopping at the juncture of her thighs.

"Oh." Heat swamped her. The thought of Noah "tending" to her *there* made her mouth go dry. And her sex pulse. "Okay."

"Then just lie back and relax."

She did as he asked, never taking her gaze from him. He was a magnificent man. Muscles rippled under his tanned skin as he moved. Dark hair swirled across his sculptured chest, then tapered down to his flat belly. Below that, his sex stirred as he settled before her. Just looking at him made her want him.

"Open for me, Sabrina."

She hesitated, suddenly feeling timid and…decadent.

"Don't turn shy on me now."

The excitement in his eyes was all the encouragement she needed. A soft moan escaped him as she drew her knees outward, welcoming him to the most intimate part of her. He knelt before her, stroking her inner thigh with the warm cloth.

"Does this make you want me again?" His voice was rough as he stroked higher, brushing lightly over the part of her that wept for him.

She closed her eyes as the cloth retreated and cool air hit her skin. "Yes."

He moved to her other thigh, caressing just to the top, then stopping. She moaned softly. "Don't tease me, Noah."

"I'll get there, sweetheart. Just being thorough."

The warmth of the cloth draped her aching center. His hand pressed into her, his fingers probing her entrance through the fabric. With a sigh, she moved against him. She wanted him again.

"You like this, don't you?"

"Yes." She shivered as he traced the cloth over her cleft. With deliberate care, he explored each fold and crease, circling her tender flesh with the warm cloth, until she moaned and rocked her hips. That delicious tension escalated again inside her, catching her breath and heightening her senses. The slightest touch nearly sent her spiraling out of control.

"Easy." When he withdrew the cloth she cried out her disappointment. "Not to worry, love. I'm not finished with you."

His warm breath fanned across her inner thigh a second before his mouth settled there. He kissed his way upward, following the same path the washcloth had taken. Sabrina closed her eyes as anticipation burned through her. She'd dreamed of this moment. He reached her cleft and she bit down on her bottom lip as he traced her nether lips with the tip of his tongue.

Her pulse thrummed and she strained against him as, with lips, teeth and tongue, he explored her most private terrain. At last, he reached her pleasure point. He teased the nub, circling it until her hips found the rhythm that brought her again to the brink. Pleasure poured through her in a wave that built, then rushed, then broke with heart-rending intensity.

"Noah!"

Noah pulled himself up beside her. He'd meant to let her

rest, recuperate after their first round, but she'd gotten so turned on as he'd cleaned her that he'd started wanting her again. Her scent had driven him to distraction, until he'd had to taste her. Oh, and the blessed taste of her! He licked his lips and cupped her breast, doing his best to ignore his raging erection.

She'd been a virgin.

That had to be why the sex was so incredible. She'd been so tight. So ready for him. So forbidden. He'd never had a virgin before. It only made sense he'd react strongly to the novelty of it.

Inhaling, he again tried to tamp down his libido. He needed to go easy on her, let her adjust. As much as he'd like to, he couldn't expect her to go all night her first time.

She rolled toward him. Her lips brushed his forehead, while her palm came to rest on his chest. "You wonderful man. Thank you."

A hoarse laugh burst from his throat. He was so hard, it hurt, but it was too soon to take her again. "You don't have to thank me. It was definitely my pleasure."

Her palm slid down his chest, then lower. His blood heated. His muscles flinched as her fingertips brushed his stomach, then continued their southward journey. "Sabrina, you don't have to—"

Her fingers closed around his throbbing length. "I want to."

She gave him a tentative squeeze, then caressed his tender flesh. "I can't get over the way it feels."

"Neither can I." He sucked in a breath as she stroked his sensitive tip.

"Tell me what to do."

It almost hurt to laugh. "You're doing…just fine."

She wrapped her fingers around him again and stroked him from base to tip. "Like this?"

"Yes." The word came out in almost a hiss.

"You'll come if I keep this up." A note of awe touched her voice. She had complete power over him and she knew it. Still, he never wanted her to stop.

"I like this," she murmured in his ear. "I like touching you this way. I like the way it feels."

Molten heat gathered in his loins, building toward an inevitable eruption. He liked it, too, very much so, but at the same time she made him feel green, out of control. He grabbed her wrist, stilling her hand, fighting the overwhelming urge to plunge himself deep inside her.

She rose to her knees beside him, staring down at him with her innocent blue eyes. "Make love to me, Noah."

Her words played like music to his ears. "It's not too soon?"

"Oh...is there a standard wait period?"

He chuckled at her worried expression. "No. I thought you might be sore."

"Well, I do ache, but I don't think that's quite what you mean." She straddled him as she spoke, settling her wet cleft against his heat.

Her eyes closed and her head fell back. Noah's breath caught as she rubbed herself along his shaft. Forward, then back, then forward again, until his blunt tip brushed her opening. "I wish...we didn't have...to stop..."

Stop? She couldn't possibly think of stopping. Not now.

"...that I could just...let you slip right inside me..."

It took a moment for her meaning to register. "Sweetheart, we'd better do it now, or it'll be too late."

Her eyes opened. "Oh."

Without leaving him, she leaned over to withdraw a condom from her nightstand drawer. Pink tinged her cheeks. "I had hoped these would come in handy."

Refusing to dwell on the fact that she had a supply of

condoms on hand, Noah took the packet and readied himself in record time. He touched her between her legs, finding her swollen and oh, so wet.

Moving his hips, he placed himself at her entrance. She eased forward slightly as he penetrated her. Shifting, she seated herself firmly on him, taking him fully into her hot sheath.

"Oohh…" She ground against him, experimenting with her hips. "It feels so good."

"Ride me, Sabrina. You'll pleasure us both."

Her muscles constricted around him. She moved, tentatively at first, then with increasing speed as a sexual blush colored her skin. From the soft planes of her face to the ruddy tips of her breasts, she presented a picture of such beauty, it burned into his memory. When he thought back to this night, this is how he'd remember her.

"Oh, Noah…it's…so good…sooo…goood…"

"Yes…yes…yes…"

She came first, her face and body contorting in a picture of ecstasy. He couldn't take his gaze from her. As she collapsed on top of him, her sheath convulsed, sending him hurtling into an abyss of pleasure so intense, he thought he might die of it. When the long orgasm ended, he cradled her, while his heart pounded, and he lay stunned, marveling over the most incredible sex he'd ever had.

At long last, she stirred, breaking their union as she rolled to his side. She nestled into the crook of his arm. "A girl could get used to this."

He kissed her forehead. "I hope so." He could get used to it himself. A restful silence cocooned them. He rubbed a lock of her hair between his fingers.

"Is it always so…so…indescribable?"

He drew a deep breath. What would she say if he told

her it had never been so indescribably indescribable before? "That was about par for the course."

She smacked his chest. "Liar. It couldn't possibly be like that all the time. Who would ever get anything done?"

Pride swelled his chest. He'd made her first...and second time memorable...for both of them. Of course, it wasn't all his doing. With her sexy moves and the way she responded to the slightest touch, Sabrina possessed enough sensuality to turn any man into the most potent lover.

"It *was* incredible," he said. "We're good together."

Her gaze met his, filled with such happiness his heart constricted. Would he ever tire of looking at her?

"Sabrina, there's something I don't understand."

She turned her face up to him, brows raised in question.

"You're an incredibly sensual woman. I don't see why—*how* you've waited this long."

She regarded him in silence for a while, then sighed. "Guess I've always had these romantic notions. I wanted it to be perfect. I wanted to wait for love. Especially after Bess's ordeal—she's the one who drove me home earlier. We've been friends forever.

"Anyway, she got pregnant at sixteen and gave up a very promising future as a runway model to marry the baby's father." She shook her head. "She was a child raising a child. She's never had a chance to really find out who she is—what she could have made of her life.

"The whole thing cemented my belief that I wanted to wait for The One—for true love."

"But after all this time, why now?"

Her dainty shoulders shifted. "I told you. At twenty-five, I felt like some kind of freak. I never realized true love would be so hard to find."

"Hasn't there been anyone else?"

"Oh, there have been a number of men—"

"A number?"

"Not as many as you—"

"Now, I've never had any men—"

"Not as many relationships. And obviously, I didn't... you know, with any of them. It never took long to figure out that a man wasn't The One."

"And tonight?"

"Well, tonight I suspended the true love prerequisite and settled for true loving." A smile spread across her lips as she ran her hand over his chest, combing her fingers through his springy curls.

"I hate to be the cynic here—"

"But you are."

"But you're more likely to find true loving like we just shared—which, by the way, is *not* so easy to find—than you are to find true love."

Her eyes darkened, and something like sadness shimmered in their depths. "You *really* don't believe in love."

He couldn't bring himself to answer her directly. "My parents had what I thought was a happy marriage. Then within a month of my fifteenth birthday their picture-perfect life disintegrated into stretches of cold silences punctuated by hostile interchanges. They divorced in record time.

"I spent a few years bouncing back and forth between them, listening to each one's bitter complaints about the other. By the time I graduated high school and moved on to Auburn, I knew I'd never marry."

She continued to stroke him, gently running her fingers up then down his chest. He set his teeth. Why had he told her about his parents? He never talked about them.

"I'm so sorry you had to go through all that." Her voice was low, soothing the hurt boy in him. "But true love *does* exist. My parents would do anything for each other.

"Once, my father drove over two hundred miles in one

day to bring my mother her favorite cheesecake from her favorite bakery in the town she grew up in."

He arched his brows. "That's dedication."

"It showed the depth of his commitment to her. She'd do the same for him. *That's* true love—taking the time and energy to drive that distance, even though you're tired and have a zillion other things to do. Losing sleep together because one of you has a problem to work out. Or giving up your favorite pet, because your love is allergic to cat hair."

A feeling of melancholy settled over him. He had tried to give to Rebecca that way. What had it gotten him? "I think giving like that is overrated. It's a rare person who appreciates it. And the one giving just risks too much."

Sabrina traced the contour of his cheek. "Who hurt you, Noah?"

He gritted his teeth, not wanting to resurrect the old wounds. Yet the softness of her tone and the compassion in her eyes loosened his tongue. "I've dated lots of women and I always kept it casual. There was *one* woman, though. I risked everything for her. Gave up my partnership with your brother, walked away from a profitable career to follow her to Denver and start again from scratch.

"I gave her everything I had. What was mine was hers. She had my time, my money, all the attention any woman could want." He paused, the old disappointment suddenly fresh.

"It wasn't enough," he continued. "In the end, she found someone with more time, more money. Someone willing to bow to her every whim."

"Sounds like you're better off without her." The protective tone of her voice had him turning to her, smiling, in spite of himself.

Her dark hair spilled in disarray around her shoulders. Her creamy skin presented a luscious vista of dips and curves, and her eyes stared back at him in rapt attention. Yes, he was much better off.

He ran his fingertips down her arm. "What kind of fool would lie here whining about the past, with a beautiful woman here at his disposal?"

"You're not disposing of anyone, bud."

"I'm no idiot." He brushed his mouth over hers and she opened to him, welcoming him again, sweeping the cobwebs of the past from his mind with the sweet caress of her tongue.

She moved against him, circling his nipple with her thumb. He grew instantly hard. He broke the kiss, needing to clear his head, but she kissed a trail along his chin, then down his neck to his chest. When her tongue flicked across his nipple, his body jerked in response.

Eyes wide, she grinned up at him. "A little sensitive, are we?"

He laughed. "You'd better watch it, or you'll find yourself the object of my lustful attention again."

She gave his nipple another pass. "A girl can only hope."

His blood raced. Could she actually be ready for round three? "First things first. A washcloth isn't going to cut it this time."

Her lower lip pushed into a pout. "No 'tending' to me this round?"

"Oh, I'm going to tend to you all right. I believe in cleaning up after myself." He let his gaze slide over her rose-tipped breasts, then down to her triangle of dark hair. "We'll have to be even more thorough than last time. Nothing short of a head-to-toe job will do."

Her eyes rounded. "Head to toe?"

"Which do you prefer, a shower or a bath?"

Her luscious breasts rose. Her pupils dilated. "I don't know. I guess a shower."

Heat filled him. What fun they were going to have showing her all the ways a man could love a woman. He took her mouth, kissing her deeply, thoroughly, until she moaned and pressed into his hardness. "Stay here. I'll get the water running, then I'll come back for you."

"Make it steamy. I like it hot."

He chuckled. "Yeah, I noticed."

Sabrina loosened her grip and Noah slipped from her arms. Would she ever tire of watching him? For the second time that night, he sauntered across her carpet, while she feasted her eyes on all his natural glory.

Sweet, sexy man. How could anyone have hurt him?

The need to erase all the pain of his past rose in her. Perhaps she'd cancel her trip to Florida. She'd spend the weekend here with him. He was a most considerate lover. Why not have her fling with Noah?

Her mind wandered over the past few hours and her skin heated. Her dream lover had become a reality.

The bathroom door opened. He emerged, the first wisps of steam curling after him. Her gaze fastened on his erection and liquid pooled between her thighs. She'd never known men could be so beautiful.

He lifted her, cradling her against his chest. A fine layer of steam coated the bathroom mirror, blurring their image as he pulled aside the shower curtain. He stepped into the hot spray, then slid her down his length, until she stood on her own feet. "If it gets too hot, just say so."

He kissed her again. Water pulsed over them as he stroked her from shoulder to hip. His hands left her. The scent of peach tinted the air.

A moment later, he cupped the sides of her neck with his lather-filled hands. He smoothed the suds up behind her ears, then down past her collarbone. "Your breasts are perfect."

"Are they? I hadn't thought you noticed."

"I was trying damn hard not to."

She brushed her belly against him as he lathered her breasts, stroking their tips with his thumbs. Desire arrowed through her. Soapy bubbles spilled down her stomach.

She gathered a handful, then returned the favor, lavishing her attention on his chest. His skin was warm and smooth beneath her fingertips, the muscle hard and defined. She skimmed her hands lower, tracing the firm plane of his stomach.

"You go any lower and we'll have round three right here in the shower."

"I thought that was the plan." She skimmed her hand lower, but he backed away.

"I haven't finished cleaning you." He squeezed more of the gel into his palm, then knelt before her.

Hot spray angled off his back, splattering the suds along her front. With long, slow strokes he lathered her legs, rubbing her first from hip to ankle, then caressing up her shins, over her knees, then her thighs. His breath warmed her belly and longing filled her as she braced her hands on his shoulders.

His palms grazed up her calves, then over the backs of her thighs. "I nearly forgot the promise I made earlier."

He cupped her buttocks and squeezed. She moaned, gripping his shoulders tighter as he kneaded her. His tongue teased her navel.

Slowly, he straightened, kissing his way past her stomach, over her breasts, stopping to lave each sensitive nipple, then up along her neck. His mouth hovered near hers, while he continued the gentle assault on her backside. She made a low sound and wriggled against him.

"You really like this," he said.

"I seem to like it all."

His erection pressed into her abdomen. She tilted her hips and her cleft met his hard flesh. Suddenly, he stilled, pressing his forehead to hers. "We didn't bring protection."

"Oh." She blinked. She'd forgotten again. "Under the sink." She braced herself against the wall, the hot spray pelting her as he made a quick exit, then returned in all haste.

A low, guttural sound vibrated from his throat, just before he captured her lips. His tongue stormed her mouth, thrusting with the same hunger burning inside her. She met him stroke for stroke, while he lifted her, bracing her legs over his arms.

He pressed her to the wall. "Tell me you want me again."

"I want you again." Her hips moved once more of their own volition.

His tip probed her entrance. She shifted, then sighed with satisfaction as he pressed into her, stretching her, filling her. Pleasure rippled through her as the water pulsed over them, sending her temperature soaring.

Noah took her with an urgency that rocked her to her core. Again, then again he thrust into her, each movement triggering waves of heat flowing through her. Incoherent sounds tore from her throat. She urged him on, moving her hips in rhythm to his steady beat.

Burying his head in the crook of her neck, he gave a muffled yell with his final thrust. She stiffened. Her orgasm hit with such force, it left her breathless and light-headed.

She went limp in his arms as he sagged against her. For long moments, they stayed that way as water ran in rivulets down their entwined bodies. At long last he stirred. "You really know how to zap a guy."

"Maybe we should take a break. Get some sleep."

He kissed her with such tenderness, her eyes burned. "Okay, but just until I get my strength back. I think we're on to something here."

Warmth, unrelated to the heated water streaming over them, filled her. With a sleepy smile, she turned off the shower, then let him lead her toward bed.

6

SABRINA GLANCED at the clock on her nightstand. 4:00 a.m. and she was wide awake. Noah lay breathing deeply beside her, his arm draped possessively across her waist.

She never wanted this night to end. Her dream lover had been nothing compared to the real Noah. He'd made love to her with a depth of caring and intensity that sent her mind reeling.

Her gaze traced the angles of his face and warmth filled her heart. She bit her lip. Good Lord, what was happening? He'd made her have *feelings* for him. How could she have gone from despising him to...to having these *feelings* in such a short time? No wonder Bess had been so apprehensive.

Panic settled over Sabrina. What was she doing? Was she falling for Noah, a self-proclaimed cynic and known womanizer, a man who'd taken a bimbo as a bribe? The shock of it left her wide-awake and staring blindly at the ceiling.

She couldn't have a fling with Noah. He *really* didn't believe in love. Now that her sexual haze had cleared, the impact hit her. She couldn't chance falling for him—she'd only get hurt.

By the time the first rays of the sun peeked through her blinds, she'd reviewed the catastrophe from every angle, trying to make some sense of it. It was simple, really. She'd waited so long for true love that her psyche had confused her rash change of plans. He was her first. Hence her sub-conscious had bestowed all those stored emotions and fantasies upon him.

She glanced at the bags she'd packed. There was only one thing to do. She had to go to Florida. She had to have a fling. Then she'd know if she had these feelings because she'd never been with another man, or because of Noah himself. If anything, her plan made even more sense now.

She eased herself from his arms. He muttered something in his sleep, but didn't wake. With a sigh, she headed for the bathroom. She had just enough time to make her flight. She'd put last night from her mind, chalking it up as another one of her fantasies. Today was a new day. Today she'd find her fling.

THE CLICK OF A DOOR jolted Noah to wakefulness. He reached for Sabrina, then frowned when his hand swept empty sheets. He rolled to his side. "Sabrina?"

She turned from her spot by the closet, a suitcase in her hand, her purse and a second bag slung over one shoulder. "You're awake."

"Are you leaving?" He frowned. This wasn't the way he'd imagined their morning. In fact, after last night, he'd envisioned a very different beginning to their weekend.

Her gaze flicked away. "Yes. I told you I had a big day planned."

He patted the bed. "Come here. I want to wish you a proper good morning."

She hesitated, her teeth worrying her bottom lip.

"Change your plans. We'll spend the rest of the weekend together."

"I can't…look, last night was wonderful, but it's over. I can't have a fling with you."

"A fling?"

She motioned with her free hand. "You know, kind of like we did last night, but over a longer period of time."

He rolled to his feet, then scooped his clothes off the floor. How could she think of leaving after last night? He slipped into his pants, while she remained still, watching him. "So, last night was just a one-time thing?"

"We agreed no strings."

"So we did. Were you going to say goodbye?"

She nodded again. "Of course."

He thrust one arm into his shirt, then fumbled a moment before finding the second armhole. "About last night—"

"Oh, it was nothing." She sighed, fidgeting with her purse strap. "I mean, thank you. It was really great of you to…you know…do that for me. I really appreciate it."

She appreciated it? He straightened. His stomach churned. That wasn't quite the reaction he'd hoped for. He forced a smile. "No problem. I'd be happy to be of service anytime."

Her eyes widened. Again, her head bobbed. "Thank you, that's very generous of you, but as I said, it won't be necessary."

He stared at her, disappointment cutting through him. What had he expected? "You know, if this is about that 'no strings' talk—"

"Oh, no. You were right. It just wouldn't do. You know Cliff would go berserk if he ever found out."

"Cliff, right." She had a point. Noah would likely find himself out of a job if her brother caught wind of this.

"I've got to get moving, or I'll miss my flight."

He nodded, then glanced around for his shoes. She held the door, while he grabbed them, then followed her out. Though overcast, the daylight stung his eyes. Leaning against the wall, he crammed on one of the shoes. "Sabrina—"

"Thanks again, Noah. I've really got to go." She gave him a tentative smile, then, before he had a chance to respond, she dashed out into the parking lot.

He stared after her as she hurried toward a blue Malibu. Grumbling, he struggled into his other shoe. Thunder rumbled as he made his way to his own car. He slipped behind the wheel, a sense of foreboding settling over him. Fat droplets splattered the windshield.

The memory of her eyes, alight with wonder, flashed through his mind. "Bloody hell."

They couldn't part like this. He turned his car around on the wet pavement, and caught sight of her taillights disappearing in the distance. Self-loathing filled him. She was upset, probably full of regrets that she'd let a cad like him touch her.

What had he been thinking? He hadn't been. At least not with his head. Not after the way she'd looked at him, touched him. He shook his head. *Love me, Noah.*

What man could have refused?

An honorable man. He frowned at the small voice of his conscience. She hadn't wanted an honorable man last night, damn it. She'd wanted *him.* And he'd pleasured her well. No, she couldn't have been disappointed there. No woman had ever responded like that to his every touch. Desire shuddered through him at the memory.

He'd never known being with a woman could be so...fulfilling. She'd taken everything out of him, but had given him her all. He glanced again at her car as it drew further ahead of him. Damn it, he couldn't let her go.

He checked the oncoming cars, then merged into the lane behind her. Could he give her all the things she wanted? Guilt soured his thoughts. Who was he to think he even stood a chance with a woman like her? Here she was fleeing from him as fast as traffic and the bad weather allowed.

If he had an ounce of pride, he'd turn around and let her go. He pressed harder on the gas. Wherever she was headed, he couldn't let her go without knowing how she truly felt about last night.

They took the airport exit off the interstate. Noah scowled. He squeezed the wheel, oddly disturbed by the fact that she was leaving town. He followed her into Hartsfield Airport's parking garage. A moment later she lifted the large suitcase and second bag from her trunk.

After locking his car, he hurried to her side. "Let me help you with that." He reached for her suitcase.

She started, clasping her hand to her chest. "Noah, what are you doing here?"

He clutched her suitcase, suddenly feeling awkward for chasing after her. "You didn't let me say goodbye."

"Oh." She worried her lip with her teeth. "I'm sorry. I was in a hurry."

"I'll see you off."

Her gaze held his and for a moment her eyes flickered with some of the warmth they'd held last night. "You really don't have to."

"I want to." He gestured toward the main terminal.

She nodded, and they fell into step, dashing across the lanes of traffic, and dodging raindrops on the way to the building. Early-morning travelers hurried about the busy area.

"So, where're you going?"

She threaded her way toward a baggage counter. "I'm headed to the beach. Florida. Thought I'd get away for a few days."

Images of Sabrina dressed in scant swimwear flashed through his mind. "Want some company?"

Her smile froze. "You mean, you?"

He glanced around. "I don't see anyone else." He wiggled his brows. "You might need someone to fight off all the weirdos."

A blush appeared on her cheeks. "Well, actually, I do hope to make some new acquaintances."

"Acquaintances?"

She straightened, lifting her chin in the air. "I suppose I should thank you. You helped me reach a decision." Her round lips curved into another smile. "I feel liberated, really."

Blood pounded in his ears. She couldn't mean what he thought. "Liberated?"

Her brows rose. "Yes, what you did for me last night. Well, it gives me so much more freedom."

He narrowed his eyes. "I know I don't have any right to ask, and God knows, I don't think I want to hear the answer, but freedom to do what?"

She moved into a line that stretched before one of the counters. "If you must know, I'm going in search of a weekend fling."

His insides heaved. "What?"

"A fling. You know, like last night, only longer."

He stared at her, speechless, a sick feeling swirling in his gut. "Yes, you explained that earlier, but if you want a fling, I'm more than willing—"

"No! Thank you. I want someone from out of town. Someone Cliff won't get upset about—or scare away. Besides, since we're both in the wedding, we don't want to make that awkward."

Noah stepped closer to her. "You can't be serious. What about Mr. Right and that happy-ever-after stuff?"

"Don't you see? You were right, at dinner, when you said I was wasting my time—"

"I don't think that's what I said—"

"All that stuff about my internal clock, that was true. I

guess I was mad because you were right." She chuckled softly. "The funny part is that I thought you might be Mr. Right."

His heart contracted.

Her shoulders shook as she suppressed a heartier laugh. "I really do appreciate how you helped me see that it's time I got on with my life." She shrugged again. "And of course helped me eliminate the barrier that was holding me back. I figure this'll sort of jump-start things for me."

That sick feeling mushroomed inside him. "Jump-start?"

She nodded. "Sounds exciting, doesn't it?"

"No." A kind of panic took hold of him. He grabbed her by the arm. "You can't do this, Sabrina. You'd be making a huge mistake. You'd regret it for the rest of your life."

Her eyes narrowed. "How can you know what I'd regret?" The line moved. She took her bag from him to hand it to the attendant, then stepped to the counter, setting her carry-on on the floor. Noah ground his teeth. Guilt tore at him. He had to talk her out of this ridiculous plan.

A few moments later, she turned to him, boarding pass in hand. He picked up her carry-on and followed her as she got in line to go through the security check. She faced him, and something like regret flashed in her eyes. "Look, I appreciate your concern, but I'm a big girl. I'll be fine."

His gaze fastened on her mouth. The memory of loving her washed over him, the warmth of her pressed against him, the stroke of her tongue fresh in his mind. He'd taken her virginity, and now she meant to endow all her blessings on some stranger.

Because Noah had liberated her.

His guilt and some other unfamiliar emotion he didn't

want to explore swelled in him. He stared at her, bereft of words.

Once the security attendant had checked her ticket and ID, she placed her purse on the conveyor belt. "Well, good-bye."

He straightened. "Wait. Sabrina, don't go."

"This is just something I have to do." She gave him a small smile, then walked through the metal detector.

The attendant frowned at Noah. "Sir, do you have a boarding pass?"

Sabrina retrieved her purse from the other end of the conveyor belt. Without looking back, she moved away to join other travelers heading for the concourse.

Noah shook his head at the attendant. "I just want to talk to her."

"Only ticketed passengers from here."

Noah stepped aside, straining to catch his last glimpse of Sabrina as she disappeared down an escalator. His heart hammered. He couldn't let her go. Not before he talked some sense into her.

He tightened his fist and realized he still held her bag. Determination filled him. "That's it. If I have to buy a damn ticket just to return her bag and talk some sense into her, then so be it."

A well-placed bribe to a college kid near the front of the ticket line shortened his wait. Ten minutes later he arrived at her gate. Sabrina had plopped down into a vinyl chair. Noah settled beside her. How could she contemplate this insane scheme?

She stared at him, her eyes wide. "What are you doing here?"

"You forgot your bag."

"They let you back here without a ticket?"

"It's worth the price of a ticket if I can get through to you. You can't do this."

"You bought a ticket, just to talk to me?"

He leaned toward her. "I don't get why, Sabrina. Why would you want to do this?"

She stared straight ahead. "You'd never understand."

"Try me."

Her shoulders drooped. "Have you ever felt invisible? Like you were on the outside, looking in? Like everyone else was at this wonderful party and you weren't invited?"

He slipped his arm around her shoulders, but she stiffened away from him. "Sabrina…"

"Well, it's time I threw my own party."

Anger rose in him. "What about diseases or pregnancy?"

"You sound like Cliff. Don't worry, I'll be careful. I'll use protection."

He squeezed his eyes shut. He'd never be able to live with himself if he didn't stop her.

"I'll be right back."

His eyes flew open. She stood beside him. "Where are you going?"

"To the ladies' room to powder my nose." With a backhanded wave she headed up the concourse.

Noah stared out the wall-sized window, hardly seeing the bustle outside on the blacktop. Maybe if she stayed gone long enough she'd miss her flight. He shifted in his seat and fastened his gaze to a clock hung on the far wall.

Nearly fifteen minutes later, he stood in the middle of the concourse, straining for a glimpse of her. Where was she? She really was going to miss her flight. They'd just announced general boarding. He ignored his growing unease, and nurtured the hope that her plan might fail.

Finally he caught sight of her. A tall man walked close

beside her. Too close. His hand rested at the base of her spine. The hair on the back of Noah's neck shot to attention. Who the hell was this? Had she picked up some stranger on her way from the rest room?

The couple drew near. Sabrina's unmistakable laughter reached Noah's ears. He ground his teeth. This guy could be anybody.

"Noah," she called as they approached. "You're still here. You didn't have to wait." She gave him a pointed look, then gestured toward the tall stranger. "This is Michael. He's an architect. We had a showdown over the last pack of Juicy Fruit gum and decided to share."

"How nice." Noah bared his teeth in an attempt to smile. That old queasiness hit his stomach.

"Michael Barnes." The man offered his hand.

Noah stared at it, then turned to Sabrina. "You know you don't really want to do this."

An overhead speaker announced final boarding for her flight.

Her eyes widened. "I guess we lost track. Michael, do you have your boarding pass?"

"Right here." He withdrew the paper from his pocket.

"Wait a minute!" Noah stared at them. "He's on this flight?"

Sabrina smiled. "Isn't that great? We're both headed for Destin, via Panama City." She turned to Michael. "We'd better hurry."

Before Noah could form a logical protest, she turned back to him. "Have a great weekend, Noah. I'll see you around."

See him around? Noah's blood pounded. His earlier panic returned tenfold. Sabrina walked away with the stranger at her side, his hand glued to the small of her back. What if the guy was some psycho killer?

Noah had to do something. His mind raced as he scanned the gate. Other passengers headed toward the boarding checkpoint. With a start, he realized he still held Sabrina's bag. Closing his eyes, he stepped in line behind the last passenger. Looked like he'd get his money's worth out of that ticket after all.

Shaking his head, he handed his ID and pass to the attendant. "I can't believe I'm doing this."

THE PLANE'S ENGINE ROARED to life. Sabrina gripped her armrest and forced herself to relax. What had possessed Noah to follow her to the airport? The man must be suffering a major attack of conscience. She frowned. Too bad he hadn't suffered it sooner, like before their date...before last night. The hungry stroke of his tongue, his body hard against hers and his roving hands ran endlessly through her mind.

She'd lost her virginity. The realization shivered through her. The whole evening had taken on a surreal quality, like one of her fantasies. It had been real, though. Her joints seemed stiff and her muscles ached in places she hadn't known she had.

He'd been extraordinary, but she'd been right to tell him about her plans—to let him know there'd be no repeat of the evening. Though refusing him this morning, pretending their night together had been casual—when it had been anything but casual for her—had been the most difficult thing she'd ever done.

Sure, he wanted her now, but what about tomorrow, or next week? She closed her eyes. No, only heartache awaited her if she got involved with him. If only she hadn't played that juvenile game at the party. Maybe if he hadn't kissed her, she wouldn't have craved it again when he'd arrived on her doorstep.

Michael placed his hand over hers. Her stomach knotted. Now here she'd acted juvenile again. "Nervous?" he asked.

She nodded. Flying had never bothered her. Flying in the company of a virile stranger was wreaking havoc on her nerves, though. What was she doing?

She extricated her hand to dig in her purse for her half pack of gum. It was odd, how at this time yesterday she hadn't the faintest idea how to pick up a man. Apprehension coursed through her. Her stomach tightened at the memory of Noah's stunned expression. Michael's rapt attention had certainly proven her desirability beyond a doubt.

She glanced at him. By anyone's standards, Michael was a handsome man. Every hair on his fair head lay smooth and unruffled. His blue eyes sparkled with intelligence and genuine interest, and he filled his designer suit in all the right places.

"Here, let me." He took a stick of gum from her. After unwrapping it with slow, careful movements, he held the stick to her lips.

Embarrassment flooded her. She straightened in her seat, taking his offering in her hand. "Thank you." She couldn't look at him as she bit it into her mouth.

A stewardess clicked on the intercom, and explained the emergency procedures. "Don't worry." He rested his arm along the back of her seat and leaned over her. "I'll keep you safe."

The pilot clicked on to welcome them aboard. Moments later the plane raced down the runway. Sabrina's stomach swirled as they lifted into the air, then climbed.

Michael dropped his arm around her. She resisted the instinct to pull away, and held her breath for the eternity it took for the plane to level out. The "fasten seat belt" sign went off. Other passengers began moving around the cabin.

Still, he kept his arm tight around her. She swallowed. She had to relax if she meant to carry out her plan. Maybe if they spent the day together, then had a nice dinner, she'd be comfortable enough with him by Sunday to—

"Have you ever done it on a plane?"

Her gaze flew to his. Her heart sped. "Done it?"

His eyes gleamed. He traced her arm with his fingertip. "We're both adults here, obviously attracted to each other. There's no reason to beat around the bush, is there?" He withdrew his arm and nodded toward the rear of the plane. "You head back to the lavatory. I'll give you a minute, then I'll join you."

She blinked. Goodness, she was a better flirt than she realized. Drawing a deep breath, she steeled herself. Here was her chance to jump-start her life and get Noah out of her system. Though she'd accomplished her goal sooner than expected, this was what she wanted.

She unclenched her jaw. Panic swelled inside her. "I—"

"Michael!" A dark-suited man stopped beside them. Michael stood. The man ran a curious gaze over her, then turned to pump her companion's hand. "You going down for the St. Mark's briefing?"

"You think I'd miss the beach?"

The man chuckled. "Great. We'll hit a few. You bring your racket?"

"And a fresh can of balls."

"Good. We'll do it, then." Again, the man's gaze swept her. "So, Lorraine and the kids doing okay?"

"Fine. Fine. Kids're growing like weeds."

"Great. They'll keep you hopping. See you down there." With that, the man moved up the aisle.

Sabrina stared after him. Disbelief filled her. *Lorraine*

and the kids? She turned to Michael as he sank back into his seat. "You're married?"

He shrugged. "We have an understanding."

She raised her brows. "She understands you don't wear a wedding band, so you can seduce strange women in airplane bathrooms?"

He leaned back. "Look, you came on to me. I was just giving you what you wanted."

She stared at him in shocked silence. She'd come on to him? Maybe she hadn't really wanted that Juicy Fruit. Maybe she had flirted with him to make Noah jealous. Maybe having sex with a stranger *was* on her agenda. But where did he get off thinking she'd do it with a married man, à la commode?

Disgusted, she snatched up her purse. "I can't do this. This has been a mistake."

"Your loss." He crossed his arms and let his gaze wander over her. "Let me know if you change your mind."

She rose from her seat, glancing toward the back of the plane. She'd find a seat as far away from this Bozo as possible.

Noah scrunched down in his seat and raised a magazine over his face as Sabrina stepped into the aisle. How would he explain his presence here? He couldn't quite explain to himself why he'd boarded the plane.

He dared a peek over the magazine. She was moving down the aisle toward him, probably headed for the rest room. He settled back in his seat, keeping the magazine in place. Good. She was taking a break from that Michael character.

Noah shuddered. The guy had been all over her since Noah had slipped in several rows behind them. He'd had to avert his gaze numerous times to keep from using the airsick bag. He'd not known guilt could make a body sick, but his stomach had revolted at the sight of the two of them snuggled together.

Michael rose. He stepped into the aisle, conspicuously pacing himself behind Sabrina. Noah stared in dismay as the man's gaze fastened on her backside. Good God, they were going to do it in the latrine!

Noah surged to his feet. A sound of distress tore from his throat. He strode up the aisle, toward Sabrina, his heart thudding, his gut doing the Watusi. He couldn't let her do it. Not like this. Not after last night.

She froze, her eyes rounding in disbelief. "Noah?"

With a meaningful glance at Michael, Noah swept her into his arms. There was just one way to show this jerk the lady was taken. "Darling, I was able to join you, after all."

Before she had time to react, he gathered her closer and kissed her. She hesitated for the briefest second, before melting into him, her tongue greeting his with the same fervor of last night. Noah's blood hummed.

They *were* good together. He hadn't imagined it. Why then was she so bent on finding someone else?

Michael made a sound of disdain as he shoved past. "You two can have each other."

Sabrina stiffened as though suddenly coming to her senses. She pushed away from Noah, fire burning in her eyes. "What, are you stalking me now?" She kept her voice low, though many of the other passengers openly stared.

"I'm saving you from this ridiculous plan of yours."

"I don't need saving."

"Yes, you do."

A tight-lipped stewardess approached them. "Sir, why don't you take your seat?"

Noah waved her aside, and turned to Sabrina. "I can't let you go through with this. We need to talk."

Her lip curled. She stepped back. "I don't think so. Are you insane? I thought you weren't boarding."

He strode back to his seat to retrieve her bag. "You forgot this."

"You boarded just to give me my bag?"

"You are way too reckless. Good thing I'm here to look after you. No way was I going to let *that* beanpole initiate you into the Mile High Club."

Her eyes rounded. "You all think alike, with your minds in the gutter."

The stewardess stepped between them. "Perhaps you should both take your seats."

Noah stared at Sabrina, anger pumping through him. "He *did* proposition you!"

"Sir. Miss. Please sit down." The stewardess crossed her arms. "You could discuss this later, in private."

Sabrina drew up straight, her eyes flashing. "We have nothing to discuss." She turned on her heel, then stopped and swiveled back. "And I am *not* having a fling with you!"

That said, she stalked to a section of seats beyond the bathroom. Noah stared after her. That pig had propositioned her, but she'd moved as far away from him as possible. A smile curved his lips. Maybe the woman would see reason after all.

SABRINA SHIVERED as cold air blasted from a vent above the hotel's reception counter. As she waited her turn to check in, she scanned the vast lobby with its sparkling fountain and jungle of potted trees. A dark-haired man caught her eye. She tensed, then he turned, revealing a stranger's profile. Relaxing, she turned back to the desk.

She'd lost Noah in the airport by doubling back through

baggage claim. The man was insufferable. What had possessed him to follow her?

She'd been very clear about her plans. He understood they didn't include him. How, then, had he come to be on that plane, or even on the concourse, for that matter? Another shiver ran down her spine. He'd actually thought she'd meant to join the Mile High Club with that lowlife.

The couple in front of her departed with a bellman, and a well-groomed woman in a charcoal uniform greeted her with a smile. "May I help you?"

Sabrina moved forward and set her bags on the smooth Spanish tile. "Yes, I'd like to check in, please."

"Certainly. Your name?"

Sabrina told her and a few clicks of the keyboard later, the woman nodded. "Here you are, Ms. Walker. We have you checking out Tuesday."

"That's right." That would give her a little more time to accomplish her mission.

"One moment please. Let me make sure your room is ready."

As the woman bent again over the computer, a young man, also dressed in charcoal, joined her behind the counter. Anticipation lit his face as his gaze fell beyond Sabrina. "Hello, Mr. Perry. Nice to have you back."

Sabrina glanced at a man of medium build as he peeled a number of bills from a thick roll, then handed them to a smiling valet. The valet's eyes widened and he nodded his thanks. As he scurried out the front revolving door, keys in hand, the man made his way to the counter beside her.

He was nice-looking, perhaps somewhere in his midforties. He wore a silk shirt of muted tones with olive-colored slacks, which echoed the pale green of his eyes. His arm encircled an older woman.

In spite of her age, the woman possessed a proud bearing, her shoulders back, her more-than-adequate breasts defying gravity with the help of a shocking expanse of leopard-print Lycra. Slim black slacks molded her hips, while a red chiffon scarf wrapped her shoulders. Only the telltale gray of her Southern-beauty-queen big hair hinted at her true age.

Mr. Perry smiled at the young man, the corners of his green eyes crinkling. "Good day to you, Andrew. Yvonne."

He nodded to the woman helping Sabrina and she granted him a bright smile. "It's always a pleasure to have you with us, Mr. Perry."

"I decided my dear mother needed a respite by your healing Gulf waters, so I've brought her with me this time."

He gave his mother an affectionate squeeze. "She's been pushing herself lately, but you're going to take it easy this weekend, right, Rosie?"

Rosie gave a husky laugh, "Not if I can find a robust gentleman to pass the time with." She reached her bony hand up to pat her son's cheek. "Don't you worry about me, Bill dear. I'll find my own fun."

Sabrina chuckled along with the others. What a character this Rosie was. Sabrina smiled as Bill caught her eye and winked. And what a son to treat his mother with such care. A man of strong values. Perhaps that was more what Sabrina was looking for.

She cast a covert glance at his left hand, drawing a deep breath at its barren state. Of course, Michael hadn't worn a ring either.

"We reserved you our last beach-front room." The desk clerk interrupted her thoughts. "We've got a crowd in this weekend." She slid a key card across the counter.

While she gave directions to the room, Sabrina again

caught Bill's eye and smiled. He was certainly handsome enough, with a tan that spoke of many hours outdoors, yet he had what she could only describe as a polished look about him.

His gaze assessed her from head to toe, then up again. "You're in the new tower. They were just finishing it up when I was last here. I had a personal tour of the center suites. They're well done in burgundy and gold, a striking combination."

She nodded. "Yes, I knew they were renovating the old wing, but I haven't been here in some time." She waved her key card. "As long as I can wake up to see the Gulf outside my window, I'm happy."

She thanked the clerk and moved away from the counter, her suitcase in hand, the carry-on slung over her shoulder. Bill turned with her. "Don't tell me a beauty such as you is traveling alone."

"It was a very…impromptu trip."

Rosie turned to Bill, handing him the key card Andrew had just given her. "Dear, you go on. I need to speak with Andrew a moment. I want to make sure I'm getting one of those new comfort-zone beds. He's checking."

"No worry, I'll wait with you." He murmured conspiratorially to Sabrina, "No telling what kind of trouble she'll get into on her own."

Sabrina smiled, then shifted her suitcase. She'd never dated an older man. Perhaps he'd have more insight on what women really want. Dare she proposition him in front of his mother? "Well, maybe I'll run into you again."

Warmth shimmered in his eyes. "I will make every effort to ensure it."

He held her gaze for a brief moment before returning his attention to Rosie, who had found another matter to discuss with Andrew.

Sabrina stepped away and headed for the elevator, surveying the beach through a wide window. Sun worshippers dotted the white sand. If not Bill, then certainly, another suitable prospect awaited her along the Gulf Shore.

Fortified with renewed optimism, she pressed the button for her floor, and attempted to push all thoughts of Noah from her mind.

7

NOAH BLINKED at the sunlight reflecting off the blue-green water and white sand. Even through his dark glasses, the beach dazzled. He drew in a breath of salt air, and searched the area for Sabrina. The little minx had nearly lost him in the airport. He'd hung back, though, following her to this plush resort in Destin, just west of Panama City.

The sun glinted off his watch as he checked the time. She'd been in her room fifteen minutes. If his hunch proved right, she'd head straight for the beach.

He passed a group of college kids playing volleyball, and moved toward a vacant chair beside a far umbrella. He'd have a good view of the beach from here, but wouldn't be too conspicuous.

Sabrina emerged as he settled into the canvas seat. He sat forward, his throat tightening as she sashayed to a spot near the volleyball players. A bright blue bikini top cupped her lovely breasts, while a flowered sarong hugged her hips. Ignoring the umbrellas, she spread a multi-colored towel on the sand, sparking interest on both sides of the net as she bent to straighten the corners.

When she stood and dropped her sarong, heat shot through him. Her narrow waist curved out to meet her well-rounded hips, while the long contour of her legs comple-mented her firm backside. He dug his fingers into the arm-rests, stifling the surge of possessiveness that claimed him. Somehow, he resisted the urge to dash over and cover her.

She'd made it clear his job was done and she had no further use for him.

Besides, he couldn't let her see him yet. She'd likely bolt, and he might lose her this time. Maybe if he kept his cool, he'd think up a plan.

He drew in a deep breath and forced himself to relax. She settled onto the towel, her legs stretched before her. With slow strokes, she rubbed sunscreen into her supple skin. In a matter of moments, several of the volleyball players flocked to her.

Noah craned his neck as one of the youths warmed lotion in his hands, then smoothed it over her back. The guy was as tall as that Michael jerk, and twice as fair. Noah dug his heels into the sand. What did she have against dark hair?

"College kids," a voice beside him startled him.

He tore his gaze from Sabrina. An older couple dropped their gear in the umbrella's shade. The old guy panted as he eased into one of the canvas loungers. "They're everywhere." He gestured toward the group around the volleyball net.

"Quit complaining." The woman slapped a towel onto an adjacent chair. She winked at Noah. "It isn't like he wasn't young once. He just can't remember it."

The man made a disgruntled sound. He leaned toward Noah. "We never flaunted ourselves like these young people."

The woman snorted. "You should have seen him. You can't tell by the look of him now, but that young buck," she nodded toward Sabrina's companion, "wouldn't have had a thing on my Marvin, here." She patted her husband's hand.

Marvin grunted. He nodded in Sabrina's direction. "Like honey to the bees."

Swallowing, Noah followed the man's gaze. The "young

buck'' had finished her back. He moved in front of her and reached for the bottle of lotion. Anger surged through Noah. Just where did that kid think he'd be rubbing her now?

Noah half rose from his seat before Sabrina retrieved her sunscreen and waved the young man back toward the net where his comrades had resumed play.

"Now's your chance." The old man pointed his crooked finger toward Sabrina. "Move on in there, while they're all distracted."

Noah stared hard at the man. "What makes you think I'm interested?"

Marvin elbowed his wife. The two broke out into know-it-all grins. Noah scowled. "Some of us are a little more mature here. Some of us don't have to act on every little impulse."

Laughter pealed from the couple. Nodding toward Sabrina, the old man grabbed his chest. "I don't know about you, but *that* does something for my impulses."

The woman stared, eyes wide, then slugged the man soundly in his arm. Noah swung his gaze back to Sabrina, dread creeping through him.

Sabrina had spread stomach-down on the towel. Her luscious bottom twitched as she worked the ties loose on the back of her bikini top. His throat went dry as she dropped the string, leaving her back bare to the sun. He swallowed. That smooth stretch of skin and the thought of her freed breasts *did* fire up his impulses. His mouth watered for the taste of her.

"Look at that little darling," the old woman said to Marvin. "Doesn't he remind you of our Justin at that age?"

In spite of himself, Noah peeled his gaze from Sabrina to see where Marvin's wife indicated. Two women, laden with floats and beach bags trudged beside Sabrina. In their wake trailed a toddler, gripping a pail with water sloshing over its top.

The boy neared Sabrina. He tripped. The bucket flew from his small hands. Noah sucked in his breath. Water spewed over Sabrina. She screeched and bolted upright.

The young Viking buck stopped midstride on the far side of the net. His gaze fixed on Sabrina. His eyes rounded in appreciation. The volleyball spiked across the net. With a loud *thwack,* it slammed into his temple. He crumpled to the sand.

Noah jumped to his feet. Good Lord, she'd killed him!

"OH MY GOD!" Sabrina snatched up her sarong. She jerked it around to cover herself.

Her attention flew from the little boy, who stared open-mouthed, to her new friend, Ben, lying facedown in the sand.

"Oh my God!" Horrified, she knotted the garment securely at her back. What had she done? He was just a boy himself.

"Timmy, tell the lady you're sorry." A sunburned woman pushed the boy forward.

Sabrina scrambled to her feet. "It's okay." She waved the woman and child away, then stumbled toward the crowd gathering around Ben. He'd been so sweet to rub lotion on her back. Such a nice kid, he was just finishing his first year at Florida State.

Good Lord, why had she untied her top? A little tan line seemed such a small thing, now. The crowd parted. Ben lay unmoving. She swallowed a lump of dread. "Is he breathing?" she asked, pressing past one of his teammates.

The young man turned to her. "He never misses a shot. What could have happened?"

Her cheeks burned. She opened her mouth.

Ben groaned and cupped his head. Sabrina gave a quick prayer of thanks. She dropped to his side. Scooping her arm around him, she helped him to sit. "You poor dear. Are you okay?"

He grimaced, gingerly touching his temple. "My head."

"I know." She looked around. "You need ice. Is your mother with you?"

His chin jutted forward. "She's home, in Freeport."

"Oh." Now she'd added insult to injury. It must be his first trip on his own. He was so young.

"You have beautiful breasts."

Heat suffused her face. "I'm sorry. I didn't mean to—"

"I need some aspirin. Could you help me to my room?" His green gaze probed hers.

For a second she tensed, but he groaned again and sank against her. He was in pain and it was her fault. Besides, in spite of his size, he was clearly just a kid.

"Okay." She nodded. With his friends' help she got him to his feet.

"Here." One of them grabbed her belongings—errant top and all—threw them in her bag, then slipped it over her shoulder.

With Ben leaning heavily on her, she stumbled toward the hotel. The air inside sent goose bumps rising along her heated skin. An elderly gentleman held the elevator for them.

"Four." Ben reached past her to press the button. His arm brushed across the tips of her breasts. She sucked in a breath and pulled back, her nipples tingling through the thin cotton.

"Sorry." He glanced at her, his expression contrite.

She nodded, relaxing a degree. Surely he hadn't meant anything. He was obviously still in pain. "Maybe we should have a doctor look at you."

He waved aside her concern. "I'm fine. I just need a couple of aspirin, and to lie down."

When they arrived in his room, he sank onto one of the double beds. "Could you close the drapes, please?"

"Of course." Sabrina rushed to comply, shutting out the view of the sun and surf. She turned back to him. "You have aspirin?"

He waved toward the bathroom. "Black shaving kit by the sink."

With a nod, she hurried to get them. She paused inside the bathroom door. Sand coated the floor. Wet cutoffs, trunks and briefs littered the small area. Were all college kids this messy?

Shaking her head, she reached for the little black bag by the sink. She opened the bag's main compartment, then searched inside, feeling around for the aspirin, until her fingers closed around the small bottle. After filling a glass with water, she made her way to his bedside, stepping over more clothing along the way.

"Thanks." He smiled weakly, then swallowed the pills she had handed him.

"Good boy." Taking his water glass, she set it on the table.

His gaze fastened on her chest. "So…can I see them again?"

Sabrina blinked, feeling suddenly naked in the thin sarong. Maybe he wasn't such a kid after all. "Why don't you rest? Would you like some ice?"

"Oh, babe, ice isn't gonna help what's ailing me. All I need is you, snuggling right here beside me. You're one hot enchilada, Sabrina. Don't you like me?" He leaned forward and caught her arm.

She closed her eyes. Regardless of his awesome pecs and rippling chest, Ben couldn't be more than nineteen. And in spite of his build, he just didn't compare to Noah.

The memory of kissing Noah's chest—a *man's* chest— floated over Sabrina. The feel and taste of his skin washed over her, before she roused herself, dousing the vision. She was *not* going to think about Noah. And even though he'd jumped on that plane, she was *definitely* not having a fling with him.

She looked again at Ben. He watched her with bright, hopeful eyes. How could she let him down easy? She couldn't possibly make love with him. "Look, Ben. You're really a nice guy. You're everything a girl could want. But I'm not comfortable with this age thing."

He leaned back his head and laughed. "I was afraid you thought I was repulsive, or something." He slid his arms around her, pulling her close. "I think you're sexy as hell, for an older chick. I like that you're more mature than the girls I know."

"Are you even twenty?"

His mouth quirked to one side. "Almost. But most chicks think I'm older. You know, I'm kinda built. I work out." He lowered his voice to a seductive growl. "Besides, I perform like a twenty-year-old."

She gently pried his arms from around her waist. "That's really nice. You seem fine now. I'm sorry you got whacked by that ball, but I've got to be going."

"Aww, pleeeeease?" He implored her with his puppy-dog eyes.

She moved away, slinging her beach bag over her shoulder. "Have a great weekend, Ben. It was nice knowing you." Feeling a little chagrined, she left, doing her best to ignore his pleading cry as the door closed behind her.

NOAH CLUNG to the balcony railing and glanced down at his feet dangling four stories above the ground. "Christ, how did I get myself into this?"

The whole situation was funny, really. Maybe later he'd be able to laugh about sprinting after Sabrina and her Nordic jock, then nearly breaking his leg in some kid's moat. Maybe some day he'd see having the kid's linebacker-type father threaten to pound him into the ground as amusing. For now, though, Noah wasn't laughing.

At least he'd escaped in time to overhear the jock's floor number as he raced for the elevator. After jogging up the stairs, he'd burst onto the floor as the chummy pair disappeared into a room at the far end of the hall. Luck had it that a maid's cart stood outside the room next door.

In all haste, he'd snuck through the open door, past the maid bent over the tub, then out onto the balcony. In one swift and senseless move, he found himself clinging to the neighboring balcony. With an effort, he swung one leg up and over the railing, then hauled himself to the other side. "Now what?"

Damned if he hadn't come up with a plan. The woman was going to put an end to him. Squaring his shoulders, he stepped to the balcony door and knocked. "Hotel maintenance."

The door opened. The blond jock squinted out at him.

"I'm with maintenance…we're checking to see that all exterior exits are in working order."

"She's gone, dude."

Noah relaxed. "You mean you two didn't…"

"Naw. She ditched me." He pressed a frosty can of beer to his temple. "So, what…you stalking her, or something?"

Noah blinked. "No. I am not stalking her. She's a…friend and I'm merely watching out for her best interests."

"Oh." The kid shrugged. "I saw you down on the beach, watching her. You kinda stood out. You were the only one down there with all your clothes on."

Noah glanced at his slacks and shirt, the same ones he'd

taken Sabrina to dinner in. He'd have to buy some clothes somewhere. He frowned at the sweat stains spreading under his arms. "I, uh, haven't had a chance to change."

The kid scooped a wadded pair of shorts off the floor. He held them to his nose and sniffed. "These are passable if you want to borrow them. You'll blend a little better."

"Ah, no thanks. Um, you wouldn't know where she was headed, would you?"

"Can't help you there."

Noah nodded, then he gestured toward the room. "Would you mind if I cut through?"

With a wave of his hand, the kid stepped back. "Be my guest. You know, next time you might want to try that maintenance routine at the front door."

Noah stared at him in consternation. "Right. Thanks." He crossed the room, and had his hand on the doorknob when the kid called out to him.

"Good luck with Sabrina. You just might score. She seems to like older dudes."

Noah squeezed his eyes shut. A lot of good scoring had done him. "I'm just here to look after her."

The kid had the nerve to laugh. "Right, dude, whatever you say."

Frowning, Noah stalked from the room. What did he care what that jock of a kid thought? His sole interest in Sabrina was to talk some sense into her, then get her on the next plane home. Older dude, indeed!

SWEET PLEASURE SPIRALED *through her. She rocked her hips, thrusting herself hard against him. Her breath caught. Her world splintered. She screamed.*

When she calmed, she lifted his face to gaze lovingly upon the man who granted her such ecstasy. Noah smiled down at her, his dark eyes brimming. "I need you, Sabrina. Always."

Sabrina groaned and rolled to her side. She shuddered. Opening her eyes, she gazed at the empty pillow beside her. *Noah.* Damn the man. Did he have to insinuate himself everywhere?

She punched the pillow. *I don't believe in love, Sabrina.* Even in her dream he spoke only of his need for her. She had to forget him. If she could only get on with this fling thing, she might quit having these ridiculous fantasies about the man.

A glance at the clock showed she had plenty of time to shower and change before happy hour started at the poolside bar. After her harrowing experience with Ben, she'd been desperate for a nap. Not surprising, since she'd hardly slept last night.

After a quick shower, she slipped into a pale green sundress. She'd bought it on her shopping spree with Bess. As she pivoted before the mirror, her skin warmed at the sight of her bare back and the length of leg showing below the short hemline. With a satisfied smile, she headed down to the bar.

The late afternoon sun peeked out from behind a lone puff of cloud. A seagull screeched overhead. She settled on a corner stool and smiled as a warm breeze wafted over her.

"What'll you have, pretty lady?" The bartender wiped the counter in front of her.

"Frozen margarita?"

"Coming right up." He moved away to tend to her order, and she glanced around at the other patrons.

A man and woman sat in one corner, sipping umbrella-topped drinks. A young couple, probably honeymooners, sat engrossed in each other, and a bunch of college kids clustered around a far table. Sabrina held her breath and searched for Ben in their midst. To her relief none of them looked familiar.

She really did need to find someone a little older—someone

who didn't have a wife and kids at home. Someone she wouldn't fall head-over-heels for.

The bartender slid her drink in front of her. "Here you go, miss."

"Thank you." She reached for her purse.

"Please, allow me." The man who had checked in at the same time as her slipped onto the stool at a right angle to her.

Sabrina returned his smile. "Only if you're not married. I have absolutely no use for married men this weekend."

The man's thick brows arched. He chuckled. "I'm afraid I tried that once...and once was one time too many. Besides, I stay much too busy to keep up with a wife."

She smiled and he turned to the bartender. "Put that on my tab, Mark, and get another one for me, if you could be so kind."

"No problem, Mr. Perry. Coming right up." With a quick salute, the bartender left them.

"So," Bill turned to her, "you have a distaste for married men?"

She sipped her drink, savoring the tangy cold slipping down her throat. "Let's just say they don't fit with my plans."

"Good. I don't care for the bums, either." He held his hand out to her. "Bill Perry at your service. I'm sorry I didn't get a chance to introduce myself earlier. Rosie is a bit of a handful, I'm afraid. I hoped I'd find you here, though."

She placed her hand in his. "Sabrina Walker. I think it's wonderful the way you look after your mother."

He clasped her hand in both of his. "She's taught me all I know." A quick glance at his watch drew his brows together. "She's supposed to meet me. I'd like to introduce you."

Sabrina smiled. Such thoughtful, caring men were rare these days. "I'd love to meet her. So, what is it you do that keeps you too busy for a wife?"

"I'm a producer."

"There you are." Bill's mother, Rosie, her hair as big as before, swept up to the bar.

The woman knew how to make an entrance. She'd exchanged the leopard print top and black slacks for a zebra print sheath slit up each side, revealing a shocking amount of leg. Still, those legs held enough allure to elicit open-mouthed stares from the college boys at the far table.

"Ah, Mother." Bill rose to greet her, kissing her lightly on the cheek.

He gestured to Sabrina, who slid from the barstool to stand beside him. "Allow me to introduce the lovely Sabrina Walker. Sabrina, Rosalie Perry, the most supportive mother anyone could want."

"My pleasure." Sabrina smiled, taking the woman's hand.

Rosie's grip proved surprisingly strong. She had to be somewhere in her late sixties to early seventies, but she had the figure of a much younger woman.

Tiny crow's-feet crinkled the corners of her eyes as she beamed at Sabrina. She had striking features, though the smooth tightness of her skin hinted at a face-lift. "Now, don't you fret, dear. I can vouch for my Bill here. He's a fine man. A professional."

"Rosie's my biggest fan, as well as one of my top advisors. If ever I have a problem, she's there to help me work it out."

Rosie waved her ring-studded hand in the air. "I was in the business long before you came into this world." She winked at Sabrina. "I know all the ins and outs."

She glanced at Bill and they both grinned broadly. "Did you hear that, son? All the *ins and outs?*"

They fell into a short fit of laughter as Sabrina stared from one to the other. With a sigh, she waited for them to recover. Perhaps then they'd let her in on their little inside joke.

Bill took his mother's elbow, still smiling broadly. "Let's find a table. Sabrina, you'll join us?"

"Um, yes, I'd like that." *I think.* She grabbed her drink and the one the bartender had brought for Bill. Maneuvering around another table, she hurried after them.

Bill held a chair for his mother, while Sabrina set the drinks down. He moved to Sabrina's chair and pulled it out for her.

"Thank you."

"The pleasure's all mine." He seated himself beside her, so she sat between mother and son. "Sabrina, such a lovely name. So, how is it that a beauty like you is all alone here? Are you waiting for some young buck?"

"Actually, I've had my fill of young bucks. I was hoping to find someone more mature."

Rosie nodded her approval.

A knowing light brightened Bill's eyes. He squeezed her hand. "Ahh…you are looking for a man who has a bit of experience?"

"Definitely, experience is a plus."

"I, myself, am a man of varied experience."

"Oh, yes." Rosie leaned forward. "Bill is absolutely the best at what he does."

Sabrina had to admire the woman's enthusiasm. "So, you're a producer. What do you produce?"

"Films." He took a thoughtful sip of his drink.

"He is the *best* in the industry. An award winner, my Bill."

"Let me ask you something, Sabrina." Bill's eyes shone with intensity. "You like variety? You like to try different things?"

She drew in a breath. "Yes, I guess this whole trip is about experiencing the new and unknown."

A broad smile lit his face. He patted her hand. "Yes. I knew when I saw you that you had an adventurous heart."

"You know how to pick them, son."

Sabrina ran her finger along the salt-coated rim of her glass. "I think adventure might be exactly what I want."

Bill let loose a small sound of excitement. "I have been searching for just such a woman, someone who dares to leave the beaten path, who makes her own rules, regardless of what society dictates."

She laughed. "Believe me, I have definitely not traveled the beaten path."

He and Rosie shared a knowing look. Sabrina straightened, feeling a little self-conscious. Had they guessed she referred to her long stint as a virgin?

A waitress, a young woman with a deep tan and sun-bleached hair, approached their table. While she took Rosie's drink order, Bill leaned in closer to Sabrina. He held her hand and rubbed his thumb along her palm, asking in a low voice, "And this urge to take the unbeaten path, does it apply to all areas of your life?"

Her gaze drifted over him. Could she really do it with him? She licked the salt off her finger, then took a long gulp of her drink. After a quick glance to see Rosie was still busy with the waitress, she asked, "You mean sexually?"

His gaze fell to her lips. "You are a sensual woman. I can only hope this adventurous spirit accompanies you into the bedroom."

She swallowed, and closed her eyes. Last night certainly qualified as adventurous. She shifted, still feeling the soreness in her muscles. "I suppose you could say my sexual experience qualifies as unusual."

He leaned in closer, his mouth hovering near her ear. "I understand completely. Don't you worry, I'll take good care of you."

"You will?" Surprise and relief flowed through her. She hadn't known how to address her lack of experience with her potential partner. Bill had made it so easy.

"She *is* lovely." Rosie patted Sabrina's hand. "Have you asked her about tomorrow?"

"Not yet." He flashed Sabrina an apologetic smile. "I thought we'd lead up to that."

"What's happening tomorrow?"

Bill rubbed his hands together, excitement stirring in his eyes. "We're starting a new shoot. Perhaps you'd like to come along?"

Rosie chuckled as she reached for Bill's drink. "Yes, dear, do *come* along. We'd like to show you all the *ins and outs* of the business."

The corners of his mouth twitched, until he was smiling broadly. "Yes, Sabrina, I'd really like it if you'd come."

Laughter bubbled from Rosie's throat. "Coming is optional, but certainly encouraged."

Sabrina stared at the woman. Did Rosie have a few loose screws?

Still smiling, Bill took Sabrina's hand. "You are a most remarkable woman." His gaze scanned her from head to toe. "You'll make an exciting addition to our project. I could coach you through it. I have a feeling you're a natural."

A sense of apprehension flitted over Sabrina. Addition to their project? "I'm sorry, I'm not sure I understand. Exactly what is this project? I don't have any acting experience, if that's what you're thinking."

Rosie leaned forward. "Most people don't think it's necessary. My Bill's work can be a little more demanding on the actors involved, but in your case, just being yourself should do the trick.'' Another chuckle escaped her. ''Ah, *do the trick.* I do crack myself up.''

She settled back in her seat. ''Seriously, he's famous for the depth of plot in his projects. No small feat in that field.''

Bill's chest swelled. ''Yes, well, I think it's worthwhile to engage the intellect as well as the libido, if possible.''

Do the trick? Libido? Sabrina shifted in her seat, her gaze swinging from Bill to Rosie. What were they talking about?

''Now don't be modest. He's also known for his innovative camera angles. Makes the viewer feel like they're right there.''

The noise level in the bar shot up a few decibels as two men in swim trunks entered with a dark-haired woman in the skimpiest one-piece Sabrina had ever seen. The threesome laughed and talked with much animation as two more bikini-clad women and a third man followed close on their heels. They were the most attractive—and sensual—group of people Sabrina had ever seen. To her surprise, they converged on their table.

Rosie brightened. ''Oh good, looks like you get to meet the cast.''

''Good afternoon all,'' Bill greeted them. He took Sabrina by the hand. ''This is Sabrina. Isn't she stunning?''

Heat crawled up Sabrina's neck as several of them crowded around her. *Stunning?* They all sported sculptured bodies and deep tans, with dazzling smiles. The three women had breasts the size of ripe melons.

Sabrina felt like a frumpy country mouse. What was it that Bill produced? This group didn't look like the documentary type. Her feeling of unease billowed inside her.

One of the bikini-clad women squatted beside Sabrina's chair. Her melon-breasts pressed against the armrest.

"Hello, Sabrina! I'm Tabby." She lifted a strand of Sabrina's hair. "Pretty."

Sabrina blinked, shifting uneasily. Tabby's gaze locked on hers. "Are you joining us for the shoot? Bill said he was looking for another girl."

"Well, I—"

"She's a cat, our Tabby." The blond man grabbed Sabrina's hand and pumped it in a hearty shake, using both of his large paws. "I'm Clarence," he said, winking, "but everyone calls me Thor." He stroked the length of her arm. "I like to roar," he added cryptically.

Sabrina forced a smile and pulled her arm loose. They certainly were a feely lot. "It's a pleasure, Thor."

"Yes, it will be." His gaze swept her from head to toe, lingering along the way.

Sabrina darted a glance at Bill. Was he jealous of his associate's obvious flirtation? He smiled broadly, gesturing to one of the other women. "This is Ginger."

Ginger pressed forward, her plump breasts barely confined in her top. Sabrina straightened, trying not to feel inadequate. She nodded to the dark-haired woman.

Peering over her designer shades, Ginger leveled her keen gaze on Sabrina. "I hope you don't mind we came straight from lazing on the beach. I'm conserving energy today. This kind of work takes it all out of me."

"Of course not." Sabrina smiled tightly.

Bill tapped her elbow, turning her attention toward the others. "We're missing George, my director, but there's Frank, our number-one camera man, and MoJo and Priss."

Frank gave her a two-finger wave. MoJo nodded and slid his hand along Priss's thigh. She waved, then leaned into him. She cupped his face and pressed her mouth to his. With a groan, he turned her more fully into the embrace, without breaking the kiss. Priss wriggled against him and splayed her fingers across his bare chest, kissing him with all she had.

Bill chuckled beside Sabrina. "It doesn't take much to get those two going."

With some difficulty, Sabrina cleared her throat. "You didn't say. What *is* this shoot tomorrow?"

"We were going to call it *Viking Vixens,* but the horned helmets proved a little difficult—"

"I warned you about that." Rosie shook her beringed finger.

"Yes, you did, but I liked the story idea about the sex slaves, so we kept that, did a minor rewrite, and got new costumes. I'm quite excited about it. We're not straight yet on the new title."

Horror filled Sabrina as she swung her wide gaze again from Bill to his mother, then around the group surrounding them. They were filming some X-rated movie, and they expected her to join in!

"There's been some mistake." She turned back to Bill. "I had no idea...I mean, there you were with your sweet mother...I didn't know..."

Bill's brows arched. "Actually, Rosie's one of my biggest backers."

Rosie shook her head, pursing her lips in disappointment. "She *did* seem the adventurous type."

He turned his troubled eyes to Sabrina. "Yes, what about your craving for adventure...experiencing the new and unknown...daring to break with conventionality?"

Sabrina heated to the roots of her hair. She *had* told them she hadn't followed the beaten path, but how could they have thought she meant this? "I'm sorry. This is all a misunderstanding. Believe me, I've never done *this* before."

"Ahhh!" Bill's eyes lit with understanding. "You're nervous about the camera."

"You're a video virgin?" Tabby straightened, hope gleaming in her eyes.

Sabrina flopped back in her chair. Humiliation thrummed through her. How had she gotten into this? She squeezed her eyes shut. "Something like that."

Rosie leaned across the table. "I know exactly how you feel. Tabby can guide you through it, or we could get Thor, or MoJo…or Thor and MoJo."

Sabrina shot upright. "No!"

Tabby drew back. "Priss?"

Sabrina bit her lip and shook her head.

"You're sure?" Bill frowned.

Averting her gaze, Sabrina nodded vigorously.

When she dared to look, Bill wore an expression of pure distress. "I've bungled this. I thought we were of the same mind."

She tamped down on her anger. Hadn't she said she was looking for adventure? "It isn't your fault. I came here wanting excitement."

He leaned toward her. "If *Viking Vixens* isn't your kind of excitement, we can fix that. Tell me what you want, Sabrina. We're in the business of creating fantasies here. What is your deepest desire?"

She drew a long breath, then let it out. *Desire.* What did she know of desire? A keen ache passed through her. She sighed. "I want a man to care about me, to put my needs above his, to want to make me happy."

Rosie nodded. "You want love."

Love? She shook her head. Hadn't she changed her mind about that? She was getting too old to wait for something so elusive. "I'd settle for caring."

Again, Bill nodded. He glanced beyond her. "I'd say a man who comes to a woman's rescue is the caring sort."

Sabrina peered around Tabby as a dark-headed man stormed toward them from across the bar. Her heart thudded.

She clasped her hands to her chest, while a wave of surprise and relief swept through her. "Noah."

8

HE'D COME FOR HER. Sabrina smiled and shifted closer to Noah as the crowded elevator carried them up and away from the poolside bar. She inhaled his scent, a little salt air mixed in with his personal essence.

The elevator stopped, emptying most of its occupants onto one of the floors. A wonderful exhilaration filled her.

Why hadn't she seen it? Noah cared for her. He had to. Why else would he have followed her on this trip—arriving like a white knight to save her from the mortifying fix she'd just gotten into? This chivalry of his explained everything. Fool that she was, she'd let him think she wasn't interested. She hadn't dreamed the wonder in his eyes as they'd made love. He'd felt it too. Yes, Noah was a chivalrous knight, bent on protecting her. Of course he cared.

What is your deepest desire? Bill's question drifted back to her, along with the answer. She wanted Noah. She wanted to explore every divine inch of him, to touch, taste and feast on him. She wanted to know again the feel of him filling her, making wild love to her.

The elevator stopped again. When more passengers brushed by her to exit, she used it as an excuse to press against him. His arm came around her, and he held her close, even as the last passenger cleared the space, leaving them alone. She flattened her palm against the taut muscle of his abdomen. She felt, more than heard his faint moan.

Satisfaction rippled through her. A brazen fantasy of

making love to him in the elevator played through her mind, but she stilled the impulse to explore further with her hands. The time for that would come later. She'd make this a slow seduction.

"Thanks for getting me out of there. I got in a little over my head on that one." She tilted her head to see him better.

A shudder ran through him. "The bartender said that guy runs a pleasure boat where he auditions would-be actresses. What if he'd gotten you out on that? How would I have found you?"

"Oh, you would have. Somehow, you would have still come to my rescue. I just know it."

The muscles in his jaw bunched. "At least you have the good sense to eat in your room tonight. I need a break from fending off potential suitors."

"You'll join me, won't you?"

He huffed out a breath. "It'll make it a lot easier to keep an eye on you."

She smiled as a plan formed in her head. By nightfall, Noah would be hers.

SABRINA HUNG UP the phone and turned to find Noah. He stood past the open balcony door, admiring the Gulf from her seventh-floor vantage point. The sun had dipped below the horizon and spectacular hues of orange and red tinted the azure sky. Soft music floated up to them from the courtyard below.

Smiling, she joined him at the railing. "Food will be here in about thirty minutes."

He nodded, his gaze fastened on the horizon.

"It's beautiful."

Still he made no response. His shoulders shifted as he exhaled a deep breath.

Moving behind him, she reached for his shoulders. "You're so tense."

At last he turned to her. "And how am I supposed to be?" He gestured wildly with his arms. "I've been chasing after you all day, warding off every available guy who happens to catch your eye." His brows arched. "Me...defending a woman's virtue. And one who doesn't want it defended at that."

"But I do appreciate your efforts, Noah. Honestly, I do." She closed her eyes and let the courtyard's music flow over her. Slowly, she circled her hips, swaying to the soft strains.

"What are you doing?"

She opened her eyes as her body found its sensual beat. "I'm thanking you."

He held up his hands as if to fend her off. "You don't have to thank me. You didn't ask me to do any of this."

She moved and the soft fabric of her sundress brushed across her nipples, caressing them with every move. "Mmm...okay, then I'm seducing you."

He made a strangled sound. "I thought we weren't having a fling."

Unable to resist the sensation, she cupped her breasts and squeezed, lost in the allure of her own dance. "No. No fling," she said dreamily, imagining Noah's hands on her.

"But, Sabrina, if you don't stop, we're going to end up in that bed." He jammed his finger toward her room.

Gazing at him through heavy lids, she stroked her hands down her front, over her thighs, then back to her breasts. "If you don't touch me soon, I'll die of neglect."

With a muffled curse, he swept her up in his arms. "You are the most frustrating woman."

He tumbled with her onto the bed, his lips coming down on hers, his tongue hungry. While he foraged her mouth, his hands roamed all over her body. It seemed he touched her everywhere—her hips, her back, her breasts.

Oh, the magic his fingers worked on her breasts! Touching her through the thin fabric, he rolled her nipples between his fingers, sending shivers of molten heat straight to her core. She moved against him, pulling his shirt from his waistband to slip beneath and tease him in return.

His fingers brushed her neck, fumbling with the closure at her nape. She made quick work of the small buttons for him. The dress pooled around her waist, baring her breasts. Their gazes locked for one heated moment, then he bent his head and drew one rosy tip into his mouth.

She moaned with the sheer pleasure he gave her, as moisture gathered between her legs. "Feels…so good."

Laving her with brisk strokes, he slipped his hand up her thigh. Her panties proved an inadequate barrier as he slipped his fingers under the elastic, then eased into her entrance. "I love how you get so wet for me."

He kissed her again, his fingers mimicking the dance of his tongue as he stroked her intimately, plunging into her depths, then withdrawing, over and over again. The sensations built from deep within her this time, coiling tighter and tighter.

"I want to be inside you."

"Yes…yes." Together, they made quick work of her panties.

She reached for his waistband, but he brushed her hands away. "Another time, love, I'll let you undress me. Now, I can't wait."

To her amazement, she had the wherewithal to remember the condom. "Here." She rolled to her side, snatched her purse from the nightstand, thankful to have it close, then pulled out one of the square packets.

Flopping back on the bed, she tried to breathe and calm

her racing heart. Her nipples tingled. Blood pulsed through her sex. She nearly cried out when Noah touched her again there.

He covered her, his mouth joining with hers, while he slid inside her in one long stroke. With smooth, controlled movements he rode her, seating himself deep within her sheath, then pulling out almost entirely before stroking back again. "Yes…Sabrina…oh God…"

Desire consumed her. Her whole life spun down to this one moment, this one man and the sensations he sparked in her. Her heart swelled with the magic he worked, strumming her body to a fine pitch, until the tension broke and she contracted around him, caught in the depths of another powerful orgasm.

A low moan parted his lips and he shuddered against her, inside her. His arms squeezed tight around her and he collapsed, rolling to his side with her locked in the intimate embrace.

She clung to him, his heart pounding against her ear. Noah, her chivalrous knight. Her dream lover. That she could so affect him sent her confidence soaring.

Glancing down, she laughed at the sight they made. Her dress lay twisted and bunched about her waist. He was still dressed, with the exception that his slacks and briefs rode halfway off his finely curved backside.

"Hmm, we're going to have to do better than this." She tugged at his shirt.

His sexy mouth curved into a grin. "Sorry. It's your fault for getting me so stirred up."

He grabbed his shirt hem, but she stopped him. "Not just yet."

A knock sounded on the door and a muffled voice announced their room service had arrived. She pulled her dress back up, then shooed him toward the door. "Get your britches on, then get the door. I want dinner in bed."

She rose to her knees, shaking her hem in place as he headed toward the door. "Then *I* get to undress you, like you promised."

He grinned back at her. "Anything you want, sweetheart. Anything you want."

SOMETHING BRIGHT against her eyelids dragged Sabrina from her slumber. Yawning, she slowly stretched. Sunlight flickered in through the open curtains. A weight across her middle and warmth at her back brought memory flooding in. Heat crept up her cheeks as she rolled carefully to her other side.

Noah mumbled something in his sleep and tightened his hold. His half-erection pressed against her thigh. She smiled, in spite of herself. The man just kept going and going. Seems he was going again in his dreams.

She closed her eyes as details from the previous night spun through her mind. Embarrassment filled her. How was it she could act so brazenly, so unSabrina-like around him? It was as though he was some mind-altering drug that had her doing and saying things she dared only dream of in her normal world.

Now, here in the morning light, her actions played out for her. She'd lost her virginity to her brother's best friend, a known and admitted womanizer, a man adept at pleasuring women, a man who for some reason stirred deep emotion in her—deep emotion that filled her now as she gave in to the need to touch him and lightly traced his jaw.

Had she been so relieved to see him last night that she'd rationalized that whole chivalry theory to allow herself another night of ecstasy in his arms? *Fool!* Those emotions she'd woken with the morning after her birthday crowded in on her now doubled in intensity, choking her. She'd ignored her brain's shrill warning and had let her body lead her.

And all those *feelings* were back.

Why had she let herself believe he cared for her? Was she that lonely, that desperate that she'd come to think her fantasies were real?

"What's got you looking so serious this morning?"

Her heart pounded. He gazed at her, his eyes dark and dreamy. She forced a smile, even as his erection pressed into her. "I was wondering if you'd ever wake up."

His palm settled over her breast. "I was dreaming about you. About this." He kneaded her gently.

She swallowed past a hard knot in her throat. She couldn't make love to him now, not when she felt so vulnerable—her emotions raw.

Somehow, she managed another smile. She pushed away from him, wrapping herself in the sheet as she scrambled to her feet. "We can't spend all day in bed. It's beautiful out. The beach is waiting."

His brows arched in surprise. No doubt, rejection wasn't part of his experience. "It can keep waiting. It isn't going anywhere."

He reached for her, but she twisted away. His brows furrowed. "What's wrong?"

Drawing up as straight as she could in her sheet, she reached for all her dignity. "Nothing's wrong. I just think maybe we should clarify... Well, last night I was feeling grateful to you for getting me out of that...fix I'd gotten myself into—"

"Grateful?" His eyes widened.

"Well, relieved—"

"Relieved?" He was sitting up now, frowning. "Is that what you call it?"

She huffed out a frustrated breath. This was coming out all wrong. "Last night, in the bar, why did you come for me? I didn't know you were here. I thought I'd lost you in the airport."

He blinked, as if not comprehending.

"Why did you even hop on that plane and follow me here, for that matter?" She held her breath. Maybe she'd been right last night. Maybe he did care.

After a long pause, he cleared his throat. "Well, I felt responsible for you."

"Responsible?"

"You yourself said you had me to thank for 'liberating you.' Besides, I owe Cliff a lot." His eyes narrowed. "And apparently someone has to look out for you."

Her lip trembled. *I will not cry.* "That's it?"

He raised his hands, baffled. "It was the right thing to do. What do you want?"

"I don't want anything." Hurt and anger choked her. *Fool. Fool. Ten times a fool.* He hadn't followed her because he cared. He'd followed out of a sense of responsibility and obligation to her brother.

Her eyes misted. "I just want to get one more thing clear."

"Please do, because I'm in the dark here. One minute we're having a great time and the next, you're upset with me and I don't know why."

Having a great time. That was what their time together added up to. "I'm upset with me, not you."

"Okay. That's what you want to get clear?"

She drew a deep breath. "We are *not* having a fling."

"We're not?" His eyes rounded in disbelief.

"No."

"Well, let me tell you something, sweetheart, you may

not have a lot of experience with this, but *I* do. And *this*…"
he thumped the bed for emphasis "is a fling."

She folded her arms and glared at him.

For a moment he just stared back at her. "Fine. Does
that mean you're on the hunt again for a fling?"

She supposed she deserved that, but it still hurt. "It's
already Sunday. I don't suppose I could find a weekend
fling this late in the weekend."

His shoulders relaxed. "All right, then I suppose I should
go back to my room and get cleaned up. May I take you
to brunch?"

"Brunch?"

He glanced at the clock. "It's early yet for lunch, but
I'm guessing the restaurant does a decent Sunday brunch."

"Okay." She swallowed, surprise and relief rising in her.
"Brunch would be nice."

NOAH PRESSED his glass of iced tea to his forehead, and
cursed himself for a fool. He should have left on the first
available flight back to Atlanta, but Sabrina had been so
upset this morning. He wasn't sure what had upset her, but
he suspected he had something to do with it. Somehow, he
couldn't bring himself to leave her.

Thankfully, the tension between them had dissipated by
the time he'd returned to take her to brunch. She'd answered her door, fresh and smiling as if their earlier discussion hadn't taken place.

He shook his head. The woman had him completely off
balance. Part of him exulted in the ultimate pleasure she
dished out, the other part regretted his inability to resist her
charms. She was the sister of his best friend—the man who
was helping him rebuild his career, the man he would stand
by in less than a week. And Noah had taken her virginity.

He should be checking the later flight schedules right now, not enjoying a friendly lunch with her.

Memories of her sweet mouth roaming over him, her eyes burning with desire as she slowly stripped his clothes from him, and her nipples budding against his lips washed over him. Guilt twisted his gut. He felt anything but friendly toward her.

He ran the cold glass down his throat, then lowered the zipper on his windbreaker. In spite of the afternoon heat, he didn't dare remove the light jacket. It hid the huge tent in his trunks.

At least he'd had a chance to shop yesterday. He'd be most uncomfortable in his slacks in this state. Damn the woman. Did she have to be so sexy?

We are not *having a fling.*

How she could turn her back on the attraction between them was beyond him, but he'd honor her wishes. It wasn't going to be easy, now that he knew what he was missing, but at least one of them had come to her senses.

The memory of finding her in the bar last night shuddered through him. Mark, the bartender, had given him the rundown on the company she was keeping when Noah had entered the bar. He'd never felt more panicked and upset in his life as he did when he saw her surrounded, her eyes wide with alarm.

Now she smiled at him, all innocence, as if she'd forgotten he'd plucked her from the verge of an orgy last night. He shuddered. If that producer had gotten her on his pleasure boat...

"What's wrong?"

He pointed an accusing finger at her. "You distracted me on purpose last night, so I wouldn't think about it. If anything had happened to you—if that pervert had forced you—"

"Oh, you're back to that thing in the bar. It wasn't like that. I told you. Bill was really quite upset. It was just a little misunderstanding." A blush crept over her cheeks. "I did tell him I was looking for excitement."

Noah snorted. "Well, you got that all right." He groaned. "If Cliff hears about this—"

"My brother has to learn to mind his own business." Her eyes sparked fire.

Trying to relax, he sipped his iced tea. At least she still had her spunk. She didn't seem at all traumatized by the ordeal. He, however, might never recover. He shuddered again. To think of her in the clutches of that dirty old man.

"This is absolutely wonderful." She smiled, her gaze scanning their surroundings. At her request, they sat at a table in a covered patio area off of the poolside bar. A server cleared away their brunch remains.

"Admit it." Sabrina gestured to the Gulf of Mexico, lapping quietly at the pristine shore. "You needed a day off. A day to sit around and enjoy the scenery."

Noah's gaze strayed over her kissable lips, her delicate shoulders, her rounded breasts, just the size to fill his hands. He nodded. "I do enjoy a good bit of scenery."

Leaning forward, she toyed with one thin bikini strap. "Let's go for a swim. Aren't you hot?"

He nearly barked in laughter. He'd never been so damned hot in his entire life, but cavorting in the surf with Sabrina didn't seem the wisest choice at the moment. He'd end up begging her to let him back in her bed, and his ego hadn't healed from her last rejection. He felt good and safe with the table between them. It hid his raging desire that even the windbreaker was proving inadequate in masking.

"We need to let our food settle." He pursed his lips as a male passerby gave her the once-over. Why the woman had to strut around with nothing to cover her skimpy swim-

GIFTS
from the
Heart

Play and you can get **2 FREE BOOKS** and a **SURPRISE GIFT!**

GIFTS from the Heart

Play Gifts from the Heart and get 2 FREE Books and a FREE Gift!

HOW TO PLAY:

1. With a coin, carefully scratch off the gold area at the right. Then check the claim chart to see what we have for you — **2 FREE BOOKS** and a **FREE GIFT** — **ALL YOURS FREE!**

2. Send back the card and you'll receive two brand-new Harlequin Blaze™ novels. These books have a cover price of $4.50 each in the U.S. and $5.25 each in Canada, but they are yours to keep absolutely free.

3. There's no catch. You're under no obligation to buy anything. We charge nothing —**ZERO** — for your first shipment. And you don't have to make any minimum number of purchases — not even one!

4. The fact is, thousands of readers enjoy receiving books by mail from the Harlequin Reader Service®. They enjoy the convenience of home delivery... they like getting the best new novels at discount prices, **BEFORE** they're available in stores...and they love their *Heart to Heart* subscriber newsletter featuring author news, horoscopes, recipes, book reviews and much more!

5. We hope that after receiving your free books you'll want to remain a subscriber. But the choice is yours — to continue or cancel, any time at all! So why not take us up on our invitation, with no risk of any kind. You'll be glad you did!

A surprise gift

FREE!

We can't tell you what it is... but we're sure you'll like it! A

FREE GIFT!

just for playing **GIFTS FROM THE HEART!**

DETACH AND MAIL CARD TODAY!

PLAY GIFTS from the Heart

Scratch off the gold area with a coin.
Then check below to see the gifts you get!

YES! I have scratched off the gold area. Please send me the 2 Free books and gift for which I qualify. I understand I am under no obligation to purchase any books as explained on the back and on the opposite page.

350 HDL DNSA   150 HDL DNLV

FIRST NAME	LAST NAME

ADDRESS

APT.#	CITY

STATE/PROV.   ZIP/POSTAL CODE

♥ ♥ ♥ ♥ 2 free books plus a surprise gift
♥ ♥ ♥ 2 free books   ♥ ♥ 1 free book

The Harlequin Reader Service® — Here's how it works:

Accepting your 2 free books and gift places you under no obligation to buy anything. You may keep the books and gift and return the shipping statement marked "cancel." If you do not cancel, about a month later we'll send you 4 additional books and bill you just $3.80 each in the U.S., or $4.21 each in Canada, plus 25¢ shipping & handling per book and applicable taxes if any.* That's the complete price and — compared to cover prices of $4.50 each in the U.S. and $5.25 each in Canada — it's quite a bargain! You may cancel at any time, but if you choose to continue, every month we'll send you 4 more books, which you may either purchase at the discount price or return to us and cancel your subscription.

*Terms and prices subject to change without notice. Sales tax applicable in N.Y. Canadian residents will be charged applicable provincial taxes and GST.

If offer card is missing write to: Harlequin Reader Service, 3010 Walden Ave., P.O. Box 1867, Buffalo NY 14240-1867

BUSINESS REPLY MAIL
FIRST-CLASS MAIL   PERMIT NO. 717-003   BUFFALO, NY

POSTAGE WILL BE PAID BY ADDRESSEE

HARLEQUIN READER SERVICE
3010 WALDEN AVE
PO BOX 1867
BUFFALO NY 14240-9952

NO POSTAGE
NECESSARY
IF MAILED
IN THE
UNITED STATES

wear but that square of cotton tied around her hips was beyond him.

She pushed her chair back, then stood. "Pooh, then a quiet stroll along the beach. We can at least splash our toes in the water."

Toes. He scooted his chair back a fraction. Toes sounded safe. At least she seemed to have scrapped her plan to jump the next available male. Maybe he could keep her distracted for the rest of the day, then get her on a late flight back. "Okay, a quiet stroll."

She beamed in delight, then preceded him across the wooden walkway to the beach. He averted his eyes from the sight of her hips' supple sway, and silently recited Dow Jones Averages until the tightness in his groin eased.

The sun beat down on them. Sand crunched underfoot. He whipped off the jacket, tugged his shirt over his head, then slid off his shoes, dropping the items in a pile on the beach. He glanced longingly at the water.

"I don't want to bring all this, either." She kicked off her sandals, untied her sarong, then spread it on the sand. After digging in her bag a moment she extracted a small wallet. "Can you carry this for me? I don't have any pockets."

He swept his gaze over her scant attire—a few scraps of fabric held together with string. No, she didn't have any pockets. His pulse raced. Did the woman have to look so trusting? He held out his hand. "Sure."

She placed the wallet in his palm, and graced him with a bright smile. "Thanks. Oh, one more thing…"

Again, she fished around in her bag, this time retrieving a bottle of sunscreen. "I need to reapply. This'll just take a minute."

Noah turned to look out over the vast expanse of blue-green water. Why torture himself by watching her smooth the lotion over her creamy skin? He wasn't about to offer his services either. Let her reach every luscious curve herself. Look what'd happened to the last guy who'd helped her. No way. She was on her own.

A gull screeched overhead. Children's laughter floated on the slight breeze. Someone's stereo cranked out one of the top twenty.

"There, I'm done. You're next," she said, standing close behind him.

He started to turn, but her hand on his shoulder stopped him. "Be still. Tanned as you are, you'll burn, too."

He sucked in his breath as the cool lotion touched him. He should tell her he never got sunburned, but her gentle fingers were stroking him, rubbing his heated skin. Stifling a moan, he resorted again to silently quoting stock figures.

Her hands glided low down his spine. Her fingertips brushed the elastic of his trunks, then slid back up to his shoulders. Again, the cool lotion touched him, then her warm hands. She moved to his side, working her way over his right shoulder, then down his arm. If it had been any other woman, Noah would have thought she was trying to seduce him.

But no sexy glint sparked in her eyes. Her voice held no sultry tone. No, this wasn't some other woman. This was Sabrina with her nurturing instincts, her manner annoyingly practical as she moved to his left.

We are not *having a fling.*

A grin quirked one side of her mouth. "Almost done."

Reminding himself not to be disappointed, he stopped her before she started his other arm. "I'll take it from here."

She handed him the bottle. He squirted a measure into his palm, then made a few obligatory swipes down his arm and chest. "Done. Now can we walk?"

After stuffing the lotion back in her bag, which she left with her sarong, she turned to him. "Let's head toward the pier. If we keep a good pace, we'll get some decent exercise."

He nodded. Here he was with a desirable woman, on one of the most beautiful beaches in the world, and they were walking for exercise. He was losing his touch.

She marched straight for the water, not stopping until she waded shin deep along the shore. "Sure you don't want to swim? It feels great." She reached down and splashed a couple of handfuls of water over her face and shoulders.

He swallowed. A vision of her rising wet from the surf, tiny rivulets coursing down her body, swam before his eyes. "Maybe later."

They strode along in silence. Noah couldn't resist wading beside her in the cool water. She stumbled once. He caught her, his heart quickening, but she steadied herself with a laugh, and pushed away from him.

"Look." Pointing, she sloshed out of the water and headed toward a life-size sand sculpture of a racecar.

Noah followed. "That took some time."

The sculpture spread low and long across the sand. The artist had carved a driver's seat into the middle, complete with a steering wheel.

A young girl in pigtails ran toward them, a plastic shovel in her hand. "You can drive it."

Sabrina bent, her hands braced on her knees. A smile spread across her face. "Did you help make this?"

"Naw." The girl crinkled her nose. "Watched them. We've been here all morning." She gestured toward an umbrella-covered blanket housing a man and a woman holding a small baby.

"Two guys made it, but they left. They said anyone could play in it. I drove it for a while, but you can have a turn now, if you want." The little girl smiled expectantly up at Sabrina.

Sabrina regarded the child a moment, before reaching out, perhaps to brush a bit of sand from the child's cheek. She stopped short of touching her, though. "Thanks, maybe I will."

With a quick glance at Noah, she climbed into the car sculpture. She smiled again at the girl, and something wistful in her expression caused Noah's chest to tighten.

"I'm Sabrina. What's your name?"

"Megan. I'm six. And that's Tyler. He's my baby brother. He cries sometimes, but I help take care of him. I give him a bottle, 'cause he can't eat real food yet. He's too little."

Noah followed Sabrina's gaze as it swung to Megan's brother nestled in her mother's arms as she approached. That wistful look in Sabrina's eyes intensified. She scrambled out of the car, smiling at the woman. "Hello. Megan's been showing us the car."

"She'll talk your ear off. She's not bothering you?" In spite of her words, Megan's mother ruffled her daughter's hair with obvious affection.

"See Tyler? He doesn't look all squishy like he did at first." Megan tiptoed, peering at her brother.

Noah moved closer. The baby blinked his dark eyes at Sabrina, and his little rosebud lips curved into a toothless smile. Noah grinned, turning his gaze to Sabrina, but she didn't seem to notice him. Megan's little brother commanded her attention. Her eyes glistened soft and warm, and they were filled with...longing.

Noah's jaw went slack as the realization hit him. Sabrina wanted a child. By the look in her eyes as she gazed at that baby, she not only wanted a child, she needed one.

"He's beautiful." Her voice was low, almost reverent.

She turned at last to Noah, as though just remembering he was there. "He's an angel."

Noah cleared his throat. He leaned over her shoulder, trying to dispel the unease that had settled over him. "He's a little guy."

To prove to himself that the small bundle posed no threat, he poked at it. Five miniature fingers closed around his. An odd warmth swelled inside him. He glanced up at the baby's mother. "How old is he?"

"He'll be five weeks tomorrow." She shifted the child in her arms, but it retained its fierce grip on Noah's finger.

"You're very blessed." Sabrina's voice faltered. She blinked several times.

Regret wound its way around Noah's heart. He wasn't in any position to give Sabrina her white picket fence, let alone a baby. If he had a drop of honor in him, he'd walk away from her right now.

He freed his finger and leaned closer to her. "We'd better move on."

Her throat worked, as though she had trouble swallowing. She nodded and turned to Megan. "Thanks for the ride. You take care of your brother."

"I will." Megan waved as they turned to leave.

Noah waved back. "Cute kid."

Sabrina nodded again as she marched stiffly beside him.

He sighed. She'd been kidding herself with this fling thing. She wanted children, a husband and a home. If he had half a brain, he'd get her on the next plane home, then say goodbye to her.

Feeling inadequate, he stole a glance her way. The longing still filled her eyes, only now it was combined with a sadness that tore at him.

Surely one day, she'd find someone and have a kid or two of her own. He let his gaze drift over her. No doubt about it. Women like her didn't stay alone in this world. The mystery was why someone hadn't snatched her up already.

He swallowed and focused on the strip of white sand before them. The guy had better treat her right, though, because she deserved the best. She deserved a man who could give her the whole nine yards—picket fence and all.

Too bad he wasn't the picket fence type.

He couldn't keep from looking at her again. This time she forced a smile for him. It twisted his insides to see how it fell just short of her eyes. Without a word, he reached over, took her hand in his and gave her a comforting squeeze.

She moved a step closer to him as they continued down the beach, hand-in-hand, without speaking. A mellow feeling settled over him. Yes, it was definitely too bad he wasn't the picket fence type.

9

"THAT ONE LOOKS like a mouse in a parachute." Noah pointed to a puffy cloud above them.

They'd made it back to the spot where they'd left their belongings. Sabrina lay stretched out on her sarong, while Noah used his jacket to protect his head and back from the sand. As considerate as he'd been all day, she couldn't seem to shake a feeling of melancholy.

She cocked her head. The wind shifted the clouds. "I think it looks like one of those scary clowns."

"Ah...could be."

Casting him a sideways glance, she pointed to an indiscriminate puff. "And that one looks like a wilted rose."

"So it does."

Turning to her side, she faced him. She had to get out of this slump. It wasn't fair to Noah. He was trying so hard to pamper her.

He was close enough to touch, if she reached out her hand. Her gaze drifted longingly over him. Sunlight glistened on his tan body. The man was pure temptation. "You're being awfully agreeable today."

He'd surprised her earlier when he'd invited her to brunch. She'd thought he'd want to wash his hands of her once she made it clear they weren't having a fling. If she'd been thinking straight, she probably would have politely declined. His eyes had held such hope, though, that she couldn't refuse.

"I'm an agreeable guy."

She managed a small smile. "You do seem to be."

"No, really...try me." His eyes sparkled.

"Okay, let's go for a swim." Maybe the heat was getting to her, beating her down. A cool dip might be just what she needed.

He stilled. "That sun *is* on the warm side."

"And the water looks fresh and cool."

"Rejuvenating."

"Yeah."

He rose to his feet, brushed the sand from his backside, then extended his hand to her. "Come."

Swallowing, she placed her hand in his, then let him tow her to where the waves broke on the shore. "Come on." He coaxed her into the aqua water.

When she stood waist deep he let her go. "Okay?"

She scooped handfuls of water over her chest and shoulders. "It's wonderful."

With a small splash, Noah disappeared beneath the surf. He appeared again a few yards away, stroking smoothly across the water, his shoulder and arm muscles rippling in a show of strength. He was all dark beauty, sunbeams glancing off the water all around him, as he dipped again, then headed back.

Sabrina drew a breath, then dove shallow and long. Cool water swirled around her. She swam a few strokes, then rolled onto her back, kicking idly as the clouds drifted above her. Closing her eyes, she blocked out all thought and focused on her breathing—drawing air slowly in through her nose, then out through her mouth.

Gradually, she relaxed. A warm breeze skimmed over her. The water rocked her, buoying her along with its slow current. Music played from a radio far off down the beach.

"A penny for your thoughts."

Startled, she lurched to the side, taking in water. Salt stung her nose. She flailed about and sucked in more water, then bobbed back up, gasping for air.

"Whoa, hold on." Steady and assured, Noah scooped his arm around her, then dragged her back to where her feet touched bottom.

He brought her up against his chest, water lapping up to her shoulders. His brows furrowed as he patted her back. "Breathe."

"I'm okay." She coughed, all too aware of the hard wall of muscle bracing her. Her heart quickened, sending warmth throughout her body. "You just startled me."

"Sorry, I didn't mean to sneak up on you." Concern grooved his forehead.

She smiled and smoothed her hand across his brow, unable to keep from touching him. His chest muscles flexed beneath her other palm. "It's fine."

"You're sure?" A teasing light lit his eyes. "Because, I'd be happy to assist with a little mouth-to-mouth if necessary."

Desire filled her. Why was it she lost her head whenever he touched her? Some distant part of her screamed a warning, even as she pressed into him, her arm curving around his neck. "Well, now that you mention it, I *am* feeling a little...breathless."

She pressed her mouth to his, no more able to stop herself than she could stop her heart from beating. Slipping her other arm around his neck, she tiptoed, opening to him, rejoicing in the touch of his tongue. He kissed her gently, sweetly, as though time had stopped and all that mattered was this one drugging kiss.

The water undulated around them. A seagull cried from somewhere in the distance. The kiss continued in a slow, leisurely dance of tongues, teeth and lips. Desire heated her blood and hardened her nipples. She broke away, only to merge back again into the blissful haze.

Noah skimmed his hands up her sides to the edge of her bikini top. A slight tug at her back and the top loosened. He cupped her below the water, kneading her, while his mouth continued its tender assault.

A low moan escaped her as he rolled her nipples between his fingers. Liquid fire gathered between her thighs. Tilting her hips, she pressed into him, squirming to get closer.

Something hit the surface beside them with a loud *thwack*, pelting water across them. She pulled back, turning toward the disturbance. Noah moved with her, shielding her from the shore, though the water covered her.

"Sorry, mister. That one went way off," a boy, probably around the age of ten, called from the shore. He stood knee deep, a hundred yards or so from them. Another boy, much smaller, covered his face and sloshed toward the shore, heading toward a motherly looking figure.

A Frisbee floated in the water nearby.

"Here I go, losing my top again." Chagrined, Sabrina twisted and pulled, until she had the errant garment back in place. Hurriedly, she tied a knot again at her back.

"Hey, sport! Heads up." With a practiced flip of his wrist, Noah sent the disc flying in a neat arc back to the boy.

Confusion and sexual frustration churned through Sabrina. Now that Noah wasn't touching her, the alarms in her head rang a little clearer. At the same time, she ached for more of his touch.

He turned back to her. "Sorry, I didn't mean to get so carried away."

She shrugged, striving for her best casual expression. Embarrassment flooded her. She'd been so deep in lust, she probably wouldn't have remembered where they were until after he'd made love to her right there in the Gulf. "It's okay."

With a slow nod, he extended his hand to her. "Come on, you're getting a bit pink. Time to get you inside."

A tremor ran through her as she took his hand. Was he taking her up to finish what they'd started? He let go of her long enough to gather their belongings on the beach. Once he'd slipped his shirt on and she'd knotted her sarong around her hips, then shouldered her bag, he took her hand again.

Her heartbeat pounded in her ears as they passed through a side door, then found a back elevator. Several people crowded in with them, wet from the pool or sandy from the beach. The doors opened on her floor and Noah gave her hand a squeeze as he maneuvered them around the other passengers.

Sabrina glanced back as the doors closed. What would have happened if they'd been alone on that elevator? She closed her eyes at the thought as heat surged through her.

"Key?"

Opening her eyes, she swung her bag around to search through its contents. She found the card key by the time they'd reached her room. It seemed all the saliva had left her mouth by the time she got the door open.

She turned to him, torn between bidding him a hasty goodbye and dragging him back to her bed. "Noah—"

"Why don't you get cleaned up, take some time for yourself, and I'll check on you later?"

"Oh…" She shouldn't feel so disappointed. This should be relief coursing through her. "Okay."

He bent to plant a chaste kiss on her cheek, then turned to leave.

"Dinner?"

He stopped, then swiveled back to face her. "Sure."

"Here. I'm not up to going back out. I'd like to take it easy, if that's all right."

"Around seven?"

Now the relief flowed, coaxing a smile to her lips. "Seven's good."

NOAH WINCED as he pricked himself again with the razor. He blew out a breath, concentrating as he guided the blade around his jaw. "You're just going to keep her company, bud, cheer her up, that's all. This is not a date."

He frowned at his reflection. The truth was, he didn't trust himself alone with Sabrina, not with the memory of her sweet body haunting him. He gritted his teeth and forced away the vision.

She wasn't sure if she wanted him, and whether or not she'd admit it, she didn't really want a fling. She wanted what he couldn't give her—a happy ending.

He rinsed the razor, then set it aside, mopping his face with a towel. She'd been so down today. Somehow, meeting Megan and her baby brother had extinguished the light in her eyes.

He'd felt odd himself, standing beside Sabrina and peering at that baby. He hadn't really noticed babies before. The little tyke had been so new, so innocent.

Shaking himself, Noah threw on a pair of khaki shorts and a polo shirt. He'd taken the liberty of ordering room service to be delivered to Sabrina's room. He'd actually been relieved when she suggested staying in. At least he wouldn't be fending off any would-be suitors.

He frowned again. She seemed to have given up her crazy scheme. This was a good thing. So, why was his gut twisting in a knot?

Putting his misgivings aside, he arrived at Sabrina's door. She answered his knock right away. She'd piled her mass of hair haphazardly on the top of her head, and stray tendrils brushed her cheeks and the nape of her neck. She'd slipped into a pair of cutoff shorts and a blue halter-top that accented her eyes. A coating of pink polish on her toenails completed her attire.

Noah swallowed, his blood warming. Maybe toes weren't so safe. "Hi."

"Hi." She smiled, and stepped aside for him to enter.

Soft music played from a radio on her bedside table. Her sliding door stood open, letting in a gentle breeze and the distant crashing of the surf. The setting sun filled the sky with rich hues of orange and red. She'd had room service set their dinner on a small table facing the view.

She handed him a glass of wine. "Thanks for ordering."

He nodded, then followed as she stepped out onto the balcony.

"It's so peaceful here." She gazed over the horizon.

They watched the sun set in silence. Noah's gaze flickered over Sabrina. Somehow, the spectacular beauty of the moment seemed to enhance her melancholy. He gripped the railing, feeling helpless. How could he put the light back in her eyes?

She turned to him after the last wisps of golden-red faded and the first pinpricks of light glittered across the darkening canopy.

"Hungry?" he asked.

Nodding, she led the way to the table. The aroma of basted snapper and sea scallops rose from the dishes. He unfolded his napkin. "You know, I've enjoyed this weekend."

"I'm a little surprised Cliff hasn't shown up."

"Cliff? You think he'd track you down?"

She leveled her gaze on him. "He might, if he realized we'd both disappeared around the same time."

Shifting uncomfortably, Noah tossed back a swallow of wine. "How would he know where to look?"

"I've always favored this area...but I could be wrong. He's so tied up with Mona and the wedding these days." A heavy sigh escaped her. She lifted her glass again to her lips.

Noah nodded, but a feeling of unease crept over him.

"Dance with me?" Sabrina rose and held her hand out to him. The radio crooned a soft melody.

The sad, hopeful look in her eyes drew him to his feet. The moon had risen, casting a gentle glow. They stepped onto the balcony, and she slipped into his arms. Her fresh scent enveloped him. She smelled of soap and woman.

She tucked her head against his shoulder, and he inhaled that essence that was hers alone. She nestled her soft body into his, tripping every one of his nerves to full alert.

We are not *having a fling.*

His pulse sped. He murmured her name into her hair. He should pull away. He should leave. His hand stroked down her bare back.

Her fingers knotted in his shirtfront. She turned her face to his. Her breath feathered across his cheek, then her lips brushed his. When she pressed her mouth to his, he ignored his screaming conscience, and kissed her.

She moaned, pressing closer to him as he deepened the kiss. She opened to him, allowing him access to every sweet crevice of her luscious mouth. Her tongue stroked his with an eagerness that set his heart pounding. She tasted of wine and Sabrina—an irresistible combination.

He let his hands roam down her back to the firm curve of her bottom. With a groan of his own, he cupped her, lifting her, fitting her to the part of him that ached to fill her.

She moved against him, breathing his name in his ear.

Desire shuddered through him. Drawing back, she took his face in her hands. Her open gaze held him.

"Make love to me, Noah."

He stilled. Blood rushed in his ears. For himself, he could suffer leaving her, but in that instant he couldn't deny her as she gazed up at him. At last, he'd found a way to put the light back in her eyes.

Sabrina drew in a long breath, her heart quickening. She let her gaze drift over Noah's lips, before settling again on his eyes. Desire shone in their depths. Her pulse thrummed. "Let's go inside."

He shifted to lift her in his arms. Anticipation washed over her as he carried her to the bed. He set her on her feet, sliding her down his front and taking her mouth in another heated kiss. She stroked her hands down his back, while his lips left hers to nibble a path along her neck.

"Sabrina..." He cupped her breasts through her halter-top, then ran his thumbs over her hardened peaks. "You don't know what you do to me."

She sighed, and tugged his shirt from his waistband. "I think I may have some idea."

"I want to see you...all of you." He pulled his shirt off, then watched her, his eyes dark with desire.

With shaking fingers, she fumbled with the buttons at her back.

"Turn around. Let me help." He moved behind her, to sit on the edge of the bed.

She turned. His knuckles brushed her back as he unfastened her buttons, while she loosened the knot at the nape of her neck. Her heart raced as the top slid to the floor.

His arms came around her, and his mouth skimmed over her back to her side. He ran his hands up to knead her breasts. "Look how beautiful you are."

She raised her eyes. Her heart thudded at the sight re-

flected in the mirror hung across from them. Noah's tanned
fingers contrasted sharply with the pale skin of her breasts.
She muffled a groan, unable to avert her gaze, as he stroked
her hardened nipples.

"Now these." He undid her shorts, then tugged them
down her hips.

Heat pooled inside her as she turned to face him, wearing
nothing but white cotton panties. His gaze drifted over her.
He hooked his fingers in the elastic waistband.

"All of you." With one smooth motion, he slipped the
garment down her legs.

As she stepped from the panties she braced her hands on
his shoulders. His skin was warm and smooth beneath her
fingers, his muscles hard and well defined. Again, his gaze
swept her, sending heat spiraling low in her belly.

"Exquisite." He ran his hand over her hip, then up to
cup her breast. Once more, he stroked his thumb over the
swollen peak. Then leaning forward, he captured her in his
mouth.

"Noah." She sank her fingers into his hair, while waves
of desire rippled through her. As before, her body's response was immediate. Moisture gathered between her
thighs, the ache there intensifying with each pull of his
mouth.

When he moved to her other breast, she gasped, aroused
almost beyond bearing. "I need you to…touch me."

Noah lifted her, then swung her onto the bed. If he
weren't so hard he might have laughed. She'd always been
incredibly bold, in spite of her innocence. Lord, she was
beautiful. He brushed his palm across her satiny belly, savoring the soft, firm feel of her. "But I *am* touching you."

She bit her lip. A blush crept over her cheeks. "Yes, I
noticed that…and I like the way you've been…touching

me, with your hands…and your mouth. But…I'm…aching.''

He smiled, awash with male pride, and nuzzled her stomach. He could tell her a thing or two about aching. After dipping his tongue into her navel, he raised his head. "There?''

She squirmed, her fingers knotting in his hair. She wet her lips. The pink in her cheeks darkened. "Lower.''

He exhaled. With his gaze locked on hers, he sifted his fingers through her tangle of curls. His heart pounded as her body trembled and she gasped.

He paused, but she nodded, encouraging him to continue. Nudging her legs apart, he slid down to explore her more intimately. He breathed in her woman's scent, and touched her.

She moaned, sliding her knees upward to grant him better access. "I feel so…so hot.''

A choked laugh lodged in his throat. He was a bit on the flammable side himself. He dipped his head to taste her.

She moved against him. The sexy sounds she made sent desire surging through him. She responded to every touch, every stroke of his tongue. He loved her with his mouth and his hands, seeking her hidden treasures as he savored her sweetness.

She shifted her hips, and his finger slipped inside her. She was so tight. He glanced up. Her eyes were wide, her lips parted. He pushed further into her, reclaiming her, exalting in the knowledge that no other man had touched her this way.

He pressed a kiss to the inside of her thigh. She sighed as he moved his mouth back over her, teasing her with his tongue and teeth. He slipped a second finger inside her to join the first, stroking her until she moaned and her lovely breasts rose and fell with her rapid breath.

He reached his other hand beneath her to squeeze her firm buttocks, while lifting her again to his mouth. He groaned, losing himself in the taste and feel of her.

She rocked against him. A low moan tore from her throat, then she tensed and cried out. He coaxed her with his tongue and the steady thrust of his fingers as her hips arched off the bed.

Not until she stilled did he move beside her to take her in his arms. He kissed her hair and stroked her back, while she clung to him. For long moments he held her, an odd warmth spreading inside him.

Unbidden, her look of yearning as she watched that baby on the beach flooded back to him. He swallowed. She wanted so much. She deserved a man who could give her the whole shebang. He kissed the top of her head. The regret he'd felt earlier returned with a vengeance. If only he were the marrying kind.

Guilt rode on the heels of his regret. He should leave her now. He had no business being with her like this when he couldn't offer her forever.

She stirred, smiling up at him, light dancing in her eyes. She tapped her fingers against his chest. "I believe it's your turn."

Lowering her head, she laved his nipple, while her palm roamed down his stomach. He swallowed. If he had an ounce of honor in him, he'd stop her. She kissed a path across his chest, her mouth hot against his skin.

He closed his eyes. "Sabrina, you don't have to do this."

She gave him a disapproving frown. "Come now, I let you have your way with me. It's my turn to ravish you."

She brushed her lips over his, then kissed him, her tongue massaging his in a way that had him pressing her close. As she rubbed her breasts against his bare chest he fought for control. Somewhere, somehow, he needed to dredge up some willpower.

She slipped her hand down his front. Her fingers drifted over his shorts. Desire seared him. He leaned back, and drew in a ragged breath. Gripping her wrists, he pulled her hands from him. "Maybe that's not such a good idea."

"I just want to touch you. I want you to make love to me."

He blew out a breath and let go of her. "I care about you, Sabrina."

"I care about you, too, Noah." She cupped his jaw and kissed him then, with such heat and passion he knew he couldn't deny her.

Just one last time to remember and treasure, then I'll leave her alone.

He rolled her beneath him, covering her with his body. He savored her mouth, cataloging every taste and texture, while his hands memorized the landscape of her body. A dip here, a curve there. Soft, sensitive nipples that stood at attention to greet him as he brushed his fingers over them in a long farewell caress.

Pulling back, he shifted. *And a slow, goodbye kiss there.* He drew the rosy tip into his mouth, stroking her with his tongue, until she pulled at his shoulders.

"Oh, God, Noah, don't make me wait anymore."

Four hands divested him of the rest of his clothes in no time. Sabrina came up with a condom from somewhere and he chastised himself for not even thinking of it. In her haste, she tore open the packet. Her fingers tripped over his as she helped roll it on.

He met her gaze as he slipped into her welcoming heat. She fit him so tightly, he sighed with sheer pleasure. Never would it feel this good again. Her body was made for his. Every contour a complement to his form, sheathing him, caressing him, sending him to a place of ecstasy he had never dreamed existed.

Her hips met his at every thrust. Her breathy cries piqued his desire, urging him on. He kept a steady pace, not wanting this time to end, suspending them in the ebb and flow of their loving.

"Oh...oh...ooohh, Noah." She clutched him, too soon, moving against him as her body convulsed first once, then again, then again in an orgasm that stole his breath and triggered his own climax.

He shuddered inside her, then fell trembling over her. Her inner muscles continued to quake around him in little aftershocks as he lay dazed. A sense of irony filled him. What god had made a woman so perfect in body for him, yet so emotionally out of his reach?

She wanted too much. God help him, he just wasn't her man.

He slid off her, full of bitterness and regret. He'd never live up to her expectations. This had to be the end of it.

"All right, so maybe we *should* have a fling."

"What?" He turned to her, his breath catching at the sight of her. Her eyes glowed, her cheeks were rosy, her lips swollen with his kisses. She looked thoroughly tousled and thoroughly loved.

She'd never been more beautiful.

She snuggled up closer to him. "I could really get used to this."

His heart lurched. "Sabrina, that...isn't what you really want."

"I know that's what I've been saying—no fling—but you were right. We keep ending up in bed together. Must be a fling."

"Sabrina—"

"It'll be fine. Actually, the wedding is in a matter of

days and the festivities start almost as soon as we get back. I was thinking it might be awkward, but if we just extend this through next weekend, it could actually be a lot of fun.''

''Sabrina, we can't. I can't. It wouldn't be right.''

''Why not?''

He took her hand. ''You don't want a fling. You want so much more. You deserve more.''

She made an exasperated sound. ''What makes you think you know what I want?''

''I saw the look in your eyes today, with that little girl and her baby brother. That's what you want, sweetheart.''

She blinked, catching her bottom lip between her teeth. Then she looked away, grabbed the sheet, then bunched it around her. ''We agreed no strings.''

''Yes, we did.''

Her beautiful eyes misted as she gazed at him. ''You don't think I can do that. Have a no-strings relationship with you.''

He brushed his fingers against her cheek. ''I think it's your nature to feel things deeper than that.''

She blinked, as though she were fighting back tears. ''Why did you follow me here? Why did you rescue me last night?''

His throat tightened. So she was back to that. ''I told you. I feel responsible for you.''

''Responsible?'' Her voice cracked around the word.

He gestured with his hand. ''All that talk of how I liberated you. If I'd have known you'd react like this to being made love to…''

''You'd still have made love to me. You wanted me. I think you still want me. You've just got some chivalrous idea in your head that you've got to be noble.''

Noble? Him? His heart thumped against his rib cage. Of

course he wanted her. He'd wanted her from the moment he entered her shop and found her with her hips swaying in that sensual dance. He wanted to devour her hot mouth and sink himself so far inside her he might never find his way out.

But she was a dreamer. A dreamer who believed in love and happily-ever-after. It wasn't anything so noble as chivalry that kept him from committing to a fling. It was a sense of self-preservation.

He dropped his gaze to the rumpled sheets. "You've got me all wrong."

"I don't think so."

He looked up to find her mouth a hair's breadth from his. "Have a fling with me, Noah."

A deep sadness crept over him. "I can't. I'd be doing you a great disservice."

"You wouldn't be. I can handle it."

With a weary shake of his head, he let his gaze wander over her one last tortuous time. What was it about this woman that tempted him beyond endurance? Hurt and hope shimmered in her eyes, piercing his heart. To stay meant hurting her more.

His heart, if he had one, thudded dully. "No, Sabrina. I'm sorry."

Her eyes widened, but she said no more as he turned from her and gathered his things. He dressed, then left, letting the door click shut behind him. When the hell had he developed a conscience?

10

SABRINA ROLLED to her back and stared up at the ceiling. Damn the man. How could he have walked out on her like that? Her heart contracted.

I care about you, Sabrina.

How could he care about her and leave? A pox on his chivalry. She didn't need him to be noble. She needed him naked beside her—inside her.

She clutched her pillow and moaned. To think she'd let him touch her—kiss her—everywhere. Sure, he'd given her what had to be the mother of all orgasms. Many times over. Sex with Noah had surpassed her wildest fantasies. Yet, he'd left her wanting more. She wanted to experience again the mind-blowing release they'd shared that first night. Sighing, she smacked the pillow into the mattress.

Who was she kidding? She wanted him to care for her, really care for her. *I want a man to care about me, to put my needs above his, to want to make me happy.*

Wasn't that exactly what Noah had done?

From the start, everything he'd done had contradicted the picture she'd held of him before they met. Noah, the lady-killer, couldn't have had a chivalrous bone in his body, unlike her Noah—the Noah she'd come to know over the past week.

Her Noah. Sabrina closed her eyes. When had she come to care so much for him? Here she was trying to defend his actions, as though she were…falling in love with him. She straightened, her heart thudding.

Love? Was this sick feeling love?

She sank into the bed. A kaleidoscope of memories flashed before her—Noah appearing out of nowhere to kiss her senseless in front of the married jerk on the plane. Noah arriving like some avenging angel to sweep her from the clutches of the questionable producer and his crew. Noah holding her, bringing her pleasure she'd never imagined.

I care about you, Sabrina.

He had a funny way of showing it.

What had made her go through with seducing him? After their walk she had decided to abandon her plan. Seeing Megan and her brother had reminded her she hadn't changed what she wanted in life. Seducing Noah wouldn't have gotten her any closer to her goals.

Asking him to dinner had merely been a ploy to stave off her depression. He was supposed to keep her company. Then the moon and the wine combined with his irresistible attraction and her tripping hormones had conspired against her.

She'd known all along what he was. He hadn't made her any promises. He hadn't led her on in any way. She'd been foolish to glorify his behavior. He'd obviously suffered a severe case of guilt, nothing more.

Gritting her teeth, she strode into the bathroom to turn on the shower. She stepped under the hot water. With brisk movements, she scrubbed every inch of her body, as if she could wash away the memory of his touch.

Can you do this without being emotionally involved? Bess's words rang in Sabrina's ears.

"I am *not* emotionally involved!" She stepped from the shower and jerked a towel around her, her hands trembling.

She clenched her fists, and moved to the outer room to

dress, her gaze falling on the curtains as they fluttered in the light breeze. Moonlight glanced off the tiny balcony, casting a soft glow over the small table where she and Noah had shared their dinner.

She swallowed. Her gaze swerved to the bed, with its disheveled comforter and rumpled pillows. Her stomach churned. She couldn't stay here. Not for one more minute.

She strode to the closet, then yanked her suitcase from the top shelf. As far as she was concerned, this fling was flung.

THE PLANE DIPPED then leveled, its engines vibrating in a steady hum. Sabrina turned to look out the dark window. Clouds had moved in to obliterate the moon and stars. She sighed.

After rousing a tired desk clerk she'd made a hasty escape from the hotel. Driving her rental all out, she'd arrived in Panama City in record time. To her profound relief she'd caught this midnight flight to Atlanta.

Home. Her little apartment had never sounded so good. One of her full time employees was scheduled to open the bookstore in the morning. Sabrina could sleep in and lick her wounds.

She closed her eyes, resting her head against the high back of her seat. Her limbs seemed too heavy to move. She grimaced. The muscles in her inner thighs and buttocks were sore—no doubt from her earlier acrobatics with Noah—and for some inexplicable reason, her chest ached.

"Sabrina?"

She started at the masculine voice. Her pulse pounded. A dark-haired stranger slipped into the seat beside her. For the briefest milli-second, she entertained the hope that Noah had followed her.

But this man peered at her with clear, blue eyes, and his

hair held a hint of auburn. She straightened. "Do I know you?"

He shook his head. "We haven't met, but I've heard all about you."

She cocked her head, frowning, while he searched his coat pockets for something. After a moment his face brightened. "Aha, here it is." He held up a battered envelope.

"I'm sorry, I don't—"

"I'm John Dalton. I'm more or less related to Mona. She's got me flying in to help tie up loose ends for the wedding."

"So, you're related to Mo—*Uncle John?* You're Mona's *Uncle John?*" She gazed at him in disbelief. The man couldn't be much older than thirty-five. "How can that be?"

He laughed and his smile transformed his rather ordinary looks. His eyes shone and his face took on a new appeal. Sabrina shook herself. She was checking out Mona's uncle.

John opened the envelope as he explained, "My sister, who is a good ten years older than me, married Mona's father, who's a good twelve years older than my sister."

"Your sister is Mona's stepmother—"

"So, we're not blood related, but since we were closer in age, and since she doesn't have any other family, Mona and I just hit it off. She thought it would be funny to call me uncle. I guess it stuck."

He shook his head. "I've always been there to help her get organized. I wasn't surprised when she asked me to come up early."

He handed Sabrina a photograph that he'd removed from the envelope. The picture was of her, Cliff and Mona. Their waiter had taken it while they were out at dinner one night. Mona and Cliff sat snuggled together, all smiles, while Sabrina perched stiffly to one side.

She handed the picture back to John. "That was taken at Blarney's. It's a little pub Cliff and I used to hang out at." She closed her mouth, surprised at the resentment straining her voice.

John's attention remained on the photograph. "I wish I'd been there." He raised his head. His gaze connected with hers. "I wouldn't have let you feel like a third wheel."

"I…" Sabrina slumped back against her seat.

How had he done that? She'd been disgruntled for months, unable to admit to herself the reason. He'd just hit the nail on the head. She'd felt like a third wheel. Ever since Mona had dropped into Cliff's life, Sabrina had felt extraneous.

She peered at her new companion. "So, you're bound for Atlanta at this ungodly hour."

"I'm thinking of moving my business there. I wanted some time to meet with some of my contacts, and check out the area. And there's the wedding, of course."

"What kind of business?"

He tucked the photo into its envelope, then stowed it back in his pocket. "Advertising. I already spend a good deal of my time in Atlanta."

"Why the red-eye flight?"

He shrugged. "It was the best I could work around my schedule. I could ask you the same question."

She puffed out a breath of air. "You don't want to know."

He leaned in closer. His spicy cologne swirled around her. A sympathetic glow filled his eyes. "Sure I do."

Something about him had her shifting forward. Maybe it was his sincerity, or his empathetic gaze, or perhaps the fact that though he was a total stranger, he elicited a trusting response in her. Talking to him felt as comfortable as talking to Bess. Whatever it was about John Dalton, he made Sabrina feel safe.

The lure of spilling her guts proved irresistible. She told him everything. Of course, she left out any mention of the raw emotions she'd experienced over the weekend. Explaining her plan and its utter failure shed a pitiful light on her life.

Her depression descended heavier than ever. Could Noah be right? Was true love a figment of her imagination? Would she never find The One?

John patted her hand, his brow furrowed in empathy. "I know it's difficult to see now, but this is all for the best. You'll find someone deserving, someone to love, who'll love you in return."

Sabrina narrowed her gaze on him. "You believe in love?"

He regarded her a long moment, then nodded, something warm stirring in his eyes. "You could say I'm a believer."

"So, you've experienced it firsthand?"

The warmth in his eyes seemed to glimmer and grow, holding her transfixed. "I guess that answer would be yes."

She stared for a moment, tensing under his gaze. All that warmth couldn't possibly be directed at her. The memory of some other woman surely sparked that heated look.

Sighing, she turned to gaze out the window as lights glittered far below them. They neared their destination. "You're lucky."

"Tonight I am."

She turned to give him a questioning look.

"I've been dying to meet you, ever since Mona sent me that picture. I couldn't believe it when I saw you. It must be fate."

A feeling of unease shifted through her. *Fate.* She frowned. "Maybe there is no fate. Maybe there is no rhyme or reason to the universe. The world and our lives are ruled by chaos and random happenings. Nothing matters. Nothing we do or believe has significance.''

''I'd heard you were a hopeless romantic. That doesn't sound very romantic to me.''

The pilot clicked on the intercom to let them know they were approaching the airport. Sabrina fiddled with her seat belt. ''Maybe I've finally come to my senses.''

''Oh, I hope not.'' The comment was so faint, she wasn't sure she'd heard him.

The plane started its descent, and she turned to him. ''Don't tell me you're a true romantic?''

A slow smile curved his lips, and she couldn't help noticing again how it transformed him. He'd make some woman happy.

''I've been known to spout a line or two of poetry.''

''Really? Poetry?'' In spite of her melancholy, her heart gave a little thump.

''And I definitely believe in happy endings, so if that makes me a romantic, I plead guilty.''

Sabrina cocked her head and regarded him. The man was too good to be true. He believed in love and happily-ever-after. If she could have designed the perfect man for her, John might have been the one.

The plane hit the runway, then glided to a stop. He squeezed her hand. ''This has been great, Sabrina. No matter what you say, I believe fate brought us together on this flight.''

He cocked his head thoughtfully. ''You'll have lunch with me tomorrow—'' He glanced at his watch. ''I mean today, won't you?''

She swallowed at the unconcealed hope in his eyes. How could she turn down a guy who believed in happy endings?

"Sure." She ignored the way her gut clenched. "Lunch would be great."

THE ELEVATOR DOOR OPENED. Noah squared his shoulders and stared down the long hallway leading to the suite of offices he shared with Cliff. Drawing a deep breath, he stepped onto the carpeted walkway. He'd spent a good part of the morning on his trip back, but he could still put in a few hours. He had time to make a couple of trades. Besides, the sooner he faced his partner, the better.

The trip to the double glass doors took an inordinate amount of time. He paused with one hand on the brass door pull. Fluorescent light shone on the gold lettering spelling first Cliff's name, then his.

Guilt burned in Noah's belly. When he'd had his fill of Denver, Cliff had taken him back without question, welcoming him with open arms. Then, in less than a month's time, his sister had done the same. Only Sabrina had done so literally.

Make love to me, Noah.

Scowling, he pushed through the door. Now was not the time to brood over missed opportunities. He had work to do. Without a glance to either side, he strode past the reception desk, and headed for the seclusion of his office.

"Noah! Thank goodness you're here." Tiffany, who doubled as both their receptionist and secretary, surged after him, her fist full of small slips of paper. "Mr. Cramer insists you call him immediately. He's called three times. Something about Home Depot stock splitting, and—"

"Thank you, Tiffany." He snatched the stack of messages from her hand, then whirled back toward his office, his temples throbbing.

"Um, and Cliff said if you had the, uh, balls to show up, he wanted to see you pronto…in his office."

Noah stopped, then pivoted on the balls of his feet. Tiffany bit her lip. Her trim brows arched to her hairline. "He seemed a little upset. Everything okay?"

"Fine."

"Oh…should I get you some coffee?"

He shook his head. "No thanks. Guess I'd better get this over with."

A moment later, Cliff answered his knock with a sharp, "Come in."

He looked up as Noah entered. His lip curled, and his eyes narrowed as he pushed back from his desk, then rose. "Tell me, *old friend,* how is it that you and my sister both disappeared from her party at about the same time, then were both unreachable for the rest of the weekend?"

Noah planted his feet wide. "Hello, Cliff."

"You couldn't leave her alone, could you? Had to add one more notch to your bedpost, didn't you?"

"It's true, I didn't feel I could leave her alone—"

"I knew it. You've ruined her!"

A dry laugh worked its way from Noah's throat. As if anything could ruin Sabrina. The woman was perfect in every way. "Ruined her? Not in this day and age."

"Damn it, Noah! How could you?" Cliff moved in front of him. Noah's gut clenched at the flicker of anguish in his partner's eyes. The guy really cared about his sister.

"She's a grown woman. You've got to let her live her own life."

"But she's my sister, for God's sake."

"Look, there's nothing going on between us."

"You mean you didn't…"

"I mean she's special, like you said. She deserves someone who'll treat her right."

Cliff stared at him a moment. He sat back on the edge

of his desk, his arms folded across his chest. "So, you're not sleeping with her?"

Noah shook his head. "No." *At least not anymore.*

For a long moment, Cliff stared at him, his eyes narrowed. Then he shrugged. "So, how did it go with Darcy?"

"Darcy?"

It seemed a million years ago when they'd first discussed her. Had he really been interested? It seemed hard to fathom that he'd accepted the woman as a bribe to take Sabrina out. He slid into a chair facing Cliff's desk. "Look, I'd appreciate it if you refrained from matchmaking in the future."

"You didn't make it with Darcy? But I thought—"

"I changed my mind."

Cliff stared at him again. "So, what *did* you do this weekend?"

Noah shook his head. How could he explain his time with Sabrina? "Sabrina found out about our whole deal with Darcy. I don't know, she must have overheard something. She got upset and left the party. I went to see her. I had to explain." He paused. There was no sense in telling Cliff everything. It would only upset him. "I ended up following her to the airport to try to talk to her."

He rose, then paced away. "She was planning some weekend fling. She wouldn't listen to reason. Then this guy hit on her. They boarded together...I couldn't let her do anything rash. I followed them."

"A fling? She let some strange guy pick her up?"

Noah faced him and nodded. "Then there was this young jock on the beach, then this older guy at the bar."

"Good God." Cliff's face had gone pale. "She didn't...you know...with any of them?"

"No."

"You're sure?"

"Positive. I kept an eye on her. Why the hell else would I have followed her?" The half truth sat heavy in his stomach. He'd kept to the truth...for the most part.

"Why indeed?" For a moment Cliff regarded him, his eyes narrowed. Then he shifted. "I know virgins aren't your style, but after the way you two disappeared...well, I thought for sure..."

Noah stared straight ahead, guilt twisting his insides.

Cliff leaned on his desk. "So, you ready for this week?"

"This week?"

Cliff's brows arched. "The wedding shower, rehearsal, rehearsal dinner...my wedding day. You're still my best man, aren't you?"

That sick feeling mushroomed inside Noah. Cliff's wedding. How could he have forgotten? "Sure. Wouldn't miss it."

"Great. To be honest, I just want to get the thing over with."

Noah stood. "I've got to get to work."

With a glance at his watch, Cliff shook his head. "I've got a client coming in. Guess I'd better get to work, too."

Nodding, Noah turned toward the door.

"Don't work too hard, though. Mona'll blame me if you turn up exhausted at the wedding. She wants everything perfect. Can't have the best man worn out."

Glancing over his shoulder, Noah clenched his fistful of messages. "I've just got a few calls to make."

Cliff nodded and Noah turned again to leave. Maybe if he concentrated on work he'd forget the past weekend. He set his jaw and headed for his office. Somehow, he had to forget Sabrina and the fact he'd be seeing her all week. If his mind replayed those glorious hours with her one more time, he'd go insane—or worse, beg her to finish what they'd started.

"DID YOU HAVE a nice birthday weekend?" Libby emerged from an aisle, reading glasses low on her nose, a hardback in hand.

Sabrina paused on her way to her office. She was straggling in late to the bookshop. She'd lost track of time while at lunch with John.

"Hi Libby." She sighed. "It was okay. How was your weekend?"

"We had a party down at Shady Grove. I taught the Petersons how to tango." Her eyes widened. "Would you like to learn?"

"Uh, no thanks." Sabrina's cheeks heated. She would have been much better off had she not learned Libby's last dance. Mortification filled her at the memory of dancing for Noah and the disastrous results.

Libby clucked softly. "You had a bad time, dear?"

The bell on the door jangled. Trish, her part-timer, waved from across the shop as she headed to greet the customer who entered.

Turning back to Libby, Sabrina sighed. "It was…disastrous."

"Didn't you go to Florida to spoil yourself?"

"It's not worth rehashing. I don't have the energy for it."

"I'm sorry. I don't mean to pry. You're just not your usual chipper self today."

Numb resignation settled over Sabrina. "Guess I'm going through a philosophical adjustment period."

"Oh, that sounds serious. You go put your things down. Then meet me in the reading corner. I'll fix us some tea."

Sabrina opened her mouth to protest as Libby scurried away, but changed her mind. Trish could handle the small number of customers dwindling in, and the orders on Sabrina's desk would keep. Besides, tea with Libby qualified as good customer relations.

A few moments later, she settled across from Libby in one of the mismatched armchairs at the back of the store. Steam rose from the mug Libby handed her. Sabrina inhaled the citrus scent.

Libby nodded toward the mug. "Orange pekoe. Now, tell me about this philosophical adjustment."

Sabrina sipped the soothing brew. "My experience this weekend has forced me to rethink my views on true love."

"Ah, true love. A topic I'm well acquainted with. So, what conclusion have you come to?"

A bitter laugh rose in Sabrina's throat. "That all my romantic notions of finding true love have been nothing more than foolishness?"

Libby frowned. "Oh my, this *is* serious. I take it you had a romantic interlude and it proved less than satisfactory?"

Groaning, Sabrina cradled her head in her hand. "Oh, Libby, I was *such* an idiot. I actually thought he was The One." She raised her head, laughing sourly. "I have to say, though, that in certain aspects it was *extremely* satisfactory."

"Ah." Libby's brows rose in understanding. "Well, you know dear, extraordinary sex is certainly a part of a true love relationship. From the moment I met my Henry, the sparks started flying. I knew when we danced we'd be good together. Then when we actually had sex...well, I knew without a doubt he was The One. I may not have wanted to admit it right away, but deep down, I knew."

"How...how did you know?" Sabrina leaned forward, intent on Libby's answer.

A light shimmered in the older woman's eyes. "The earth moved."

With a sigh, Sabrina sank back into her chair. *The earth moved.* She could relate to that. What she and Noah had experienced qualified as a tilting of the axis. "I can see that, but love isn't just physical."

"Of course not, but often, especially if those involved are honest about things, the physical comes first. Then the rest grows from there."

"Or it's just physical and it all fizzles from there."

Libby gave her a stern look. "You must persevere! No one said it was easy. Just because it's true love, doesn't mean all the chips fall in a row. Sometimes you have to work for it."

Frustration billowed inside Sabrina. "I can't. He...he dumped me." The corners of her mouth sagged with the painful memory.

"Nonsense. I dumped Henry at least half a dozen times."

Sabrina blinked. "You did?"

"I wasn't the trusting sort. Had already had my heart broken once before. I just wanted it to be a physical thing, but knew Henry wanted more. He deserved more."

"You sound just like him...the guy who dumped me. Said he couldn't give me all I deserved." A lump swelled Sabrina's throat.

"Well, my Henry just refused to give up. He persisted until he'd worn down my resistance. Like I said, I was attracted to him from the start, but I was afraid to trust and marry him." Her lip trembled. "But wear me down he did."

Her eyes took on that faraway look. "I remember the day I accepted his proposal."

She was quiet then and Sabrina's heart swelled. Libby deserved her Henry.

After a moment, Libby blinked and turned back to Sabrina. "He'll come for me. I don't know what's keeping him, but that's the most persistent man who ever walked this earth. He'll get here one of these days, and he'll have a damn good excuse."

Sabrina's throat burned so badly, she could hardly speak. She leaned over to pat Libby's hand. "We'll persevere, Libby. We'll persevere."

11

SABRINA FINGERED HER WINEGLASS and glanced around Blarney's. The bar was quiet this evening, with only a few scattered patrons lounging about its tables and high-backed booths. A clock bearing a popular beer logo glowed in the dim light.

Where was Bess? Sabrina was near bursting with the need to talk to her. Who better than Bess to understand her remorse over giving in to her physical cravings for Noah, a man who was completely wrong for her?

Bess would know what to say to ease the sick feeling that had settled in the pit of Sabrina's stomach. Talking to her would be such a relief. Maybe all Sabrina needed was to spill the entire story about her horrid weekend—the debacle with Noah, and her subsequent run-in with John Dalton.

John Dalton. She took a sip of wine, then let out a heavy sigh. He'd taken her to the quaintest Italian restaurant that afternoon. Though her appetite had been lacking, she'd been charmed by the red-and-white checked tablecloths, the white stubby candles and the violinist who'd serenaded their table.

The round-faced proprietor had evidently known John, and had waited on them personally. The service and the food had been exquisite, and John had been warm and gracious. A nicer man had never walked the earth.

Too bad he just wasn't for her.

Sabrina shook her head. His open body language and steady eye contact clearly showed his interest. That heated look had stolen into his eyes on several occasions, and he never passed up an opportunity to touch her. In fact, he had asked to book nearly every free hour she had during the remainder of the week. It had been all she could do not to commit.

The bell over the bar's door jingled. Sabrina glanced up. Relief seeped through her as Bess made her way toward their booth.

"I was getting worried about you," Sabrina greeted her friend as she plopped onto the seat across from her.

Bess signaled the waitress, who seemed to be the only one staffing the place. "I'm sorry I'm late. The girls, for once, were peacefully ensconced in the basement with a video, and Tom was feeling a little romantic."

She fanned herself with her hand, and if Sabrina's eyes weren't deceiving her, a telltale blush crept over her friend's cheeks.

"You'd think after all these years…well, the man knows how to keep things exciting." Bess turned to ask for a glass of wine as the waitress arrived.

She waited until the waitress left, before continuing in a hushed and disturbingly breathless voice. "He actually bought me edible underwear. Can you believe it?"

"Edible underwear?"

"Uh-huh. It was incredible. He was incredible. He was so turned on, he could have gone all night. I needed a break, though. He just wanted me to keep…well, you know, again and again."

She wiped her hand across her brow. "How multi-orgasmic can one woman be? Not that I'm complaining, but I swear I almost had a heart attack."

Sabrina nodded, speechless.

Bess didn't seem to notice. "I needed a break just to catch my breath. I had to convince him I'd make it worth his while if he let me slip away for an hour." She leaned forward and dropped her voice even more. "He gets to wear the next pair." She sat back. A low giggle bubbled from her throat as she again fanned herself.

The waitress returned with Bess's wine and Sabrina took a deep swallow of hers. Ignoring the glass of chablis, Bess turned toward Sabrina once they were alone again. "I get hot just thinking about him. Ever since—my God, I haven't even told you. This has been one heck of a weekend."

Sabrina nodded. "Tell me about it. I—"

"We let my mother have the girls yesterday and we checked into one of those hotels." Bess glanced at a couple sitting nearby, then leaned further over the table. "One with videos and sex toys. At first, I was so uncomfortable, but then Tom really got into it, and well…I couldn't help myself after that."

"Bess." Sabrina stopped. What could she say? That she found her friend's behavior shocking? That the last thing she needed to hear right now was exactly how fulfilling Bess's sex life was? That until this moment she had never even heard of edible underwear?

Bess's eyes widened. "Oh my gosh. How could I have forgotten?" She gripped Sabrina's arm. "Did you have your fling?"

Sabrina paused. Did her numerous encounters with Noah constitute a full fling? She shook her head. He'd turned down her request for a fling. Suddenly, she wasn't so eager to tell her friend all. "Not really."

Bess regarded her with raised brows, then shrugged when Sabrina failed to elaborate. "Good. I really hoped you wouldn't. Believe me, Mr. Right is worth waiting for. I found mine."

She smiled. "The sex has been better than I ever dreamed lately, even before this weekend, but the best part is..." She paused, her eyes twinkling.

Sabrina waited for a moment. What could be better than incredible sex in a committed relationship? Finally, she heaved a sigh. "What?"

"We're renewing our vows."

"You're what?"

"We're getting married all over again." Bess beamed.

"Why?" Sabrina couldn't keep the incredulity from her voice.

Bess drew up a little. "Well, you remember, the first time wasn't really under the best circumstances. We were both a little...resistant, but felt it was necessary at the time. I mean, we loved each other, but the timing..." She made an off-hand gesture.

Sabrina frowned. At the time, Bess had claimed to love Tom, but Sabrina always felt she said so in order to convince herself she was doing the right thing. She'd only been sixteen, after all. What could she have known about love?

"Bess, you cried for weeks before the wedding."

"Exactly." Bess relaxed, seemingly relieved that Sabrina understood, which she didn't.

At all.

"Why on earth do you need to renew your vows? It isn't as though those things expire."

Bess cocked her head. "My, you're not sounding at all like yourself, Sabrina. Of course they don't expire, but we want to celebrate the fact that our love has endured all these years, in spite of our shaky beginning."

She sighed in a dreamy, faroff way. "Ever since we decided, it's been like starting fresh again. He calls me two, three times a day. I even snuck over to his office last week while the girls were in school. Never underestimate the power of a quickie.''

"So, you two are having great sex. That's good. That's terrific.'' Sabrina did her best to force some enthusiasm into her voice.

She wanted to be happy for Bess, truly she did. It was just that Bess's frank admissions somehow made Sabrina feel as though she were weighed down. With bricks.

"Oh, it's so much more than great sex. I get so warm and tingly just sitting holding hands with him in front of the TV.''

Feeling decidedly unsettled, Sabrina shifted. "Bess, are you trying to tell me that you're in love with your husband?''

Bess's eyes sparkled. "I've always loved him, Bree. Lately, though, it's like we're falling in love all over again. That's why we want to renew our vows.''

She twisted her glass by its stem. "It was all Tom's idea. Can you believe it? One minute I was mooning over Cliff and Mona's wedding, then the next thing I knew, he was down on one knee.''

She shook her head and sniffed. Her eyes misted. "It was the most romantic moment of my life. I'm so lucky to have him.''

Sabrina looked long and hard at her friend. "You're really happy, aren't you? I mean, all this time with Tom, you've always been happy?''

Bess nodded, then drew her brows together. "Of course. What did you think?''

"Honestly? I thought you were miserable all these years. I thought you felt trapped, that you regretted giving up New York.''

"New York?''

"The runway. *Vogue*.''

A short laugh parted Bess's lips. "Oh, that." Her shoulders rose, then fell. "That was a dream I had a long, long time ago."

"You never regretted giving it up?"

"For Tom? For my girls? Nope. Not once. I can't imagine living any other life. I can't imagine life without them."

Sabrina nodded, marveling at the revelation. Bess was happy. Imagine that. "Then I'm happy for you."

Bess reached across the table to squeeze Sabrina's hand. "I knew you would be. Now, you're one of Mona's bridesmaids, but I know you won't disappoint me. You'll be my maid of honor, won't you?"

A knot formed in Sabrina's throat. Another wedding, another bride. She hadn't been to the altar once, yet Bess was ready for round two. To the same man.

Always the bridesmaid, never the bride. She drew in a deep breath and pushed back the wave of self-pity threatening to overcome her. "Sure, hon. I'd be honored. Again."

A radiant smile burst across Bess's face. "I knew you wouldn't let me down." She glanced at the clock on the wall. "Tom's counting down. I'd better go. He's promised the most naughty punishment if I'm late."

She half rose, then stopped. "Did you need to talk about something?"

Sabrina bit her lip and shook her head. "I'm fine. You go have a good time."

"You're sure? You seem a little, I don't know, off somehow." She narrowed her eyes and plunked herself back into her seat. "You're not still upset about Cliff bribing your date? Tell me you didn't spend the weekend sulking, and that's why you didn't go through with your plan."

"I...I'm just a little tired. You run along, unless of course, you're looking for a little punishment."

Bess stood, then moved to Sabrina's side. She threw her arms around her in a quick hug. "You're a peach, Sabrina. I'll let you know all the details as soon as we work them out."

She'd taken a few steps toward the door, before turning back. "I'll call you tomorrow."

Sabrina forced a smile and waved her on. "Have fun."

Long after Bess had gone, Sabrina sat staring into space. Her best friend in the world was happy, had always been happy. Sabrina was glad for her. Here was proof that love existed, that it had endured all these years under less-than-desirable circumstances.

She raised her glass, and ignored the funny feeling in her gut and the yawning emptiness in her chest. "To love," she said, then took a long swallow. "Whatever the hell that is."

EARLY THE NEXT MORNING, Sabrina grimaced and erased the entry she'd made in her day planner. Though she'd scheduled plenty of coverage this week at the store, with all the wedding festivities she still needed to squeeze in some time to review her updated budget. The problem was that between the wedding shower on Wednesday, Friday's rehearsal dinner, then the wedding on Saturday, she didn't have much left to work with.

Any spare time she had she'd need to work up her nerve to see Noah again. Why had she agreed to be a bridesmaid for Mona? Mona had obviously felt obligated to ask Cliff's only sister, and Sabrina hadn't been able to think of a single excuse that would enable her to refuse.

Now she was committed to seeing Noah at each event. A wave of agony swept through her. How could she possibly face him again?

She braced herself over the bookstore counter, and

wished fervently for a cup of coffee. She hadn't slept much last night after Bess's astounding announcement.

The shop's door chimed. She glanced up from her maze of scribbles. John Dalton stepped over her threshold, bearing two steaming cups. The aroma of strong coffee reached her, bringing a measure of comfort, just as John himself seemed to do.

She managed a small smile. The man was a wonder. Why didn't *he* make her pulse lurch the way Noah did? "Now, here's a man after my heart."

"Ah, a truly glorious prize." He set one of the cups before her, then produced several packets of sugar and creamer from his pocket.

"Thank you. I need this." She cocked her head as she sweetened her drink. "I wasn't expecting you this morning. This is a nice surprise."

"Well, it turns out Mona disapproves of my tux. She's meeting me not far from here to pick another. And the truth of the matter is I arrived early on purpose so I could start the day seeing one of the most beautiful women I've ever had the good fortune of meeting."

"Me?" Sabrina quirked her mouth to one side. She had bags the size of Texas under her eyes. The last thing she felt was beautiful. "My, we're laying it on thick today."

He eyed her with open curiosity. "You don't believe that you're beautiful?"

She sighed. Kind, and blind as Bess's Aunt Hattie. "I don't want to make an issue of it. It was a kind remark. Thank you."

His hand covered hers. Once again she was struck by his goodness—and the sad fact that she didn't go giddy at his touch. Still, a warm feeling seeped over her. He leaned close to her over the counter, his eyes full of empathy. "I know we just met, and I'm not much more than a stranger to you, Sabrina, but I want you to know that I care about you. I'm here for you, in whatever capacity you need me."

He smiled. "I've got a shoulder to cry on and ears to listen."

She shook her head. "I think I did enough of that the other night."

"Ah, but you still have something weighing on your mind. Something you didn't tell me." His brows furrowed. "A matter of the heart, I fear."

Straightening, she pulled her hand from his. "My heart is perfectly all right. I'm just tired this morning. Nothing a little caffeine won't fix." She saluted him with her cup, before taking a long swallow.

He watched her intently for a moment, then straightened away from the counter. "We're still on for the bridal shower tomorrow evening?"

At that moment she was so tired, she felt like she could spend the next several days sleeping. But when she slept the dreams came, replaying the memories of those times with Noah when she'd lost her self-control. But if she had to face him, at least she'd have John for moral support.

She sighed. "Yes, we're still on."

He nodded. "Good. I don't want to keep you from your work. I'll pick you up around six?"

"I'll be ready."

He nodded again. "There's just one thing you should know, Sabrina."

She raised her brows and waited for him to continue.

"You were right when you said I was a man after your heart."

She stared at him in surprise. She opened her mouth, but had no idea what to say to his admission, so she closed it again.

He lifted his chin. "I wanted to get that clear from the

start." His eyes narrowed. "I'm going to do my best to make you forget whoever put that wounded look in your eye, then I'm going to show you how much a man can appreciate a woman."

"John..." Again, words failed her.

"Don't say anything. It'll all work out all right. You'll see." He gave her another decisive nod, turned, then left, the door chiming behind him.

Sabrina ran her hand over her eyes. Why, oh why, couldn't she fall for the right man?

How HAD CLIFF found the right woman? Noah set his gift on the growing stack of presents overflowing a table decorated with white bells and ribbons. Cliff and Mona stood nearby, side by side, happily welcoming each guest to the shower Tiffany had arranged in their honor. The couple seemed to emanate a depressingly happy glow.

More of the fluffy bells hung across the entryway to this back room at Casey's, a restaurant of polished wood and high backed booths on the first floor of their office building. The owner, one of Cliff's clients, had conspired with Tiffany to pull off the festive occasion.

"Looks like a painting." Tiffany spoke by his elbow as she bent to straighten the bow on his gift.

"It is."

"Cool. I got them a coffeemaker with a timer." She shrugged. "It was on their list." Her gaze strayed beyond him. "Oh, there's Sabrina. Who's that guy with her? I don't remember him from her party."

Sabrina hovered just inside the room's entrance. Like a bride on a wedding cake, she stood below a pair of decorative wedding bells, her arm tucked into the arm of a dark-haired stranger. Her gaze met Noah's and time ceased.

Some obscure emotion curled through him. Her lips

parted and his gut tightened at the memory of her hot mouth. She blinked, her blue eyes rounding as she shifted her attention to her companion. Something Noah feared was jealousy boiled through him, twisting his insides. Cliff moved up beside him as Tiffany excused herself, mumbling something about punch.

"Who the hell is that?" Noah stared hard at the man standing at Sabrina's side. Had she resumed her quest for a fling? Or worse, had she fulfilled it?

"Oh, that's Mona's Uncle John."

"Uncle? He doesn't look like anyone's uncle to me."

"You sound jealous."

"I'm just curious."

"She *has* spent a lot of time with him this week."

"Good for her."

"He's really a great guy. Mona was hoping they'd hit it off. She's been trying to get him to move here for years. She thought maybe Sabrina would provide the right incentive. Seems she has."

"Oh?" Noah did his best to keep his tone and expression nonchalant. Why should he care if Sabrina got involved with Mona's uncle?

"I hear he's already found office space and put a bid in on a house, a big house. His offer was accepted late yesterday. He certainly doesn't waste time."

A trickle of unease passed through Noah. He shrugged, as if to dislodge the feeling. "Good for him. Mona must be happy."

"Thrilled." Cliff paused, raising his brows suggestively. "Seems it's a great house—Sabrina saw it. It has a huge yard, a picket fence and off the master bedroom is a nursery. He told Mona he's a man with a plan."

Noah jerked his head toward Cliff.

"Oh, I forgot to warn you." Cliff's brows arched in

apology. "I invited Darcy...you know, before you said you weren't interested."

Noah followed his gaze to where the blonde, drink in hand, threaded her way toward them. She still had all the right curves in all the right places, but somehow his hormones failed to appreciate that fact.

"Hello handsome." She slipped her arm through his.

"Darcy."

"Come on." Mona rushed over to grab Cliff. "Tiffany wants us to open the presents."

"Okay, okay..." Cliff smiled indulgently as she tugged him closer to the table.

"Isn't this fun?" Darcy murmured. She sipped her drink.

Noah nodded absently as he scanned the crowd that had assembled. Sabrina stood near the back, Mona's "uncle" still fast by her side. Her gaze remained on Mona and Cliff, though, and that same look of longing she'd had on the beach stole into her eyes as she watched them open their gifts.

Noah closed his eyes against a wave of regret. A delighted squeal drew his attention. With a last tear, Mona pulled the packing from the painting he'd bought. Swirls of bright colors danced across the canvas.

"Noah, I love it! How did you know?" Her eyes sparkled.

Sabrina had moved forward and Noah nodded in her direction. "Sabrina suggested the gallery."

His gaze met hers and for a moment he was transported to that afternoon of their first meeting. If he could go back and do it all differently, would he?

"You doll. Thank you." Mona threw her arms around him, dislodging Darcy's hold.

After a quick embrace, she released him, then turned to

Sabrina. "Thank you, Sabrina. That was thoughtful of you to suggest."

"I knew you liked contemporary art." Sabrina shifted uncomfortably as John stepped beside her, placing his arm possessively around her shoulders.

Libby's words rang through her mind. *You must persevere! No one said it was easy.*

Anger simmered through her as Darcy pressed up to Noah's side. Sabrina's gaze swept over the woman, before resting again on Noah. The man shouldn't still be able to heat her blood, especially with his bribe on his arm. "Hello, Noah."

"Sabrina. You're looking lovely as always." His gaze flickered over John, the corner of his mouth lifting in a faint movement that could have been the beginning of a scowl. Satisfaction shimmered through her. Could it be he was jealous?

She gestured to John. "This is John Dalton. John, Noah Banks."

Noah accepted John's handshake, but to her satisfaction, the muscle in his jaw worked while they shook. Was he still interested? If she pursued him, the way Henry had pursued Libby, would he eventually give in?

"And I'm Darcy Reynolds." Darcy leaned forward, clasping John's hand. "It's a pleasure."

While John was busy with Darcy, Sabrina leaned closer to Noah. "Could I have a word with you?"

He cast a quick glance at Darcy and John, who were already engaged in conversation. "I don't—"

"Please." She took his hand, giving his fingers a hopeful squeeze. She lost all reason when he touched her. Perhaps she had a similar effect on him.

"All right."

Her pulse kicked up a notch as she led him through the

crowd. Cliff and Mona would be busy for quite some time with their huge pile of gifts. Now, all she had to do was find a quiet spot where she could try to talk some sense into Noah.

Her gaze swung from side to side. A short hall at the back of the room led into the kitchen. Off to one side, before the kitchen, stood two closed doors. She tried the knob on the first one. Her heart pounded as the door swung open.

It appeared to be a pantry of sorts. Large cans, boxes, and sacks lined the floor-to-ceiling shelves. "In here," she said, tugging Noah in after her.

"Sabrina, I don't think—"

"Then don't. Just listen." After clicking on the single bulb suspended from the ceiling, she pulled the door shut.

"This probably isn't the best place to talk."

"You'd rather have this discussion out there, within earshot of my brother?"

He blew out a breath and braced himself against a shelf. "Look, if it's about this weekend—"

"Why are you afraid to be alone in here with me?"

His chin came up. "I'm not afraid."

She let her gaze travel over him. Her blood heated at the memory of his hard body, his soft touch. In spite of all that had happened between them, she still wanted him, heaven help her.

You must persevere!

"So, it wouldn't bother you if I stepped closer to you…" She moved so that her body brushed up against his. "…like this?"

His hands moved to her hips and she braced herself, but he neither pushed her away, nor pulled her against him. "You said talk."

A coarseness in his voice sent happiness blooming inside

her. He was nervous. She shifted, pressing her breasts against his chest as she ran her hands up the solid muscles of his arms. "Can you deny that you want me?"

He closed his eyes. "Sabrina…" When he opened them again, the dark depths glowed with the desire he'd shared so freely with her only days before.

"I knew it. You *do* still want me." She pressed her lips to his, willing him to kiss her back.

For a heartbeat, he stood rigid, then he swept his arms around her, delving into her mouth with all the passion of their previous encounters. His tongue stroked hers with a hunger that matched hers. She drank in his kiss, savoring the delicious heat skimming through every cell in her body.

He broke away to murmur her name, then took her mouth again, while his hands retraced her body. One hand slipped up under her dress to cup her bottom, while the other kneaded her breast. Desire spiraled through her. She gloried in the feel of his hands and mouth on her.

"Noah," she gasped as he broke the kiss, trailing his lips down her neck to her collarbone.

She worked the buttons free down the front of her dress, clearing a path for his mouth. A quick tug at the front clasp of her bra and his tongue claimed her nipple, laving it into a peak. She buried her fingers in his hair and cradled him to her breast, his mouth eliciting a dampness between her thighs.

"You make me so hot." He moved to her other breast, using his teeth and tongue as he had with the first.

She moved against him and moaned. "Oohh. You make me hot, too. Touch me." She guided his hand to her aching center.

He needed no further encouragement as he slipped his fingers beneath the elastic of her panties to tease the swollen nub of her desire. With his mouth and his fingers working their magic, the tension built and swirled within her. She cupped his hardness through his slacks and rocked against him.

A soft rap sounded on the door. Noah stilled and she muffled a cry of frustration. The knock sounded again and he straightened, setting her back, so he could begin putting her clothes to rights. Blood pounded through her ears. Her body ached with unresolved passion.

"I'm sorry," he murmured.

Her throat tightened. She pushed his hands away, finishing the rest of her buttons in silence. Noah moved as far from her as the small space allowed. Mortification filled her at his stony expression. He didn't look at all pleased to have been caught with her.

His jaw set, he opened the door.

"Um, excuse me." Darcy peered in at them. John stood close by her side. "Cliff is looking for you, Noah."

Sabrina didn't know whether to be thankful or not that Darcy had developed this annoying habit of interrupting them. She did serve as a blatant reminder why Sabrina should quit throwing herself at Noah.

"Thank you. I'll be out in just a second." As Noah turned back to Sabrina, she was surprised to see John's hand at Darcy's waist as they turned to rejoin the party.

Any guilt she may have felt evaporated in that moment. Perhaps she'd imagined John's interest in her, or perhaps he'd come to realize they'd never be more than friends.

Noah stood braced in the door. "I should have shown more restraint."

She opened her mouth to protest, but he pressed his finger to her lips. "You were right before. We are *not* having a fling."

A sense of outrage filled her as he turned, then walked away. She might not know much about these things, but she had a good idea all this hot and heavy time together constituted a fling. His stubborn attitude hardened her resolve. He certainly wasn't making it easy, but she'd persevere, all right.

She found John a moment later. "Would you please take me home?"

He glanced at Darcy, then back at Sabrina. "Of course."

A small pang of guilt plagued Sabrina at taking him away from the party. Had he been interested in Darcy? Well, Sabrina would worry about that later. For now, she needed the space and solitude of her home. She had plans to make.

Next time, she'd have Noah to herself and she'd make sure no one could interrupt them.

12

THE AMBER LIQUID SWIRLED, then settled in Noah's glass. He lifted it for another long swallow. He closed his eyes as it burned down his throat, then shook his head. He could still remember the look of outrage on Sabrina's face as he'd left her.

When she'd walked out with John, Noah had quietly slipped from the back room to the bar at the front of Casey's. He caught the bartender's eye as he glanced up from filling a mug of beer. "Another!"

The man frowned, but after serving the beer, brought Noah another drink. "You look like you've lost something pretty special."

"Maybe." Staring into his glass, Noah set his jaw. A vision of Sabrina, her eyes wide, her lips parted in invitation, flitted across his mind's eye. He'd lost big time.

"Loser," he muttered to the scotch whiskey as another patron called the bartender to the far side of the brass-railed counter.

What did Noah know about giving a woman like that all she wanted in life—a home, children…love? How could he give her something that didn't exist?

He tossed back another swig, then flexed his hand. Numbness permeated his fingers. He grunted in satisfaction.

"I'll have whatever he's having," a feminine voice said beside him. The adjacent stool scraped across the floor. A flowery scent wafted over him. He swatted at his nose, then grinned when he hit his mouth instead.

"So, what's up, big guy?"

He turned to face the newcomer. She was blond and curvy, and disturbingly familiar. His gaze dropped to her backside. He frowned. "Darcy."

Her face brightened. "That's right. It was very naughty of you to disappear again with Cliff's sister. Good thing I found you before he did."

She leaned close to him. His gaze latched onto her breasts hanging heavy in her thin-strapped camisole. He glanced down at his lap. Nothing. Not a stir. He cocked his mouth. Either he'd drunk himself into oblivion, or Sabrina had ruined him for other women.

"So, what's up with you and Sabrina?" Darcy accepted her drink from the bartender, then took a cautious sip.

"Who wants to know?" Annoyed, Noah squinted, trying to bring her into better focus. His eyelids grew heavy.

She slipped her arm in his. "Why don't we get you home? You look like you're about to fall down."

He blinked at her. The bar spun for a dizzying moment. *Sleep.* He nodded. Sleep sounded good. With a great deal of difficulty he got to his feet. He fished his keys from his pocket. They tumbled over his fingertips, then onto the floor.

She bent to pick them up, then straightened, tucking them into her own pocket. "Why don't I navigate?"

Standing proved taxing, so he let her drape his arm around her shoulder. He told her his address as they left Casey's. Outside, he glanced up at the sky. The street light tilted and swirled. He closed his eyes. *Sleep.* All he needed was a little sleep. Everything would be fine in the morning.

SABRINA LAY AWAKE, staring at her ceiling. It seemed to be a habit since meeting Noah. He had said he cared about her. Could it be he somehow didn't think he was worthy—that his past tainted him in a way that kept him from allowing himself to be happy with her? If he cared about her, could he also learn to love her?

Throwing the covers aside, she rolled to her feet. She had to find out. The only way she was going to get any sleep was to go see him and clear the air. She had a lot of questions and no answers.

Besides, in the privacy of his home, she might find a way to convince him once and for all that they should have this fling.

She found his address in the phone book and hesitated briefly, before deciding not to call first. She had the element of surprise on her side. No sense blowing that.

Moments later, she headed for her car. The ride across town seemed to take forever, but determination spurred her toward his midtown home. Once there, she paused, her heart pounding. Then, drawing a deep breath, she rapped on his door.

The dead bolt scraped. The door swung open. Sabrina blinked. Darcy stood in the doorway, clutching a man's robe around her plentiful curves. Noah's robe.

Her brows arched. "Sabrina? This isn't—"

"No." Sabrina opened her mouth, but no other words came out. Pain tightened her throat as she backed down the steps.

"Wait!"

Without looking back, Sabrina fled.

A LOUD POUNDING echoed through Noah's eardrums. He rolled to his side, wincing with pain. His head throbbed, his stomach heaved and his mouth tasted like something had died in it.

The pounding sounded again.

"What the hell?" He grabbed his head and groaned. Even his hair hurt.

"I'll get it. It's the pizza man. I ordered us some lunch. You slept through breakfast." A feminine figure clad in a familiar-looking robe cut a path in front of the bed, heading toward the door.

His heart thumped. A vague memory of Sabrina, her eyes dark with passion, flitted across his consciousness, then he squinted, making out the blond tresses trailing down the woman's back. "Who..."

Blurry recollections of the previous night crowded into his brain—Sabrina's shocked expression as he'd left her, him swigging back drink after drink at Casey's bar, then a rounded backside that hadn't impressed him the way he'd expected.

"Darcy," he mumbled, then groaned again, and threw his arm over his eyes.

"Good afternoon, handsome." The side of the bed dipped a short while later as she sat on it. The scent of pepperoni hung in the air. "Cliff called. He was majorly pissed when you didn't show up at the office this morning, but was relieved that I was here looking after you. I pacified him by telling him you were under the weather and I was nursing you back to health."

She chewed quietly on a bite of pizza, then whistled softly. "I thought you were a goner."

He moved his arm and opened one bleary eye. "Cliff?"

She quirked her mouth to one side. "Mona's got him running ragged. He asked me to ask you if you'd tried on your tux and to remind you that rehearsal's tomorrow night, followed by dinner."

Damn. He had to face Sabrina again, and so soon.

His gaze swept over Darcy. Her hair hung in disheveled

spirals. The opening of her robe revealed a good measure of cleavage. "We didn't…"

She cocked her brows. "Listen, honey, if we did it, you'd remember. Coffee?" She popped the last bite of crust in her mouth as he nodded.

A few moments later, he sat up and accepted the steaming cup, though the coffee's strong aroma churned his stomach. "Thanks."

"So, I hope you don't mind my prying, but what *is* going on between you and Cliff's sister?"

He glared at her.

"Not that what you do between the sheets is any of my business—"

"It isn't."

She surveyed him over the rim of her cup. "It's just that she showed up here last night while you were passed out. By the way she took off when I answered the door, dressed like this, well…"

"Damn." His temples throbbed. His whole body tensed. How was it possible he felt worse? Sabrina had come to see him last night after he'd walked away from her—and she'd found Darcy in his house.

"Why *are* you dressed like that?" he asked.

"We took a spill down the front lawn on our way in. My dress got all mussed. You're a big guy, you know."

He ground the heels of his palms into his eyes. This just kept getting worse. "I'll pay for your dress."

"No problem. It'll clean right up. I tried to explain, but she bolted. Sorry."

Great. She'd probably come to tell him what a slimeball he was. Now she'd never speak to him again. It didn't matter that he hadn't been with Darcy. Under normal circumstances, he wouldn't have hesitated in toppling the buxom blonde into his bed.

Hell, if he hadn't wanted to do just that he wouldn't have made that stupid deal with Cliff in the first place. He never would have had that date with Sabrina. This whole week would have been completely different. Who could say he wouldn't have ended up in a hotel somewhere with Darcy?

"Here, aspirin for your head. I never travel without them." She held her hand out to him. Two white tablets rested in her palm.

After a moment's hesitation, he slipped the pills into his mouth, then swallowed them with a sip of coffee. Grumbling under his breath, he reached for the phone to punch in Sabrina's number.

He had to talk to her. What the hell he would say to her eluded him at the moment, but he waited with his heart pounding somewhere in his throat. After a number of rings, her message center answered.

He hung up, his heart still thumping, and a dull ache filling his chest. He rubbed the spot. It was Thursday. The wedding was in two days. It made perfect sense that she wouldn't be at home. The woman had a life after all.

And it didn't include him.

Regret choked him. Sabrina hated him, no doubt. She'd probably never speak to him again, which was just as well.

"Look, Noah," Darcy shifted beside him on the bed. "I'll talk to her if you'd like. Explain how I was just trying to help out."

He raised his head and stared at her a long moment, filled with self-loathing. "Thanks, but I think it's best to let it alone."

"You're sure?"

Nodding, he reached for his pants, which were thrown over the back of a chair. Somehow Darcy had gotten him out of his clothes last night.

She moved up behind him. "Too bad things didn't work out between us. It could have been fun."

He blew out a breath and faced her. Darcy was a beautiful woman, no doubt about that. God had blessed her in abundance, in all the right places. Too bad Noah couldn't work up any enthusiasm. He leveled his gaze with hers. "Perhaps in another place and time."

Her brows arched. Her mouth rounded in a little pout. "Well, I did meet someone last night and there seems to be a mutual interest." She moved toward the bathroom, grabbing a dress hanging on the doorknob as she passed.

"Well, good luck. I think I'll pass on relationships for a while. They're just too complicated." He pulled a clean shirt from his drawer.

"You've really got it bad."

He narrowed his eyes. "Got what bad?"

"You've got it bad for her—Sabrina. Maybe you two should just have a wild affair and get it out of your system."

He frowned. "I haven't got her, or anybody, in my system."

She wriggled into the dress. The garment clung to her. "Whatever you say. All I know is the last time I got passed over, the guy turned out to be head over heels for a stripper. Poor guy, she ran off with a vacuum cleaner salesman.

"Anyway, you've got that same kind of forlorn look in your eye."

"And you're an expert on the subject?"

"I know a case of lovesickness when I see one." She gave him a pointed look.

Noah didn't respond. From what he could tell, Darcy didn't exactly qualify as an expert on love. He moved around the room, gathering his tie, socks, then shoes.

Once he was dressed, he stopped beside her. "I've got

to get to work. Thanks for looking out for me last night. Do you need a ride?''

"I have a friend coming. Is it okay if I finish getting ready? I'll lock up."

"I guess any woman who'd leave the party to look after a falling-down drunk has proven herself trustworthy."

"Thanks."

"Thank *you*. I don't normally drink like that. A shot of tequila, that's it."

She glanced up from applying mascara. "Maybe you should just tell her you're in love with her."

He grabbed his briefcase, and made a derisive grunt. "I don't believe in love…or happily-ever-after."

"Oh." She went back to the mascara. "Must just be the hangover, then."

He nodded. *Right*. It was the hangover. He gave Darcy one last glance before opening the door to leave. One thing was certain. Just because he'd suddenly lost his taste for buxom blondes, didn't mean he was lovesick.

No doubt about it. It was definitely the hangover.

THE SUN SHONE through overhead branches, dappling the asphalt as Sabrina forced her feet in the direction of the main doors of Saint Peter's Catholic Church. She took a deep breath and squared her shoulders as she headed up the wide steps guarding the front. Her legs wobbled unsteadily and she wished desperately that John was by her side. He wasn't part of the rehearsal, though, and had in fact gone to meet with his Realtor to finalize the contract on the house he was buying.

Dread filled her at the prospect of seeing Noah again. Fresh pain seared through Sabrina at the memory of finding Darcy at his door, dressed in nothing but his robe. What an idiot she'd been. Humiliation filled her at the thought of all the times she'd thrown herself at him. Deep down, she'd convinced herself that he really did care for her.

She had only herself to blame. In his own way, he probably cared for all the women he slept with. He'd never made any promises and had been honest about his intentions. Like a fool, she'd let her emotions get all blown out of proportion, convincing herself he simply hadn't yet realized his true feelings.

She paused before the double wooden doors. Why had she listened to Libby? Persevere? How could anyone persevere through this? Sadness weighed heavy in Sabrina's heart. It wasn't as though Libby were living her happily-ever-after. A tear welled, then raced down Sabrina's cheek. Was she supposed to persevere through the next twenty some years, waiting for Noah to come to his senses?

"Sabrina! Over here, darling!" At the sound of her mother's voice, she brushed the wetness from her cheeks, then turned toward the parking lot.

The sight of her parents, smiling broadly as they approached arm-in-arm loosened the knot in her stomach, and sent a small measure of reassurance flowing through her. How could she not be heartened by their evident fondness for each other?

Yes, true love lived in the hearts of her parents. Even Noah, jaded as he was, should be able to see that. She'd been blessed to be raised by such paragons. Shoving aside her own upset, she plastered on a smile.

Gabriella threw her arms around Sabrina before she reached the bottom step. "My beautiful girl. Let me see you." She leaned back, frowning. "Why, look at those bags under your eyes, aren't you sleeping these days?"

"She looks wonderful, Gabby, for God's sake. Do you have to start picking at her right away?" Don Walker shook his shaggy head, his mouth twisted in disapproval.

"Dad." Sabrina released her mother to burrow into her father's bearlike embrace. "You've been at the weights again, haven't you?" She squeezed his bulging bicep.

He grunted in reply, stepping back.

"I don't know why he's so fascinated with working out. Joining a gym at his age. Why can't he join the group I walk with?" Her mother surveyed her father through narrowed eyes.

Don glared back at her. "They're a bunch of old coots! Why would I want to be seen with them?"

Dismayed, Sabrina stared at her parents. What had gotten into the two of them? She'd never seen them bicker like this. "We should get inside. We're late. They may have started already."

Gabriella's shoulders sagged. "Excuse us, dear. We're tired from the long drive."

"You *drove*?" Again, Sabrina stared in dismay.

Three years ago, her parents had retired to West Palm Beach, in south Florida. They'd made the long drive back to Atlanta on only one occasion since then. Her mother had been so ill during the ten-hour trip that she'd sworn never to come by car again. After nursing her for two days, Sabrina had agreed.

"Your father, who doesn't mind paying a personal trainer, said it cost too much to fly."

Before Don could utter a rebuttal, the church door opened. Cliff greeted them with a hurried wave. "I thought I heard someone out here. Come on, Father O'Connal is starting."

He hugged each parent in turn as they hastened inside. Sabrina blinked as her eyes adjusted to the dim lighting. She pressed up against a wall to keep out of the way of the number of people crowding the small vestibule. A young girl in pigtails and boy of about the same age—

presumably the flower girl and ring bearer—scampered in and out of the cluster of adults. Father O'Connal stood in their midst, talking with much gesturing.

Mona emerged from the gathering, her eyes warm and welcoming. "Sabrina, I was afraid you might have gotten caught up somewhere."

"Traffic was pretty heavy on 400." She studied the tip of her shoe.

She couldn't very well admit that since discovering how incredibly stupid she'd been to have a nonaffair with a dedicated playboy, the simple act of crawling out of bed each morning had become the most daunting task. Actually making it to the church where she'd face Noah had taken every ounce of her resolve. She'd been thankful for the heavy traffic.

Mona squeezed her arm. "In case I haven't said so, I'm so grateful that you agreed to be one of my bridesmaids. I know how busy you are. It means a lot to me."

"I'm happy to do it, Mona." *Even though it's so very hard to be here.* Out of the corner of her eye she caught a glimpse of Noah. He was talking to a redheaded woman Sabrina didn't recognize. Her throat tightened. *So very hard.*

"Well, I've kind of been foisted on you. I know we haven't really had much chance to get to know each other, but I'm hoping for that to change."

The depth of sincerity in her gaze touched Sabrina. "I did always want a sister."

Mona's eyes misted. "Me too."

Father O'Connal clapped his hands. "Okay, let's get everybody lined up. You two gentlemen," he indicated Cliff and Noah, "will be up front with me. The procession starts with the ushers in single file, then the bridesmaids, followed by the maid of honor." He gestured to the redhead.

"What about me?" The little girl in pigtails bounced excitedly on the balls of her feet. She couldn't be much older than four.

Father O'Connal smiled benevolently and ushered her into line behind the redhead. "You're here."

"And then me?" the boy asked.

"Yes, you're next."

"And I won't lose the ring."

"No, I'm sure you won't." The priest ruffled his hair. "Now, let's try this with the music. Mary?" Father O'Connal cued a stout woman who scurried away.

A sudden feeling of awareness prickled the hair at the nape of Sabrina's neck. She glanced up. For a sickening moment she stood frozen as her gaze locked with Noah's.

"Up front with me, gentlemen. This way. Noah?" The priest waited patiently.

Sabrina cast her gaze to the floor, willing the buzzing in her ears to quiet. She clasped her hands to keep them from shaking.

To her relief, the music started. For the next few minutes, she concentrated on putting one foot in front of the other, pacing herself behind the other bridesmaid and keeping in step with the music. Sunlight slanted through large stained glass windows that rose high above them along two sides of the pew-lined interior. She faltered once, when she glanced up to find Noah watching her. He stood rigid and tall beside Cliff.

After they'd all found their designated places up front, Mary struck up the "Wedding March." Even in her street clothes, Mona proved to be a beautiful bride. Her eyes glowed with warmth and her smile grew wide as she caught sight of Cliff.

He in turn beamed, his excitement almost a tangible thing. Sabrina's heart filled as Mona joined him before the altar. They were so obviously in love. As they practiced their wedding vows with Father O'Connal, the depth of emotion the two shared seemed to reach out and touch everyone. Sabrina's mother sniffed loudly from the front pew. The redhead sighed and glanced toward Noah, but he seemed intent on Mona and Cliff, his gaze dark and serious.

Tears brimmed in Sabrina's eyes. She'd been nothing but a hormonal mess lately, crying at the drop of a hat.

"Here." The other bridesmaid, a petite brunette, handed her a tissue. "I always cry at weddings. And rehearsals." She laughed lightly and dabbed her own eyes. "Wait until tomorrow. I'll be like Niagara Falls."

Sabrina nodded her thanks, then discreetly wiped away her tears. Again, the prickling of awareness swept over her. Slowly she raised her eyes to find herself the target of Noah's intent gaze. The compassion brimming in his eyes had her blinking back fresh tears.

Thankfully, the priest began organizing the procession to withdraw. Cliff and Mona preceded everyone, their faces wreathed in smiles. The flower girl skipped after them, strewing imaginary flowers, while the ring bearer hurried to keep up with her. Noah followed, the redhead clinging to his arm.

Sabrina took the arm the usher offered and let him escort her leaving the last bridesmaid and usher to follow.

"I'm Antonio. I've known Cliff since high school. Now I understand why he never let any of us meet you."

Sabrina's cheeks heated. "I'm sorry about that, Antonio. Cliff was always way too protective."

Maybe if Cliff had introduced her to more of his friends she would have found someone and settled down long ago. She heaved a sigh as the organ played its last note.

Antonio stopped, stiffening beside her as they reached the vestibule. Noah stood before them, the redhead close by his side. He steadied his gaze on Antonio. "Antonio, you can release Sabrina now. Rehearsal's over. You know how protective Cliff can be. You wouldn't want him to get the wrong idea."

Sabrina's companion frowned, glancing from her to Noah, then to the redhead. Sabrina held her tongue, annoyed with Noah's highhanded tactics. She would *not* make a scene and embarrass Mona and Cliff, but where did Noah get the idea he was her guard dog?

"It's okay, Antonio." She gripped his arm tighter, even as he tried to pull away.

"I don't know. Noah's got a point. Your brother can be really irrational. I knew him for years before I even knew he *had* a sister. I need to, um, check on something." He gestured lamely and Sabrina let go of his arm.

"Well, it was a pleasure finally meeting you. Guess I'll see you tomorrow."

Antonio cast one last wary glance at Noah, then shrugged. "Sure. I look forward to it. You're going to dinner?"

"Yes." She couldn't miss it. She'd made all the arrangements.

"Would you like a ride?" Antonio asked.

"She's got a ride. Right, Sabrina?" Noah arched his brow, as if daring her to say differently.

"Actually, I'm driving my own car. The restaurant's on my way home."

"Well, I'll see you there, then."

"Right." Sabrina nodded and the usher faded into the crowd. She turned to the redhead. "I'm sorry, but could you excuse us for a moment?"

The woman cast Noah one more longing glance, then shrugged. "Sure." She disappeared in the direction Antonio had gone.

The vestibule was emptying out as the members of the wedding party departed for the restaurant. Sabrina stalked out onto the front steps. Noah followed her until she reached a secluded spot near a cluster of trees along one side of the church.

She whirled on him. "What was that?"

"What?"

"That whole guard dog attitude of yours. If I want to hold Antonio's arm, if I want to ride to the restaurant with him, that's my business."

Noah's eyes darkened as he leaned in closer to her. "Like I said before, someone has to look out for you. You have a tendency to get into trouble."

Anger burned through her. "You are *not* my keeper. You are *not* my anything. We are *not* having an affair!"

The spark in his eyes faded. "No, we're not."

"Okay, well...good then. I'm glad we've got that straight." She should have felt some satisfaction as she turned to walk away, but during the drive to the rehearsal dinner all she felt was misery.

THE NEXT MORNING dawned sunny and bright. John called to say he'd be a little late, but they'd make it in plenty of time. Just hearing his voice was balm to Sabrina's aching heart. He'd shown up for the rehearsal dinner and she'd made it through by keeping her smile plastered on and nodding and agreeing with everyone. It was amazing how so many people could carry on a one-sided conversation with the slightest encouragement. She'd left as soon as politely possible, feigning a headache.

John arrived close to the time he'd promised. They'd just entered the vestibule when they ran into Sabrina's parents. Gabriella fussed with her husband's tie. "Why did you wear this one? I had a nice one picked out for you. This one has a funny roll to it. I don't think it's cut on the right grain. What'd you do, buy seconds?''

With an impatient grunt, Don batted her hands away. "This is a fine tie. Gloria bought it for me for my birthday. At least *she* had the decency to celebrate with me.''

"I was ready to celebrate with you. You just chose to go off with that hussie trainer of yours before I got back from my group walk.''

Sabrina reached for John's hand, her stomach sinking. She cleared her throat to get their attention. "Mom, Dad, I'd like you to meet a friend of mine. This is John Dalton.''

As one, Gabriella and Don shut their mouths and turned to stare at John. A pink flush crept over Gabriella's cheeks. She opened her mouth, then closed it, blinking rapidly.

Don shoved his hand forward. "Pleased to meet you. Excuse our rude manners. This is our first wedding for one of our children.''

"Yes,'' Gabriella added, "we're just a little nervous. Everything's fine.''

John stepped forward and clasped her hand. "I've been looking forward to meeting the two of you. Sabrina tells me you're getting ready to celebrate your thirtieth wedding anniversary.''

It was Don's turn to flush scarlet, while Gabriella became engrossed with the pattern in the carpet. Sabrina's former unease gripped her, only now it had grown in intensity. Something was terribly wrong with her parents.

She hurriedly changed the subject and after a few moments her parents were again arm in arm, both smiling broadly. Sabrina slipped her hand through the crook of John's elbow and sighed. Perhaps her parents were still strained from their arduous journey. Also, like they'd said, the wedding could have them a bit stressed.

Sabrina smoothed her bridesmaid's dress. Mona had chosen peach satin with a dropped waist and low scooping neckline. Sabrina had been pleased that hers hadn't needed adjusting after the first fitting. "I want to find Cliff, then I should check in on Mona. See if she needs anything."

John nodded, squeezing her hand as they pressed through a small cluster of wedding guests milling about in the vestibule. She bit her lip as she glanced over the unfamiliar faces. Somehow, she had to make it through this ordeal with minimal contact with Noah.

"Sabrina? You look great." Brendan, one of Cliff's friends from her party, touched her arm. He gave John a curious glance.

Once more, Sabrina oversaw the necessary introductions, then turned to Brendan. "Have you seen that brother of mine anywhere?"

He nodded toward a short hall off to one side. "I think I saw him slip back that way. Try the door to the right."

"Thanks." She turned as her parents moved up beside her. "Maybe we can say a quick hello before the ceremony."

Without waiting for a response, she steered her small party toward the door Brendan had indicated. Perhaps Cliff could do something to mend things between their parents. She knocked softly at the door.

A muffled "Come in" was her response. She twisted the knob, then pushed open the door. Sunshine filtered through a gauzy curtain hung over a tiny side window. Before an aging cheval mirror, Mona stood fiddling with the veil that flowed down her back over a gown that seemed to shimmer in the light.

She turned, and Sabrina drew in a breath. Mona looked every bit the fairy-tale princess. Longing welled in Sabrina's chest. To her horror, the room blurred. She blinked.

Good God, of all the days to get hormonal, this was not one of them.

"Mona, dear!" To Sabrina's further dismay, her mother raced across the room to throw herself into Mona's arms.

Mona's eyes widened in surprise. "Mrs. Walker!" She raised her gaze to Sabrina and her companions.

"You look so beautiful," Gabriella sobbed into the translucent veil.

Sabrina stepped forward. "Mom. You'll ruin her dress." She cast an apologetic glance at Mona, moving to extricate her mother. Obviously, this hormonal thing was hereditary. "I'm sorry. This is an emotional day for her."

"There, there." Mona soothed the older woman. "I've been a little teary myself this morning."

Gabriella straightened, and dabbed at her eyes with a tissue she produced from a tiny purse hung from her wrist. "Oh, let me help you with this." She instantly brightened as she began adjusting the veil.

"Could you? Thanks." Mona turned again to the mirror, while her mother-in-law-to-be fussed and primped over her.

Sabrina's throat burned. Again, she blinked the annoying moisture from her eyes. She glanced at her father and John, who stood on either side of the door. John raised his hands in a questioning gesture.

"We were looking for Cliff." Sabrina still wanted to spend a little time before the ceremony with Mona, but she'd wait until her mother was through.

Mona looked up and caught her eye in the mirror. "He's across the hall."

"Thanks."

"Tell him I'll see him later." Her mother waved them on, her eyes shining. "I'm taking care of his bride."

Sabrina nodded stiffly, hating the jealousy burning through her. John draped a comforting arm around her shoulder as they crossed the hall. Her father rapped sharply at the door.

Cliff answered almost immediately. "Pop!" He clapped his father's shoulder as they embraced in a quick hug.

John stepped forward to clasp Cliff's hand. Sabrina relaxed. With her mother absent, the tension melted from the small group.

"Good news on that house, John. Congratulations." Cliff's smile spread wide. "I guess you know how thrilled Mona is. She's looking forward to having you around."

"Well, she'll be seeing lots of me now. I plan on rushing the closing. I can't wait to get settled here."

Sabrina's heart thudded. Had she made a mistake in not pursuing John? He had so much to give. The memory of his hand at Darcy's waist flitted across her mind and she frowned. Was John interested in the woman?

Sabrina's head pounded. She couldn't think about that now. She had to concentrate on getting through the next few days. Hopefully John would find a deserving recipient of the fairy-tale life he seemed so eager to bestow on one lucky woman. It was such a shame she wasn't that woman.

Cliff glanced at his watch. "Listen, you'd better get seated. It's almost time."

He looked at Sabrina, and opened his arms. She walked into them, letting him enfold her in his strong embrace. "Be happy, Cliff," she murmured.

He pulled back and nodded, then chucked her under her chin. "You, too, Bree." His gaze strayed to John, then back again to her. "You, too."

Her cheeks warmed. Couldn't Cliff see they were nothing more than friends? At least John hadn't made good on his promise to win her heart.

They filed out into the hall. Sabrina stopped by Mona's door. "You go ahead. I'll see how Mona's doing."

To her disappointment, Mona was surrounded by help. The other bridesmaid and the redheaded maid of honor had joined Gabriella in fussing over the bride. Sabrina stood awkwardly in the doorway, before Mona turned and beckoned her in.

"Sabrina, come in. I don't think in all the bustle yesterday I properly introduced you. I thought maybe you'd met at the shower. This is Heather and Connie." She indicated first the redhead, then the cute brunette.

Sabrina nodded. "We sort of met." She'd been too distracted by Noah to notice the other guests at the shower.

Heather was undoing tiny buttons at the back of the gown, releasing the long train. Sabrina shifted, feeling a little out of place, but wanting to make everything right between her and Mona before the ceremony. Somehow, it seemed important.

"Mona..." she fiddled with the bracelet at her wrist. It was one her mother had given her on her twenty-first birthday. "If you don't have anything borrowed, I'd love for you to wear this."

Mona's eyes widened as she took the bracelet. "No, I don't. I'd forgotten, actually. Thank you."

"I brought you a blue garter." Connie jumped up to rummage in her purse that lay on a nearby table.

"And your gown is new, right?" Gabriella smiled.

"That's right. And my necklace is old." Mona slipped the garter on under the ivory satin. She sucked in a nervous breath as Heather gave the train a final fluff. "Guess I'm all ready."

"I'll go tell Father O'Connal." Heather strode gracefully from the room.

Connie took Gabriella by the elbow. "Let's go find one of the ushers to get you seated." She glanced at Sabrina. "We should probably get in our places."

"I'll be right there. I want to wish Mona luck."

With a nod, Connie left with Sabrina's mother. Sabrina turned to Mona. "Well...good luck."

"Thanks. I feel so honored to be a part of Cliff's life."

"Actually, I really wanted to apologize for not being more welcoming toward you before. I think in a way I resented that you were taking Cliff away from me."

"Oh, Sabrina, I would never want to do that. I envy your relationship with him. He talks about you—worries about you all the time. I think *I* get a little resentful once in a while."

"You have no need to. Anyone can tell my brother is head over heels for you." Sabrina clasped Mona's hands. "I'm so happy for you. I'm so happy for me. I'm gaining a sister."

"Me, too." Mona opened her arms and Sabrina hugged her, careful not to dislodge her veil.

She straightened, smiling a real smile for the first time in days. "Ready?"

"Ready."

ORGAN MUSIC filled the air, mingling with the scents of myriad flowers. Clusters of blooms adorned several side tables and even the pews. At least fifty guests sat on either side of the ribbon-strewn aisle. Many murmured softly to one another. Toward the back, an older woman shushed a couple of young boys.

John was seated in the bride's section.

As much as she hated to admit it, she needed his moral support right now. If only she could be seated beside him. The organ struck up the processional music and Sabrina jockeyed into place behind Connie. She deliberately kept her gaze averted from the front of the church as she moved slowly down the aisle toward the altar where Noah stood solemnly beside Cliff.

As she passed John, she turned her head to catch his reassuring eye, but his gaze was fixed at the front of the church, and the look in his eye was anything but friendly.

Puzzled, she turned her head to follow his stare. Her heart skipped a beat. Noah stood off to one side of the altar, his feet planted wide, his arms by his sides, his hands fisted. She drew in a sharp breath. He was devastating in his tux and his dark gaze was fixed on her.

13

NOAH'S HEART THUDDED as Sabrina moved down the aisle. Why was it that now that she was so beyond his reach she'd become even more beautiful? His gaze swept over her slim form in the satin dress. Mentally, he traversed each hollow, each curve of her luscious body.

Cliff coughed beside him, jolting Noah back to the present. Good God, he stood before the altar of a church, lusting after Sabrina. If there was a hell, he'd just gained entrance.

She stepped up onto the raised platform, then maneuvered into place beside the petite brunette. Once Heather joined them, the organist broke into the "Wedding March." Cliff's bride appeared at the back of the church, radiant in a pearl-colored gown, her father at her side.

Clamping his mouth shut, Noah stood stiffly beside Cliff as Mona approached to the organ's triumphant strains. The ceremony itself proceeded in a blur. Concentrating on the nuptials proved impossible for Noah, when all he could think about was Sabrina and her man with the plan.

He clenched his fists and forced himself to focus on Mona, as she smiled and gazed at her groom. Her eyes sparkled, and her face lit with a becoming radiance. Cliff, too, had a certain glow about him.

Frowning, Noah steeled himself against an unfamiliar pang of envy. Obviously, these two shared some emotion deeper than lust. Had good old Cliff actually found love?

Feeling more unsettled than he cared to, Noah breathed

a sigh of relief when the priest pronounced them man and wife. Grim determination alone got him through his stint of picture taking with the newlyweds. And with Sabrina. He'd been fortunate in keeping a number of people between them at all times. She, too, seemed bent on keeping her distance, though he'd been painfully aware of her the entire time. At last, the photographer requested shots with just the bride and groom.

Noah wasted no time in heading for the exit. He needed air. Ignoring all else, he focused on a patch of daylight streaming in through one of the opened double doors. As he pushed through the crowd of milling wedding guests, a streak of chestnut hair caught his eye.

He slowed, and turned. Sabrina had somehow beaten him there. She stood on the far side of the vestibule. As though she sensed his gaze, she straightened and looked up at him. Again, their gazes locked, her blue eyes widening, her lips parting.

Noah's heart pounded. She had rolled her hair, then twisted it artfully atop her head, so that it spilled down in a tumble of curls. Light from the opened door glanced off the silky strands. The close fit of her dress accented her curves in a way that sent heat spiraling through him. In the same instant she appeared both innocent and sexy as all hell.

Before he realized what he was doing, he had pushed through the tangle of bodies toward her. What he meant to say or do when he reached her escaped him at the moment. Somehow, just getting close to her seemed more important than anything else.

He was a step away when Dalton appeared, again at her side. With a warning glance at Noah, he dropped his arm around her. Blushing, she tore her gaze away as Dalton turned her toward the door.

Noah stared after them. This time he had to be honest with himself. The blistering sensation twisting his gut was nothing short of jealousy. And it had everything to do with the fact that Sabrina had found a man capable of providing her happily-ever-after.

"WOULD YOU LIKE something to drink?" John rested his arm on the back of Sabrina's chair.

She drew her gaze from Mona and Cliff as they circled the dance floor. "How about vodka and tonic?" She might as well wallow in her despondency.

Her parents had gotten into it again shortly after the ceremony, and her mother had refused to ride to the reception with her father. Since arriving, neither had spoken to the other. Cliff had eyes only for Mona. He was oblivious to their parents' odd behavior.

John gave her a quick kiss on the cheek, then left for the buffet and bar on the far side of the ballroom. As promised, Mona and Cliff's wedding proved to be an event to put all others to shame. Sabrina watched as John melted into the crowd.

The man was perfect. He was a rock. He'd been an anchor throughout the ceremony, casting her supportive glances whenever she'd been in danger of falling apart.

She thought she'd been ready. She'd mentally steeled herself, but nothing could have prepared her for the sight of Noah in that tuxedo. When she'd looked up and her gaze had collided with his, she hadn't been able to breathe, let alone look away. Her heart had quickened, and heat had flooded her system.

It was all she could do to keep walking. Even now, her cheeks heated at the memory. How could Noah affect her that way, from across a room, no less?

Later, as people streamed out of the church, Noah had

made a path toward her. Like an entranced fool, she'd stood rooted in place, until John wrapped his protective arm around her and steered her clear. What must he think of her? By now, he'd surely guessed the part Noah played in her story.

Yet he refrained from mentioning her inappropriate fascination. Good old John. He kept her safe and secure. It was comforting just having him near her. How lucky she'd been to meet him, even though they'd never be more than good friends.

Perhaps he was right. Maybe fate had brought them together. Had they not met on that plane at a time when she'd been so emotionally wounded, she probably wouldn't have unloaded her sad tale on him. They would have met eventually, but under different circumstances they wouldn't have bonded as quickly. In the short span of a week, she felt as if she'd known him all her life.

"What happened to your guard dog?" Noah spoke quietly at her ear.

She started, nearly knocking into him. Her heart surged into her throat. "Noah! You startled me."

She pressed her hand to her chest, and cast her gaze about for John, looking everywhere but at Noah. "You mean John? He's gone to get us something to drink. He'll be right back, though."

"Not with the lines as long as they are." He pulled out the chair beside her, then draped himself over it. "So, who is this guy, anyway?"

Straightening, she moved her knees away from his. After drawing a deep breath, she spoke as calmly as possible, while her blood pounded through her ears. "His name is John Dalton. He's more or less related to Mona. He owns an advertising agency in Panama City that he's moving here to Atlanta."

"And he believes in fairy tales."

Sabrina glared at him. She was immediately sorry. He rewarded her with one of his devastating smiles. Her pulse kicked up another notch, and she scowled harder.

His broad shoulders shifted. "Okay, well, maybe just in white picket fences and happily-ever-after."

"So what if he does? Lots of women find that extremely appealing."

"Ah! But what exactly is it that appeals to you? The shiny fairy tale, or the man, himself?"

She hesitated. Noah thought she was interested in John. "The man, of course."

Noah's thick brows rose. His dark gaze delved into hers. "Of course."

"What do you want? Couldn't your precious Bambi make it?"

"You mean Darcy?"

"Whoever." Where was John?

"She told me you stopped by the other night."

She faced him, her cheeks burning. She'd forgotten how direct he could be. "Look, as far as I'm concerned, that night never happened. In fact, this entire week didn't happen. Got it?"

"Why did you come to my house? What did you want to see me about?"

Anger steeled her against him. It swelled inside her and helped her remember how shallow he was. The memory of Darcy answering the door in his robe burned into her mind. "It was nothing. I was mistaken."

"About what?"

Narrowing her eyes, she leaned toward him. "About you. About the misguided notion that there might be a heart in that shell you call a body. And the ridiculous idea that perhaps that heart might be noble." The words poured from her before she could stop them. "About the ludicrous thought that maybe we might have shared more than a would-be fling."

His mouth thinned into a line, and his eyes darkened, but he took his time before responding. "I see." He pushed his chair back from the table. "I'm sorry you feel that way, but it's just as well, seeing as we're not...suited for each other."

He stood and stared down at her. "I'll tell you one thing, though. You can forget what happened between us if you want to, Sabrina, but God knows, I never will."

After he turned then walked away, she closed her eyes. *I will not cry.* Why did he upset her? She'd made a mistake, loaded her foolish head with notions, when she'd known all along what he was. All she had to do was put it behind her, and set her sights on the future.

The future. What did it hold for her? *What exactly is it that appeals to you? The shiny fairy tale, or the man, himself?* She drew in a ragged breath. Air, she needed air. She had to get away from this noise, the crowd.

Glancing around one last time for John, she wove her way around rows of tables to a set of doors that opened onto a terraced area. She tipped her face to the warm sun, and gulped lungfuls of air.

"I have had it, Gabby. I'm sick of your holier-than-thou attitude. The sooner we get this thing over with, the better." Her father's angry voice drifted to her from around a corner.

Frowning, Sabrina stepped toward the sound, then hesitated as her mother chimed in. "That's fine with me. I can't take this bickering anymore. We'll call the agent when we get back."

Her voice wavered. "Let's just sell the condo. I don't want it. I never wanted it. I'll take my half of the proceeds and move back here, where I'm wanted, where I can watch my grandbabies grow up.'' A loud sob muffled her last word.

Shocked, Sabrina rounded the corner. ''What is going on here?''

Her parents turned to her, their eyes wide. ''Sabrina...'' her father started. Her mother dropped her face into her hands and cried, her shoulders heaving.

''Aw, hell.'' Don roughly put his arm around her shoulder and patted her. ''It'll be all right. Maybe we can at least be friends again once we both get situated. Maybe all we need is a little distance.''

Gabriella wailed all the harder.

''What is going on?'' Sabrina repeated, looking from one to the other. ''What do you mean, sell the condo?''

Her father's mournful gaze met hers. ''Isn't it obvious, Bree? We're splitting up.''

''No.'' Sabrina shook her head. ''You can't do that. You two love each other.'' She pointed to her mother. ''You always said she was your Buttercup.''

Gabriella took the handkerchief Don offered. She blew her nose with a hardy blast. ''It's true, darling.'' Her eyes glittered. ''I'm sorry. We didn't want you to find out this way. We were going to tell you and your brother sometime after the wedding. We didn't want to spoil things.''

''Spoil things?'' Sabrina's throat burned. She blinked, but this time her tears refused to be tamed. They spilled down her cheeks in hot torrents. ''You're ruining everything!''

She was acting like a spoiled child as she turned, then ran from them. All she wanted to do was throw herself onto her bed, then kick and scream until she had no breath left in her.

How could they? Had the world conspired to prove to

her Noah was right? Happy endings didn't exist. Love really was a figment of her imagination.

She stopped and leaned against a low brick wall. A nearby door creaked open, then shut. She wiped a hand across her eyes, then glanced up to find Noah standing before her. His devil-dark eyes stared down at her with an unnerving amount of compassion. Of all the people in the world to see her at the dregs of her despair, he was her last choice.

Her spine stiffening, she lifted her chin high. "I hope you're happy now."

His thick brows drew together.

"You were right." She lifted her arms, then dropped them in defeat. "About everything." Her voice cracked as fresh tears streaked down her cheeks.

"Sabrina, don't." His voice, rich with concern, rumbled through her. He reached out his hand.

She flinched backward. "No, *you* don't." She straightened, then pushed past him. "Just stay away from me, with your damn eyes."

"Sabrina." This time, he reached out and caught her arm.

She jerked from his grip. "Don't."

The door creaked open again. Throwing a dark look at Noah, John rushed to her side. "Sabrina, what's happened?"

Tearing her gaze from Noah, she turned to John. "Could you take me home, please?"

He hesitated, glancing back at the door leading to the reception. Then he squared his shoulders. "Of course."

With his arm secure about her, he guided her to his car.

THE SMELL OF CHLORINE burned Noah's nostrils the next morning as he maneuvered past the pool at his father's condominium complex. Workers had removed the pool covers, evidently getting ready for the swimming season. Spring was winding to a close.

Stepping around several rows of potted plants, he headed for his father's unit at the end of a short passageway. David Banks answered his ring almost immediately.

"Noah. Come in. I just put on some coffee. Want a cup?"

"Sounds good. How you doing, Dad?" He stepped over the threshold. As usual, his father's place smelled like a fumitory in a tobacco shop.

"Not too bad. My ticker's been giving me a little trouble." He led the way back to his small kitchen, then proceeded to fill two mugs.

Lifting the cups, he nodded toward the deck that wrapped around the back of his unit. "Let's sit outside. Doc says I need more fresh air."

Noah followed. They settled in wrought iron chairs set at a matching table. "What kind of trouble?"

Dave waved a hand in dismissal. "Nothing serious. Just getting old, I guess. Parts are wearing out. Got to watch my diet, not get too stressed." His brows knit. "I've got to give up smoking. And drinking."

Noah sipped his coffee. Knowing his father, his situation had to be serious for him to even mention it. "You got a good doctor?"

"Yep. The best. He's been patching me up for years. Dr. Stevens. Your mother used to see him, too, before she ran off to those damn mountains. Insane woman."

"Well, you look hardy enough."

"Sure. Been walking every day. Like to play a little golf still. Tennis every now and then, when I can find a player worth his salt." He sighed. "I guess I don't have much choice, but to live a good life these days."

"Funny." Noah shifted in his cushioned seat. "I've been thinking a lot about that lately—what constitutes a good life."

David's brows rose. "I get the feeling we're not talking about giving up tequila."

"I used to think all I wanted in life was a good shot of tequila, a challenging career and a fine woman to date, but lately…I don't know what I want anymore."

"I know what I want." His father gazed off over a grassy slope.

"What?"

He was silent for so long, Noah thought he wouldn't answer. Then he folded his hands in his lap, and looked intently at his son. "I want your mother back."

Noah widened his eyes in surprise. He stared at his father, not sure how to respond.

"It's foolish, all these years wasted. She's alone. I'm alone. I'd hoped she'd give in long ago. Stubborn woman."

"Give in? What do you mean? You two hate each other."

Dave's eyes gleamed with memories of a happier past. "We loved each other. Make no mistake about that. Ours was a love for the storybooks."

"Please. I was there, remember?"

He cocked his head. "You're just remembering those last few months. Think back to when you were younger. Remember?"

Furrowing his brows, Noah tried to remember. Foggy memories surfaced in his mind—his father playing catch with him, while his mother looked on, her eyes shining, his parents necking in the kitchen, whispered endearments in the night. All this time had he been focusing on a few bad months?

Dismayed, he looked at his father. "But things were really bad near the end.'' So bad, he'd apparently blocked out all the happier times.

''That was a mistake, my mistake. I admitted it, too, apologized until I was blue in the face, but that woman has a hard heart. Once she shuts you out. You're out.'' He made a cutting motion with his hand. ''Don't ever get on her bad side. Not that I ever gave her much reason to forgive me. Can't say I've forgiven myself.''

''What kind of mistake?''

David shrugged. ''A minor transgression.''

''You mean an affair?'' Noah stared, disbelieving.

''Not an affair, really. There was only that one time, well there was the time in the locker room at the club, too.''

''You had an affair.'' He'd never once thought of the possibility. His father was an honorable man. At least Noah had always thought of him that way. He'd never been the type to chase women, not even since the divorce.

''You have to understand. I was having a midlife crisis or something. I needed to prove that I was still young and attractive. The young woman, she made me feel invincible again.'' He tilted back his head and gazed at the sky.

''Who was she?''

Straightening, his father leveled his gaze on him. ''She was a waitress at the restaurant in our tennis club. She had…'' He motioned with his hands, cupping them to show the size of her breasts.

''Good God.'' Noah pressed his hand to his forehead. ''Bonnie, or something like that. I remember her.''

''Yes. That was her. You know, the way she looked at me made me feel ten years younger. Made me feel like I was a hero or something. The stress of work, the day-to-day stuff of marriage didn't exist for that time I was with her.'' He stopped, a pained look on his face.

''The second time was in the locker room. Your mother

walked in on us. I knew the moment I saw her that it was over." He shook his head. "I could have torn my heart out for the hurt in her eyes. I loved her...I still do."

"Dad..." Noah was at a loss for words.

"That waitress meant nothing to me. She was just this woman that momentarily distracted me from what was really important. I can't forgive myself for causing your mother so much pain. If I had the chance, I'd do it all differently, show her how much I really loved her. I'd give anything for a second chance."

They sat a moment in silence. The wind ruffled by, sending a nearby set of wind chimes tinkling. Noah leaned forward, placing his hand over his father's. "I'm sorry. I hadn't realized how much you loved Mom."

"Ah, I don't know why I'm telling you all of this now. Just feeling a little melancholy lately. Maybe you won't make the same mistake, huh?

"If you find someone to love, hold onto her. Keep her foremost in your thoughts. Don't lose her to some fleeting fancy. A little fling is one thing, if you're free and single, but it isn't worth giving up a good woman for."

He lifted his coffee mug, then paused before taking a sip. "Nothing beats a good woman who loves you."

Noah nodded. The wind chimes sang softly. His father was right. Maybe Noah had known the truth of those words all along. Maybe he'd begun to sense it when he met Sabrina.

By far, she was the best woman around. Damned if he couldn't get her off his mind.

He'd watched her slip out onto the terrace during the reception, knew he should leave her alone, but something in her expression had sent him out the door after her. When she'd raised her tear-filled eyes to him, he'd almost lost it.

All he wanted to do in that moment was to take her in his arms and soothe away her hurt.

But she wasn't his to hold. He'd had his fling—that too-brief interlude that left him aching and wanting. Even now, he couldn't forget the way it had been with her.

"Don't ever underestimate the power of love." His father's voice broke into his thoughts. "It can turn into one powerful hate. I'm living with that one. She hates me now. Will probably go on hating me until we're both too old and decrepit to care."

Noah cocked his head. "How can you be so sure? Have you talked to her lately? Time heals. Maybe she's of a more forgiving frame of mind these days."

A short laugh burst from his father's lips. "She won't listen to me. Why do you think she moved up on that mountain? She couldn't even stand being in the same state as me."

"I'm sorry, Dad. Maybe things'll work out one day."

His father grunted, then set down his cup with a bang. "Enough brooding. How 'bout hitting a few balls with the old man?" He motioned to the tennis courts beyond the pool area.

Noah stood. "Not today. Maybe next time. I've got some serious thinking to do."

"Thinking about giving up tequila shots?" David's eyes twinkled.

After regarding him a long moment, Noah nodded. "Yeah, maybe something like that."

14

THE CONSTANT MURMUR of voices mingled with the clink of silverware against fine china. Sabrina set down her water glass, and pasted on a brave smile for John. "What will I do until you get back? I've gotten so used to having you around."

He reached over to squeeze her hand. "I'm glad I was here for you this week."

"It wasn't one of my better ones. I hope you know you caught me while I was a little off. I'm not usually so mopey."

"You had your moments. I saw enough sparkle in those baby-blues to get the idea, anyway."

"I hope so." She pulled her hand from his to fiddle with her fork. "You're going to be so busy with your upcoming move."

"I like being busy. It'll make the time go faster. I'll be back before you know it."

Her throat tightened. How would she have survived this past week without him? "I'll miss talking to you."

His eyes warmed. "I'll miss you, too. Don't worry. You're not getting rid of me. I hope we'll still see each other when I get back."

She nodded as sadness settled over her. She felt like she was losing a dear friend.

"Sabrina, do you mind if I ask you something?"

The serious look in his eyes sent a ripple of apprehension through her. "Not at all. What do you want to know?"

He scooted his chair closer. "It was Noah, wasn't it?"

She blinked. "Noah?"

"Noah, as in Noah, who followed you to Florida to stop your plan to have a fling. As in Noah, the man you couldn't take your eyes off at the church yesterday. As in Noah, the man who took your virginity."

"Oh. That Noah."

He kept his voice calm and matter-of-fact, as though they were discussing the weather. "Something happened between you two in Florida, didn't it? I mean, something besides the physical thing."

Swallowing, she grabbed her napkin, then began twisting it into a rope. "Not what you think...exactly."

He stared at her a long moment. "You know, I wouldn't even ask any of this, except that I've come to care for you. Now that Mona and Cliff are married, I feel like we're family."

"I care about you, too, John." A short laugh bubbled from her. "You know, I'm a little relieved to have this conversation. About us being like family, I mean. I felt that way from the moment we met, like we had this connection already. Then you were paying me all that attention and I was afraid...well, that you were interested in me."

He ducked his head. "Actually, I was interested."

"Oh."

"But I think maybe we're just too much alike. We do seem to make really good friends. Besides, I think I've met someone."

The memory of Darcy answering Noah's door flashed through Sabrina's mind. Her initial impulse was to warn him away from her, but both Darcy and Noah were single. Had there been anything wrong with them being together, other than that it had devastated Sabrina? She and Noah had agreed on a no strings arrangement. She had no right being hurt.

"You mean Darcy, don't you?" she asked.

His eyes brightened. "Yeah. I don't know, there's just something outrageous about her. I can't get her off of my mind."

Should she tell him Darcy had been with Noah? Would it accomplish anything, other than to discourage John? Maybe Darcy hadn't known of his interest at the time.

"She's a lucky girl. You're everything a woman could want. I was beginning to think men like you didn't exist. Too bad you don't have a clone for me."

His fingers curled around hers. "No, you need a clone with black hair and dark eyes, but with a heart that sees the wonderful prize just waiting for him to claim."

Tears gathered in her eyes. She nodded, unable to speak.

"Want me to rough him up for you?"

"No, but thanks for offering."

"It'll happen for you, Sabrina. I can feel it. You're destined for a great love."

She had to laugh at that. "You are good for me."

He leaned forward to take her hand again. "You're sure you're okay with me and Darcy?"

She nodded, while a lump formed in her stomach. Was she fated to always be on the outside, looking in? "Positive. I wish you all happiness."

"And we pledge to always be friends?"

"Oh, yes. I wouldn't have it any other way."

DUST MOTES FLEW in every direction as Sabrina swept her feather duster over a row of books. She sneezed violently, squinting to keep the dirty specks at bay. Great. Today she couldn't seem to manage even the simple task of dusting.

Without warning, tears welled in her eyes. Goodness, not another bout with her hormones. That was all she needed. Why was she such an emotional wreck these days? She'd survived Mona's fairy-tale wedding. Somehow, she was dealing with her parents' imminent breakup. She'd even managed not to think about Noah for most of the morning.

The bell over the shop's door tinkled. Wiping her face, she stepped from the stool she'd used to reach the top of the bookcase. A young couple sauntered in, their arms wrapped around each other, their heads close together. How they walked without stumbling was a mystery.

"Good morning," she greeted them, pasting on her best smile.

The girl appraised her with her huge, round eyes, while the young man returned the greeting. "Is it okay if we just browse?" he asked.

"Of course. I'm Sabrina. Just give me a yell if you have questions, or need anything."

The girl tugged on the boy's collar, then whispered in his ear. He smiled and turned back to Sabrina. "Do you have any books of poetry? Elizabeth Barrett Browning, or maybe some Keats?"

Sabrina's throat tightened. "Certainly, right this way." She led them over a few rows, then down a short aisle. "All of our hardbacks are here. I have a few paperbacks in the used section."

"Cool." The girl let go of her boyfriend long enough to snatch a book off a shelf.

Sabrina nodded as the two bent their heads over the volume. Sighing, she headed back toward the counter. Why should she be upset over a couple of kids mooning over Keats and each other?

The bell above the door again drew her attention. She looked up as Libby Conrad swept in. She had her bright curls tied back in a turquoise scarf, and she carried a small basket over her arm.

"Good morning!" she called.

Nodding, Sabrina moved from behind the counter. Morning it was, but she had yet to find much good about it. "Morning, Libby, how are you today?"

"Wonderful, dear. I found a bluebird singing on my windowsill at sunrise. I just know it's a good omen." Her eyes brightened. "My Henry'll call today, for sure."

Sabrina pressed her hand to her chest. How would she get through this day? "I truly hope he does." Her voice quivered.

Libby set the basket on the counter, then turned to Sabrina. "Goodness, dear, what's got you all down? Are you missing John already?"

"Yes, I do miss him." Perhaps that was all. She was just missing John.

He'd only been gone for four days, but he'd called twice, doing his best to cheer her, though she tried to put up a happy front. He and Darcy were already busy planning their happily-ever-after life. At least someone was getting the white picket fence.

Truth was, Sabrina really was happy for them. Their relationship reinforced her sagging belief in true love. If only she could share John's optimism that she was destined to find love herself.

"Here. I made these to cheer you." Libby passed her the sweet-smelling basket. "They're Every Chip Cookies. They have chips flavored in three kinds of chocolate, vanilla, peanut butter and butterscotch."

She pulled a cookie from the folds of a napkin arranged to keep them warm. "They're for the person who can't make up her mind."

Sabrina studied the cookie as Libby placed it in her hand.

"Too bad you can't do the same thing with men—bake them all into a single cookie, so you don't have to pick just one."

With her eyes wide, Sabrina stared at the older woman. "I don't have any men to pick from."

Libby tucked a stray curl back into her scarf. "You will, dear. And if I'm not mistaken, there is someone. Not John. He was interested there for a bit, but that one wasn't right for you. There's someone else, isn't there?"

Sabrina's throat constricted. "I assure you, there are no other men in my life."

"You're sure?"

The emptiness of her days pressed down around Sabrina, threatening to suffocate her. The room blurred. Her throat burned as if she'd swallowed knives of fire.

Libby watched her intently. "Not even that lovely Mr. Banks, who came calling a couple of weeks ago?"

A sob burst through Sabrina's thin resolve. It led the way for a virtual waterfall. She sagged onto Libby's comforting shoulder and let the storm take her. After an endless amount of time, the heaving spasms subsided to intermittent hiccupping.

Libby produced an embroidered hankie, and dabbed lightly at Sabrina's cheeks. Good Lord, when had she evolved into such a pitiful specimen?

"There now, dear. That's better." Her eyes filled with concern, Libby guided Sabrina to a stool behind the counter. "A broken heart is a tough thing to mend."

"A broken heart?" Sabrina stared at the crinkled handkerchief Libby had given her. Why was it she was always the last one to discover what was troubling her? Of course she had a broken heart. She'd found the wrong man, then had been foolish enough to fall in love with him.

Libby placed her hand over her own heart. "I wish I

could say that time heals all wounds." Her eyes misted. "But I'm afraid I'm still waiting on this one."

A lone tear streaked down her cheek. Sabrina reached over to clasp her hand. "Oh, Libby, what will we do?"

"Well, first you're going to sell those young people that book." She gestured across the counter.

Sabrina turned her head to find the young lovers staring at them, wide-eyed.

"If that's okay..." The boy set the book on the counter, then pulled a wad of bills from his pocket.

"Yes, of course." Sabrina sprang from the stool to ring up the purchase. "I'm so sorry to have kept you waiting."

The young man scratched the side of his head. "Have you told the guy?"

Receipt in hand, Sabrina stared at him.

"That you love him," the girl piped up from her spot at his side.

The youngsters turned and gazed into each other's eyes. "Love has such a transformational power," he said.

"It can heal any hurt, right any wrong," she added.

Sabrina dropped the book into a bag, then handed it to the young man. She had to clear her throat twice before she got his attention. He smiled and tucked the bag under his free arm. "Thanks. And good luck."

All she could do was nod as the two left, arm-in-arm, nose-to-nose. How was it they walked that way?

"Out of the mouths of babes." Libby picked up another cookie.

Sabrina turned to her. She pointed after the lovebirds. "You think I should listen to those two?"

"They seem to be experts on the subject." She handed Sabrina the cookie.

Sabrina stared at a cluster of dark, semi-sweet chocolate melted into the golden cookie. Could she do it? Could she ell Noah she loved him? All the hurt and anger she'd felt when he'd walked out on her in Florida rolled back over her. "I can't."

Libby pursed her lips. "What will you do?"

"I'll pick up the pieces and move on."

"Good girl. You'll see in the long run that's best. The hurt may never go away completely, but it does get easier."

With a heavy heart, Sabrina nodded.

"And chocolate, lots of chocolate, helps."

Forcing a smile, Sabrina grabbed another cookie.

A LIGHT BREEZE ruffled Noah's hair as he paused inside the threshold of Sabrina's shop. A feeling of déjà vu shifted over him as the tones of a jazz number filled the air. He glanced toward the space in front of the long counter, where he'd first laid eyes on Sabrina. The memory of her supple hips swaying to the sax's wail curled around him. Then a second memory followed in its wake. Sabrina seducing him with her siren's dance that final night in Florida. He closed his eyes.

"Hi," a friendly voice broke his reverie. A sturdy brunette approached, bearing a plate of sweet-smelling cookies. She extended the plate in offering. "They're everything cookies, or something like that. Loaded with chips of every kind. I've never tasted anything so decadent."

He held up his hand, fending off the plate. Decadence had gotten him into enough trouble already. "No thanks."

She shrugged, then nodded toward a far corner. "The ladies will devour them, no doubt. We always provide a little something for them to nibble."

He followed her gaze to a cozy sitting area, furnished with numerous mismatched, but comfortable looking chairs, as well as a stout love seat. Nearly a dozen women filled the area, all chatting at once. A center coffee table already held a tray with a pitcher and glasses of what appeared to be pink lemonade.

"Our reader's group," the brunette supplied without his asking. "They're a loyal bunch. Gobble up the romance novels."

Brows raised, Noah nodded. "That must be good for business."

"Oh, yeah. Plus they get a discount on meeting days."

Again, he nodded, impressed. Not only was Sabrina a knockout, she had a good head for business. "Is your boss around?"

"Sabrina? She's in back. Let me drop these off, then I'll get her for you. Feel free to browse in the meantime. We're running a sale on selected hardbacks. They're on that table there." She nodded toward a table to the right of the counter, then turned with the cookies.

While he waited, Noah perused the books, intent on keeping his mind from his real reason for coming. Truth was, he wasn't exactly sure why he was there. He'd held off as long as he could, but once again, he'd let his impulses get the best of him.

All he knew was that he couldn't forget the pained look in Sabrina's eyes when he'd found her crying outside the reception. Though Cliff had explained about his parents' breakup, Noah couldn't shake the feeling he was somehow partly responsible for Sabrina's grief.

He just had to see that she was all right. Besides, he needed some closure to his time with her. Maybe then she'd leave his dreams and he'd get on with his life.

"Noah?"

His pulse tripped at the sound of her voice. He turned. She stood a few feet away, her hands clasped at her stomach, a wary look in her eyes.

"Sabrina—"

"Why are you here?" Her brows rose with the question.

He cleared his throat, momentarily stumped. "I was passing by…"

She folded her arms across her chest.

"Could we go somewhere, get a cup of coffee?"

"Why?"

"I just…" He shook his head, then tried the truth. "After the reception…well, Cliff told me about your parents. I just wanted to make sure you were all right."

She dropped her arms to her sides. Surprise flickered in her eyes, before she looked away. "I'm fine…thank you."

He eyed her a moment, frowning. "You look tired."

Actually, she looked tired and alarmingly fragile. His protective instincts kicked into gear. "Come on, you could use a little coffee break."

Her gaze swung to the group of women in the corner. "I really shouldn't. I have to leave early."

"We won't be gone long. There's a quiet spot not far. We could walk." Determined, and seeing she was wavering, he flashed his best smile. "The fresh air would do you good."

After a moment of indecision, she called to the brunette. "Trish, I'm taking a break. I'll be back shortly."

Trish saluted. "I'll hold down the fort."

A measure of optimism passed through him as he took Sabrina's elbow to steer her from the shop. "I like the idea of a reader's group."

She kept her gaze ahead, on the sidewalk. "I shouldn't be doing this."

"Why not?"

She ignored his question and they continued the half block to the coffee shop in silence. Once they'd received their orders, Noah followed Sabrina to a small table and chairs. He pursed his lips, eyeing the comfortable sofa by the unlit fireplace. Evidently, she intended for the table to keep some distance between them.

Just as well, this was all about closure, after all. She stirred sugar into her cappuccino, then blew on the hot brew. He swallowed, unable to take his gaze from her round lips.

"You looked really nice in that tux."

He gripped his cup. "So did you…in your dress, I mean."

She took a sip, letting the beverage slip down the long column of her throat. Her tongue flicked a speck of foam from her lip. "You…were alone."

He nodded as his throat went dry. *Closure.* "I didn't think a date was mandatory."

"Oh, no." That becoming shade of pink tinged her cheeks.

Frowning, he set his cup aside. "Look, Sabrina, I owe you an apology."

She stilled, her gaze fastened on her drink. "And what are you apologizing for?" Her voice sounded forced, as though she spoke with her jaw locked.

He shifted, cursing the overwhelming sense of ineptitude stealing over him. "Hell if I know. I suppose I should apologize for taking advantage of you that night after your party. I should apologize for our fling—which we did have, whether or not you'll admit it. But I've got to be honest. I just can't make myself feel sorry for any of that."

After drawing in a deep breath, he continued, "But I feel that I've wronged you somehow, so I guess I'm apologizing for that. And for not being sorry it happened."

Raking his fingers through his hair, he stole a glance at her. She watched him with her lips pressed into a thin line, her eyes guarded.

"You didn't take advantage of me. I offered myself, well knowing the consequences."

A knot formed in his stomach. Sweet Lord, she had offered herself and he had partaken of all her magnificent wonders. He was overwhelmed by the memory of her soft cries, her body convulsing around his, taking him over the edge. He could still feel her, taste her...remorse flooded him. If only he were worthy. "Still, I shouldn't have taken advantage of your generosity."

"Okay. Apology accepted." She held his gaze as she pushed back, then rose. "I've got to go."

His heart thudded. "Wait. That's not all."

"Noah, I don't see the point. You said yourself we're not suited."

"I said a lot of things. I guess I also came here to tell you I may have been wrong about most of them."

Slowly, she sank back into her chair. "Such as?"

His heart raced. What was it he was trying to say? Since he'd met her he'd been dazed and confused? He'd been wrong not to believe in fairy tales, because suddenly he wished with all his heart they were all true?

He shrugged. "I was wrong about happy endings, I guess. Maybe sometimes they do happen."

Her eyes misted. "Like when, Noah?"

"Well, look at Mona and Cliff."

"That wasn't an ending. That was a beginning. My parents started the same way."

He nodded, feeling as though he were drowning. "Well, I'm sure there's someone, somewhere that's living happily ever after."

She was silent a long moment. "So, the happy endings are reserved for a chosen few."

If he'd been near a wall, he'd bang his head on it. This

conversation wasn't going the way it should. "I don't know. I suppose."

"And that's all? That's all you wanted me to know?" The mixture of hope and sadness in her eyes drove him to distraction. He was blowing it, but he couldn't for the life of him figure out how to fix it.

He drew a deep breath. "I just wanted you to know that at the reception, when you said you hoped I was happy, that I was right about everything...well, I wasn't."

She nodded. "Okay." She rose, then paused. "Thank you for the coffee."

He sat motionless as she turned, then left. He stared after her for an interminable amount of time, with his chest so constricted it ached. A feeling of utter loss swept over him, and at last he knew.

He'd been wrong about the damn closure, because that was really the last thing he wanted with her. He'd been wrong to ever let her go, either in Florida, or just now. But most of all, he'd been wrong to ever doubt the existence of the most powerful emotion of all. He'd been wrong not to believe in love.

NOAH PACED across Cliff's carpet, an empty shot glass in his hand. "So, what does she say about the guy? Is she happy he's moving here?"

"Mona?"

Noah turned, waving his hand in frustration. "Sabrina. Does she like him?"

With his arms crossed over his chest, Cliff eyed Noah a moment before answering. "We've been over this before. I'm still not sure I trust you around my sister. Why should I answer all these questions?"

Groaning, Noah set the glass on Cliff's desk. "You have every right to give me flack. I admit it. In the past I've regarded women in a different light.'' He shrugged. ''Maybe I never took them seriously, but lately I've been seeing things from another perspective.''

''What kind of perspective?''

The chair in front of Cliff's desk protested as Noah dropped into it. He never thought he'd be having this conversation. ''Well, look at you and Mona. You two have a good thing going—love, marriage, the possibility of children. Maybe I'm starting to think about those things.''

Cliff's jaw dropped. ''You're thinking about love…and children?''

''I'm not as shallow as everyone thinks! Okay, maybe I've been skeptical about this whole love thing, but I'm willing to admit I may have been wrong.''

''I'm listening.''

''I'm thinking about all these things, and about how I don't want to look around twenty or thirty years from now and discover I'm a lonely old man, with nothing but what-ifs and a long string of meaningless relationships to show for my time.''

''Wow.''

Noah heaved a breath. What exactly did he want? ''I'm going to want memories, lots of happy memories of a family and home. I'm going to want to surround myself with a loving wife and kids, who'll still care about me when my hair falls out and my savings dry up.''

Cliff leaned forward and peered at him from across the desk, his brows forming a deep V. ''Are you saying what I think you're saying?''

Leaning forward, Noah stared back. ''I'm saying it's time I made a few changes in my life.'' He grinned. ''In my personal habits.''

''No more women of the week?'' Cliff's brows scraped his scraggly hairline.

"Who needs them with one good woman around?"

"And you think Sabrina's the one good woman who can keep you from straying?"

Noah drew a deep breath. He'd been fighting his feelings since the first moment he saw her. Suddenly admitting them didn't seem as frightening as he'd thought. "Without a doubt."

"Really?"

"Really."

Cliff pushed back his chair. He rose, then paced over to the window. "How can I be sure you're serious about changing your ways?"

Noah threw a meaningful glance at the shot glass he'd set on Cliff's desk. "Ever known me to let a bottle of José Cuervo go unopened?"

Cliff's eyes widened. He walked over and picked up the glass. "I'll be damned. I never thought I'd see the day. Guess you're serious about changing your ways." He shook his head. "I still don't know how I feel about this. You and Sabrina, huh?"

"If she'll have me."

"She'll want the whole shebang, you know."

A shiver of anticipation ran up Noah's spine. He squared his jaw in determination. "I'm counting on that."

"I guess you're going to need help."

"I know. I know. She thinks I'm the scum of the earth."

"We can fix that whole Darcy thing. I'll take the heat. I put her onto you in the first place."

"What about Dalton?"

"I think he's out of the picture. Mona says they're just friends."

Relief flowed over Noah. "And Sabrina's good with that? She isn't pining for the guy or anything?"

"Not that I know of. You've still got a major problem, though."

The chair creaked as Noah leaned forward. "What's that?"

Cliff screwed up his mouth and raised his brows. "You, of course."

"Me? What do you mean, me?"

"To win Sabrina, you've got to turn into a true romantic, bud."

A feeling of unease settled over Noah. He stared at his partner, confounded. "How the hell am I supposed to do that?"

15

WITH A SCOWL, Noah adjusted his sunglasses. June had hit Georgia with a vengeance, rolling in with record-breaking highs. The sun beat down on him. Heat shimmered off the road as he peered across at Sabrina's shop.

He'd been a dedicated cynic for most of his adult life. How was he going to change into a true romantic overnight? Pacing the length of Cliff's office, while racking his brain hadn't gained him anything but his partner's frustrated glare.

Noah had meant to escape to his favorite thinking spot, the roof, but lost in thought, he'd stepped onto an elevator headed for the street level. He'd exited, then kept walking.

He hadn't realized where he was headed, until he arrived at this place. Somewhere along the way he'd lost his tie and rolled up his sleeves. In spite of that, sweat soaked his shirt. All that walking, and he still hadn't come up with a fail-proof, knock-her-socks-off kind of plan.

He squinted, straining for a glimpse of Sabrina through the shop's window. "Christ, I am turning into a stalker."

Clenching his fists, he stifled the urge to storm the shop, kidnap her, then take her to his place to make wild love to her until she promised to spend the rest of her days with him. Though the idea had a certain appeal, she'd likely consider him more a caveman than any kind of a romantic.

He'd save that as a last resort.

Shoving his hands into his pockets, he rocked back on

his heels. To prove he was a true romantic, he had to show he believed in love and happy endings. The truth was, that even though he'd finally come to believe in the darn things, he'd yet to find one.

Trying his hand at playing Cupid, he'd traveled to see his mother, to convince her to give his dad another chance. He'd left, feeling that he'd mucked things up worse than before he'd interfered. In spite of that, though, he couldn't shake the notion that his best bet was to help create a happy ending for someone close to Sabrina.

He shuddered at the thought of interfering with her parents. They needed a professional, not an inept Cupid. No, her parents were on their own. Who else, then?

Frustrated, Noah raised his gaze to the sky. "Lord, I know you're shocked to be hearing from me, but I could use a little help. I'm not asking for a miracle, though I won't object to one. I'd settle for just a bit of inspiration."

For long moments, he focused on the bookstore, his mind a chaotic jumble. So much for divine intervention. Maybe he should give Cliff another shot. He'd have the inside scoop on all of Sabrina's friends. Surely one of them could use a happy ending.

As Noah turned to leave, an old Mercedes rounded the corner. Hitting the curb, it bumped into a parking spot in front of the store. With a creak, the driver's door flew open. Libby Conrad, her red curls tamed in a violet scarf, stepped from the vehicle. As if it were an everyday occurrence, she straightened and waved at Noah.

He lifted his hand to return the gesture, suddenly remembering the photo of Henry in her locket. A slow smile curved his mouth. "Bingo."

NOAH'S HEART RACED as he stared at the slip of paper Tiffany handed him. "How long ago did he call?"

She pointed to a notation on the message. "Not five minutes ago."

"Great, maybe I can still catch him." He was halfway down the hall before he remembered to yell back a thank you.

Once in his office, he punched in the number she'd written on the paper. The line rang once, twice. By the fifth ring he was ready to hang up, then a voice finally answered.

"Hello?" It was a crackly, old man's voice.

Noah smiled. This could be it. This could be the one. "Hello. Is this Mr. Henry Thomas Watson?"

"Henry, you say?"

Raising his voice, Noah tried again. "I'm looking for Henry Thomas Watson. I was told I could reach him at this number. I'm returning his call."

"One moment." The phone clunked. A murmur of voices traveled across the line. Noah held his breath.

"Hello?"

"Hello. My name is Noah Banks. I'm from Atlanta, Georgia, and I'm looking for a Henry Thomas Watson, who once lived near here in Decatur."

"Oh, yes, Mr. Banks. Well, my name's Henry Thomas Watson, and I lived in Decatur many years ago."

"Were you acquainted with a woman by the name of Libby Conrad?"

Henry let out a soft sigh of pleasure. "Young widow with hair the color of the setting sun? One of the prettiest women to ever walk the streets of Atlanta?"

Noah bit his lip, and said a quick prayer of thanks. "That's her. Tell me, Mr. Watson, would you be interested in seeing Mrs. Conrad again?"

A moment of silence stretched between them, then, "Good Lord, are you saying she's *alive*, that she's still there?"

"She is, and I assure you, she remembers you."

"My Libby's *alive?* How can that be? I've mourned her these past thirty years. They told me she died in that fire."

"Well, I don't know about any fire, but I promise Libby Conrad is alive and well. She must be your Libby. She wears a locket with your picture in it."

"The locket!" Excitement trembled in Henry's voice. "God Almighty, I've dreamed all these years about what it could have been like."

A smile curved Noah's lips. "Then, Henry, I suggest we arrange a little reunion. You with me?"

Henry responded with a delighted cackle. "I'm with you, Mr. Banks, just tell me when and where."

Two DAYS LATER, diesel fuel scented the air by the back door of Sabrina's shop. She checked off a final carton of books a burly deliveryman hauled into her stockroom. After scribbling her signature, she handed him a copy of the receipt voucher, then sent him on his way, locking the door behind him.

With a deep sigh, she rolled up her sleeves and faced the twenty or so cartons that had come off the truck. She couldn't complain, though. She'd wanted to stay busy. She had too much on her mind these days.

Her mother had called that morning. Her parents were delaying their separation while they sought help from a marriage counselor. Though this development eased some of Sabrina's stress, they weren't out of the woods yet. With another sigh, she ripped open a carton.

The door to the shop opened. Toby peered around it at her. "Sabrina? There's an old guy out here. He needs to see you."

"Okay, Toby." She followed him to the front, making mental notes about where she'd stock the new merchandise.

Toby led her to their reading corner, then left to tend to another customer. An older gentleman sat perched on the edge of an old wing-backed chair. When he saw her, he rose slowly, then straightened, shifting his shoulders back, and raising his chin. He ran a shaky hand over the ample amount of silvery waves covering his head.

"Are you Sabrina Walker?" he asked, his eyes bright.

"Yes, sir. How can I help you?" Sabrina cocked her head. Something about the man seemed familiar, yet she was sure they'd never met.

"I do hope so. I've come all the way from California."

She raised her brows. "California?"

"Yes, ma'am. It's a long story, but I've come to settle a thirty-year-old misunderstanding. I'm told you're the one to help me put things right."

"I'm sorry, I don't follow."

He frowned. "I'm not doing this right. You have to excuse me, I'm a little nervous."

She furrowed her brow. "I assure you, Mr..."

"Watson." He held out his hand. "Henry Thomas Watson, originally of Decatur, but I've been in Los Angeles these past thirty years."

For some reason she couldn't place, his name roused a sense of recognition. She shook his hand. "Have we met, Mr. Watson?"

"No, ma'am. Like I said, I've been in California these past thirty years."

She nodded. "Yes. Well, I assure you I'll help in any way I can, if you could explain what it is you've come for."

He sighed and a toothy smile lit his face. "Now, that part's easy. I've come for my bride."

She quirked her mouth to one side. Not another bride.

"Well, there seems to be an abundance of those around. Were you looking for one in particular?"

His eyes sparkled. "Yes ma'am. I've come for Libby Conrad. I'm thirty years late, but I'm here at last."

Sabrina stared, her eyes wide as the realization struck her. She gasped. "Oh my God, you're Henry! You're Libby's Henry!"

His smile deepened. "She's mentioned me, has she?"

"Mentioned you? She comes in daily and asks if you've called." Though it really wasn't any of her business, Sabrina couldn't help blurting, "What on earth happened to you?"

He chuckled softly. "Did you know that thirty years ago this place used to be a coffee shop?"

She gazed at him, a sense of wonder swelling inside her. "No, I hadn't realized that. I've only been here for about four years. It was already a bookstore then."

"Well, this is where we met, in the coffee shop, that is." His eyes took on a faraway look. "She was the sweetest thing I'd ever laid eyes on. She worked here."

He glanced up and pointed across the room. "There was a long counter over there. I used to come by after work with my buddy and sit and drink cup after cup, just to watch her. It took me nearly two weeks to work up the nerve to ask her out. I knew I was a goner when she poured that cup of coffee in my lap."

"But, what happened?"

"She tried mopping it up with a towel."

"No, I mean why didn't you two marry?"

He shook his head. "Stupid thing, really." His brows furrowed. "We got into this doozy of a fight. The church double booked us. I wanted to elope, but Libby wouldn't hear of it. She had to have her church wedding."

He paused, dragging his ragged hand over his face. "I

thought she was getting cold feet...stalling. All the churches around were booked solid for months.

"You see, my brother was already out in L.A. He had a coffee shop, not like this one. It was bigger, fancier. Libby and I had already decided to follow him out there. She was going to work for him. He had a little apartment over the shop he was going to rent to us. I was in sales back then, and I did quite a bit of traveling. There was a company out there willing to take me on, where I wouldn't be traveling so much. But I had a trip over to Houston to make first, the week before we were supposed to move."

He sighed. "Libby still wasn't speaking to me when I left. I was just so impatient for us to marry. I didn't like the idea of being separated. I had to start my new job. An elopement made sense to me, but I couldn't bear her being mad.

"So I called my brother and asked him to check on churches out his way. Then I said a quick prayer. I couldn't believe it when he called back saying he'd found one to do the ceremony that weekend. Libby's phone had already been disconnected, so I wired her airfare and left an urgent message for her at the coffee shop."

He paused. "Don't think she ever got that message, though. They had a terrible fire here. Gutted the place from what I heard." His voice cracked. "They told me Libby had been working at the time—that she hadn't made it out."

He swallowed and wiped his eye. "I thought I couldn't go on for the longest time." His gaze fixed on Sabrina. "If it hadn't been for my brother, I think I would've lost my mind. I just couldn't accept that my Libby was dead."

Blinking back tears, Sabrina placed her hand on his arm. "She wasn't. She's been waiting for you, all this time." She drew in a quick breath. "We have to call her." Excited at the prospect of seeing the two lovers reunited, Sabrina hurried to the counter to drag out her customer log. "I'm sure I have her number here somewhere."

While she flipped hurriedly through the pages, Henry went on in a dreamy kind of way, "What a woman. I never quite understood how she fell for the likes of me."

Sabrina found the listing. She grabbed the phone, punching in the number as Henry continued his reminiscing.

"She had a passionate soul, my Libby."

The phone on Libby's end rang.

"She would do this dance for me, while I played the harmonica." He raised his arms. Slowly, he gyrated his narrow hips, while mimicking the strains of the harmonica.

If Sabrina had had any doubts as to whether this was truly Libby's Henry, they vanished in that moment. Her eyes never leaving him, she waited as Libby's phone rang for an annoying sixth time. Disappointment flooded her. "She's not answering."

The tinkling of the bell drew her gaze to the door. Libby Conrad breezed in, her red tangle of curls held back as usual in a tidy scarf. Her gaze fell on Henry as he twisted across the floor. Sabrina held her breath, while surprise, then recognition registered across the woman's expressive features.

"Henry?" Libby took a shaky step forward.

Henry pivoted toward her. He stilled. "Libby?"

"Oh my word!" With a cry of joy, she launched herself toward him. "I knew you'd come! You're damn late, but I knew you'd come!"

He met her halfway, lifting her with a strength Sabrina wouldn't have thought possible, then swinging her in a wide circle. Her laughter sent warmth swirling through Sabrina's insides. The scene before her blurred as an incredible happiness overtook her. She didn't even try to stop the tears cascading down her cheeks.

Libby had found her Henry.

He set her down, his smile wide. "God, Libby, you're as beautiful as I remember."

She swatted his arm. "You old goat. I've aged and so have you. What took you so long?"

"Why, I thought you were dead. I called here to tell you I'd arranged a church wedding out in L.A. When you didn't show, or cash in the wire, I called your landlord. He told me you'd died in the fire that took this place. I guess I was too stricken to check with the authorities. I took his word."

Libby shook her head. "Poor dear. I left early that night to move my things in with my sister. I didn't know about the fire until about a week later. I had no idea anyone thought I was dead.

"I never got your message, and I guess you missed mine. I called that hotel in Houston and told them to tell you I was ready to elope." She smoothed her hand over his cheek. "I hated fighting with you. I figured God would understand. All I wanted was to be your bride."

With a wide grin, Henry hugged her to him, then pulled back. "Well, thanks to that nice Mr. Banks, you're going to have another shot at that."

She smiled up at him, her eyes brimming with love. "You really arranged a church wedding for me?"

"Excuse me." Sabrina rounded the counter, her heart palpitating. "Did you say, Mr. Banks?"

Henry turned to her. "That's right. Noah Banks. Says he's a friend of yours. Told me he was happy to help get me and Libby together again." He scratched his head. "Something about having to prove to someone that he believed in happy endings. Do you understand any of that?"

Sabrina swallowed past a knot in her throat. Maybe she

did understand. "Oh, I hope so. Would you excuse me? I've got something to do."

She glanced around for Toby. As usual, he was busy rearranging the sci-fi area. "Toby, can you stay and lock up tonight?"

He swept a streak of blue hair from his eyes. "Sure. What's up?" He raised his brows suggestively. "Got a hot date?"

Laughter bubbled from her. "Maybe I do."

After grabbing her keys and purse, she hurried out the door. If Noah truly believed in happy endings, did that mean he also believed in love?

"WHERE IS HE?" Sabrina bit her lip and leaned through Cliff's office door.

He turned from his computer screen. "Hey, sis. You mean Noah?"

She nodded. "He's not in his office."

Shrugging, Cliff glanced at his watch. "He's been like a caged animal today." He eyed her with open curiosity. "Got a lot on his mind. He was driving me a little nuts with all his pacing. I told him to go home."

"You sent him home?" Her heart pounded. She twisted her purse strap in both hands.

"I made the suggestion. Noah doesn't take any orders from me. He wasn't getting any work done anyway. He left about an hour ago."

"But wait," he called as she turned.

He rose, then came around to perch on his desk. "I need to talk to you."

"Can we do it later?"

"No. This won't wait."

Grinding her teeth, she waited for him to continue.

"So, things are off with Dalton?"

"They weren't ever really on. Seems he and your friend Darcy have become an item." She blew out a breath. "He's just not the type of guy for me."

"Good." Cliff's brows drew together. "I want to talk to you about this whole Darcy thing."

Her old anger resurfaced. "I don't care to get into it right now, but I still haven't forgiven you for that."

He raised his hands, palm out. "I take all the blame. It was my idea completely. Noah only agreed because I begged. You know, he never did sleep with her."

A heavy sigh escaped Sabrina. The one dark cloud in her time of hope was Darcy. Noah had been with her that night.

"She was with him the night of your wedding shower. I saw her, but—"

"They didn't do anything."

"She was wearing his robe, Cliff, his robe."

He drew back a little. "Really? Well, they still didn't do anything. He was falling-down drunk by the time she found him in the bar. She was just helping him out. Apparently he was all torn up about what happened between you."

"He told you what happened between us?"

"He didn't tell me squat. I pieced it together on my own, and Darcy had a few theories."

She glared at him. "You have got to learn to mind your own business."

"I know. I'm an interfering bastard, and I've promised my dear wife all that is going to change." He gave her a hopeful grin. "But I meant well. I thought I was protecting you."

"We don't have time to discuss this, but if you ever interfere in my life again, I will disown you as my brother."

"Bree, come on! He's nuts about you."

Hope washed over her. "Really? He told you that?"

"Practically wore a hole in my rug trying to figure out how to win you."

She frowned. "Then why did he let me think he'd been with Darcy?"

"Who knows? Maybe he didn't think he was good enough. You do ask a lot from a guy."

"I've got to talk to him."

Cliff nodded.

She turned, then scowled at him over her shoulder. "I'll get back to you later."

He grinned. "Go get him."

NOAH PACED to his front window and stared blankly at the maple tree in his yard. His temples throbbed. So much had happened lately, he hadn't had time to assimilate it all.

Yesterday, his father phoned to say his mother had called and they were getting together to talk. Noah's trip to the mountains had paid off, after all. Maybe this was a good omen. If his parents could come to terms, he, too, had a chance of mending things with Sabrina.

Henry should have made it to her shop by now. Maybe Noah should have gone along to see how things worked out.

He glanced nervously at the flickering candles he'd scattered throughout the house. He'd placed them in every room, anticipating Sabrina's wonder when she saw them. Surely she would come to him. Soft music played on the stereo in the front room. He shook his head. If she didn't show, he'd feel like the biggest fool for creating such a romantic environment.

What if Henry and Libby's reunion went sour in some way? What if Libby didn't get her happy ending? Why hadn't Noah thought of a back-up plan? He could always throw himself on Sabrina's mercy, spill his guts, beg.

The bell on his front door sounded. Noah's heart contracted. Swallowing hard, he opened the door. Sabrina stood on the other side.

"Sabrina, come in."

Her eyes narrowed and her mouth thinned as she stepped over the threshold. His hopes sagged as he shut the door behind her. Looked like he'd be begging, or maybe now was the time to try that kidnapping ploy.

"You, sir, are an imposter." She lifted an accusing finger in his direction.

He cocked his head, keeping his voice calm. "How so?"

She stopped a few feet in front of him. He stayed the impulse to throw her over his shoulder. Her lips softened into a slow smile. "You found Libby's Henry. That was *not* the work of a cynic."

Hope flared in his heart. He shrugged. "I've seen the error of my ways, turned over a new leaf."

"Henry said you told him you wanted to prove to someone that you believed in happy endings."

His gaze drifted over her face. "That's right."

She took a step closer and peered up at him, her eyes shining with that purity that shook him to his core. "Why?"

"I met a woman who believes in love and happily-ever-after. She helped me to see the world in a new light. She made me want things I never thought I'd want."

Something softened in her eyes. She reached up and laid her hand on his chest. "Such as?"

"A home, a wife...children."

She was silent for a moment, then she turned from him. He clenched his fists to keep from grabbing her back. She had to come to him on her own.

When she again lifted her gaze to him, he read the doubt in her eyes. "Why did you let me believe you'd been with Darcy? Don't you know how much that hurt?"

He couldn't resist the urge to comfort her. He closed the gap between them and put his arms around her, not too tight. He held her loosely, so she could break free with minimal effort. To his profound relief, she made no move to do so.

"You wanted so much in life. I felt so…jaded. I didn't think I had it in me to give you all you deserved. I thought I could do the noble thing and let you go, until you found Dalton and he seemed only too willing to give you everything. Please tell me you're not seeing that guy."

"I'm not seeing that guy."

He closed his eyes, relieved beyond measure. When he opened them, she watched him closely. "I've been miserable since I left you in Florida. You're all I think about, dream about. I want to make you happy in every possible way. God help me, I love you, Sabrina."

Her eyes glistened. He held his breath, waiting for her response. When it came, it wasn't exactly what he'd hoped.

"Prove it."

He paused a long moment. "I've given up women and tequila." He paused again. She watched him expectantly. He continued, "I could give up Monday night football?"

Still, she stood silent, her brows raised.

He brightened. "I'll take out an ad…get a tattoo?"

She shook her head. "No, that won't do."

"What, then?"

She raised her arms, looping them around his neck, pulling him closer. "I don't need anything quite that elaborate. I was thinking of something a little more…personal."

His pulse quickened. "Such as?"

"Make love to me, Noah."

He crushed her to him. "Good God yes, a thousand times yes."

She nipped at his lips and rubbed against him. "I've been having the most wicked dreams about you."

He closed his eyes and smiled, letting his fingers stray down to cup her bottom. "I lit candles for you and put on soft music."

"Yes, I noticed. You really are a true romantic."

His gaze captured hers. "You've taught me true love does exist."

Sabrina smiled, as anticipation rose inside her. Yes, true love *did* exist. She should never have doubted it. Standing on tiptoe, she pressed her body into Noah's. "This is the part where you ravish me. I need to know that I really please you in bed."

"You don't doubt it, do you? Not after what we've already shared. You have to realize it's *never* been like that with anyone else."

"Well, you're so much more experienced than I am. I do wonder..."

A deep light shone in his eyes. "Then, let's put that worry to rest."

He leaned down to scoop her in his arms. As before, he carried her to the bed. He kissed her slowly, deeply, then peeled her clothes from her, tracing his lips and tongue over each inch of skin he exposed. She trembled.

He drew back to meet her gaze. "See how you respond to every touch?"

She nodded, then let out a low cry as he flicked the pointed tip of his tongue over her peaked nipple. He took her in his mouth, suckling her until she clung to him, moaning softly. "Of course I respond. You know what you're doing."

He undressed, then stretched beside her, cradling her

with his body. "It's your responsiveness that gives me pleasure."

"It pleases you to please me?"

"Something like that. It really turns me on to see you enjoying the way I touch you."

She ran her finger down his chest. "That's nice."

"Trust me, Sabrina. You have nothing to worry about. I promise."

Smiling, she pushed him onto his back, feasting her eyes on his carved planes and hollows. He was glorious, every masculine inch of him. "I think it pleases me to please you, too."

She stroked her hand down his front, over the washboard muscles lining his stomach, to the mysterious part of him that stood rigid, beckoning her. She moved over him, touching him first with her fingertips, then growing bolder, she took him in her hand.

His chest heaved. He gazed down at her. "Well, you are most definitely pleasing me."

Confidence bloomed in her, but she shook her head. "I'm not quite convinced. I think I need to please you some more."

She stroked her hand up, then down him. "It's so hard, yet silky at the same time, and…" She traced the bulging head. "It's so beautiful."

He sat forward, cupping her breasts, but she brushed away his hands. She bent low over him, her hair sweeping his thighs. "I've wanted to do this since that first night in my apartment. I want to give back some of what you gave me."

"You don't have to, Sabrina."

She paused as her breath fanned his heated flesh. "You don't want me to?"

"Yes," he gasped. "If you really want to. You'll definitely please me."

She pressed her lips to his smooth skin, marveling at the underlying steel. Slowly, she explored him inch by inch, using her lips, her tongue, even her teeth as he'd done. Pleasing him indeed pleased her. Her pulse beat low, between her thighs, swelling her, moistening the folds of her femininity.

When she took him fully into her mouth, his hips rose off the bed. He groaned, pounding his fist into the mattress.

She pulled back. "Did I hurt you?"

He choked out a laugh. "You're killing me...but no you didn't hurt me."

She frowned. "You sound strained."

Sitting up, he grabbed her by her arms. "I need...to be...inside you."

"Oh." She gazed longingly down at him. "But I wasn't quite finished." Heat spread throughout her. "As I recall, you kissed me that way for quite a long time. On several occasions."

"You'll have to take a rain check." He pressed her to her back, parting her legs and nestling between them. His erection pressed into the juncture of her thighs. "If you'd kept that up, I wouldn't have made it inside you."

"Oh." She arched up as he kissed her breast, rubbing her taut peak with his lips. "Oohhh."

He touched her everywhere, suckling her nipples and burrowing his fingers through her triangle of hair to that part of her that quivered at his caress. He stroked her until she thrashed her head on the pillow.

"Noah, I...I need you...now."

He brought his mouth over hers, kissing her deeply, while he parted her soft folds. His blunt tip probed her entry. She shifted, welcoming him, wondering at the feel of him stretching her, filling her. He made one quick thrust with his hips, then was seated deep within her. Slowly, he coaxed her body to join his in a rhythmic dance, his movements bringing ripples of pleasure.

"Oh, Noah, it always feels so good."

He chuckled. "This is the part where we both take pleasure."

She murmured her agreement. Words escaped her from that moment on, as desire rose and billowed inside her. Sounds of ecstasy tore from her throat. She found her release a second before he did, their cries mingling as night blanketed the room.

For long moments they held each other, his heart beating beneath her ear. Candlelight flickered across the walls. She stirred, leaning up on one elbow to smile down at him. Warmth swelled her heart. "So, guess we're having that fling after all."

He raised his thick brows. "Absolutely not! I wouldn't dream of it."

Alarm rose in her. "What do you mean, no fling?"

"I mean…" He nestled her into the crook of his arm. "We have a lifetime of loving ahead of us. I won't settle for a mere fling. Surely you don't mean to trifle with me."

Happiness filled her. "What exactly are you saying?"

"I'm saying, marry me Sabrina. I really won't settle for anything less."

"Then I suppose I'll have to. How else will we live happily ever after?"